# Star
# Craving
# Mad

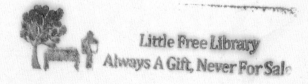

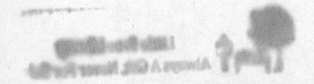

# Star
# Craving
# Mad

Elise Abrams Miller

*To Donna! Thanks for coming out in the storm! Elise*

**WARNER BOOKS**

New York   Boston

Warner Books

Time Warner Book Group
1271 Avenue of the Americas, New York, NY 10020
Visit our Web site at www.twbookmark.com.

Printed in the United States of America

First Printing: May 2004
10  9  8  7  6  5  4  3  2  1

Library of Congress Cataloging-in-Publication Data

Miller, Elise Abrams.
  Star craving mad / Elise Abrams Miller.
    p.  cm.
  ISBN 0-446-69284-0
  1. Manhattan (New York, N.Y.)—Fiction.  2. Motion picture actors and actresses—Fiction.  3. Children of celebrities—Fiction.  4. Fans (Persons)—Fiction.  5. Women teachers—Fiction.  6. Single women—Fiction.  I. Title.
PS3613.I535S73 2004 813'.6—dc22                              2003018898

Book design and composition by Stratford Publishing Services
Cover design by Brigid Pearson
Blackboard photo: Barry Rosenthal/Taxi

*For Bryan. Without you, none of this
would have been possible.
I love you.*

—E.M.

# Acknowledgments

To the celebrities who have enthralled and inspired me and Maddy B., I thank you.

Jennifer Unter at RLR, you are amazing. And my editor, Caryn Karmatz Rudy, thank you both for helping to make my dreams come true. Thanks also to Heather Kilpatrick, Carol Edwards, Harvey-Jane Kowal, and Megan Rickman at Warner Books for all your wonderful work on this project.

Without the Little Red Writing Group there would be no *Star Craving Mad.* Mari Brown (you started it all), Melanie Murray, Savannah Conheady, and Ingrid Ducmanis—your gossip, mimosas and hummos, heart-shaped cut-out of Colin Farrell, and always illuminating critiques kept me going and made sure it was a blast along the way. Thank you also to Rebecca Traister at the *New York Observer,* and Heather Cabot and Gena Binkley at ABC News for featuring LRWG and for spreading the "chick-lit" word.

To the ladies of PE who kept me clothed and fed while I wrote, thank you for the laughter through the fluorescent-lit years: Libby, Nadine, Paula, Randy, Stephanie, and Susan. Every hour should be happy hour. Thanks also to the Manhattan-based LLPs and LLCs who graciously if unwittingly paid me to write *Star Craving Mad* on their time clocks. Who says a hundred lawyers at the bottom of the ocean is a good start?

Thank you to my friends, too numerous to list, who've supported and inspired me throughout this process. Thanks especially to: Lane Nicole Addonizio, Joe Cilibrasi, Stacy Danon, Nara Garber, Kim Kenseth, Jason Kornblatt, Michael Kurhajetz, Peggy Leggat, Nick Martucci, Danielle McGurran, Leslie McKeown, Cathi Murphy, Kristen Olson, Chalkley Calderwood Pratt, Dempsey Rice, Tori Rowan, Joanna Sausa, Ken Vale, and Ned Vizzini.

Many thanks to all the talented writers and musicians who have taken part in East Side Oral, "the reading series your mother warned you about." And to Karen Lord and Jen Gilman at The Living Room, thank you both for providing my series a fabulous home.

Thank you, family! Mom and Joe, Dad and Shirl, Judy and Nancy, Dick and Ca' and the rest of you super-size bunch of hooligans, you witnessed the journey, believed in me even when I didn't, and never called me insane, at least to my face. I love you all. For real.

And lastly, thank you to my beautiful husband, Bryan, for seeing the potential in me before I saw it in myself, for loving me the way I needed to be loved, and for your sharp editorial eye. I love you with every nutty-buttery cell. *Sniff!*

*Charlie looked down at the candy bar. He ran his fingers slowly back and forth along the length of it, stroking it lovingly, and the shiny paper wrapper made sharp little crackly noises in the quiet room.*

*Then Mrs. Bucket said gently, "You mustn't be too disappointed, my darling, if you don't find what you're looking for underneath that wrapper. You really can't expect to be as lucky as all that."*

—ROALD DAHL,
*Charlie and the Chocolate Factory*

# *Chapter One*

*I* walk into the classroom, Styrofoam cup of coffee from the faculty lounge in one hand, class list in the other, cheapo Chinatown sunglasses slipping down my already-sweaty nose. Before I battle it out with the giant windows, sealed shut with a summer's worth of Manhattan grime, I perch on the edge of a table, shove the glasses up on my forehead, and study the column of names.

My new assistant is still not here and it's almost 8:40, the witching hour. That's what I get for being here for so long, for not quitting last June, when I promised myself I would. They always give me the first-year assistants because by this point it simply doesn't matter anymore. They could stick a Seeing Eye dog in here and it wouldn't faze me. I could teach first grade with my eyes closed.

Between checking the clock, glowering at the windows, and sipping from my cup of overly skim-milked coffee, I see a name on the list that sends my heart into a spasmodic fit. Seabolt. I count the names on the list. Nineteen. I could have sworn there were eighteen just a week ago, when I got my information packet in the mail.

I walk over to the wall phone and dial the headmaster's extension.

"Arthur Wilcox's office," says his very young, very beautiful assistant, the senior he handpicked from last year's graduating class. The school year has barely begun and already scandal is in the air at City Select Academy. Score one for the head molester.

"China, hi. It's Maddy. Is Arthur around?"

"Nope, sorry." She sighs, bored already with her first real job in the real world.

"Then maybe you can help me. I have a new kid in my class? Do you know anything about this?"

"Oh, didn't you get the letter?" she asks absently. I did not get any letter. I take a deep, mindful Buddhist breath, get in touch with my anger and frustration, and smile.

"No, China. I didn't get it. Could you tell me what it said, please?" I say, hoping she will grow out of her surly teenage ways before Halloween.

"Um, Lola Seabolt just moved here from L.A. and she's in your class."

"Are her parents—"

"Uh-huh. Nick and Shelby."

"Okay, China. Thank you. No message for Arthur."

I hang up the phone and wish I knew the first thing about composing oneself. One of my kids is a Seabolt. Daughter of Nick and Shelby, one of *Celeb File Weekly*'s hottest celebrity couples. I can't count how many times I've lain in bed fantasizing about Nick Seabolt, his nose a little too big, his lips a little too thin, his eyes a little too sad, but when you put them all together, your crotch ignites. Nick and Shelby are one of those rarities, like albino rock stars or loyal cunnilingus-loving boyfriends, who've been together forever and are somehow always being interviewed by Barbara Walters, gushing that they're more in love than ever. They're the couple the public roots for, like Hawn and Russell, Robbins and Sarandon, Witherspoon and Phillipe. I'm not sure the public actually roots for Aniston and Pitt. A little domestic tragedy might be beneficial for everyone in their case.

I notice that the paper in my hand is vibrating in time with my racing heart. I take a gulp of lukewarm coffee and wonder how I'll ever be able to concentrate this year with a bona fide princess of

Hollywood royalty in my class. Over the past five years, I've stayed awake at night wondering what it would be like to teach a mini Moore-Willis, a pint-size Wright-Penn or a Seabolt. I felt gypped all these years when the most famous kid I ever got was the son of a weekly columnist for the *Daily News.* Now that my wish has come true, I feel less like celebrating and more like breathing deeply into a paper bag.

City Select Academy in Greenwich Village is a different kind of school, what some people call "progressive" and others dub an "elitist hellhole." Either way, it's a magnet for the rich and famous, although Nick and Shel, as the media affectionately calls them, are unusually famous, even for CSA.

As I tack the class list to my bulletin board, I force myself to remember how experienced I am, how easily the kids warm to me, how the parents write me glowing notes at the end of the year, thanking me for working magic on their little Emmas and Eamons. I repeat these affirmations to myself, nodding my head with vigor for each one, because if I don't, I will have a nervous breakdown right here on the checkered linoleum floor.

After a couple more repetitions, nods, and prayers, I am convinced that once we get into the swing, I'll be too busy to obsess about Nick and Shelby Seabolt. Showing the eager beavers how to carry tens will leave me no time to imagine kissing Nick's lips or pressing my face to his well-muscled chest. Teaching the secret mystery of the silent *e* won't spare me a minute to imagine Shelby's inevitable disappearance/death/descent into madness.

The shrieking bell wakes me from my reverie. Five minutes to go before the kids arrive, and my assistant is still not here. My eyelid starts to twitch, making me feel slightly crazed. Usually, it's at least Yom Kippur by the time my eye spazzes out.

I throw my sunglasses in my hopelessly outdated Manhattan Portage bag and race around the room, taking chairs down from the tables and putting them on the floor. Voices and footsteps inch closer, echoing up the stairwell and through the hall. The clock says 8:55 and I decide at this obscenely late hour that I loathe my new assistant more than ever, and that he'd better have a damn good reason for being inexcusably, unforgivably, *unacceptably* late.

The first child to arrive is Kylie Passwaters, Martha Stewart in miniature, hopefully without the rap sheet. We shake hands and then she rolls up the sleeves of her linen smock dress and gets right to work in the doll corner, setting the tiny kitchen table. Her parents look at me, their mouths pressed into tight, expectant smiles. I smile back and shake my head at Kylie's enthusiasm.

"She's wonderful," I gush.

More kids and parents trickle in, and I scan them all with my fame radar, waiting in suppressed agony for Lola to arrive, in suppressed rage for my assistant to appear.

"Hi, it's nice to meet you. I'm Maddy Braverman. I'll be Julia's teacher this year. . . . Yes, six years! I know, I just keep coming back! I love that skirt, Eden. . . . Sure, Max, you can go in the block corner. Make yourself at home. . . . No, he's not here yet, subway delay," I say, lying. Grinning, shrugging, I try to look inconspicuous every time I glance at the door or the clock.

It goes on like this, my face aching already from all the smiling, my mind reeling from practicing a favorite distraction: mentally adding up the prices of the parents' and children's clothes. Lots of Prada ballet flats this year, I see. When I get to a bazillion, I feel less like a teacher and more like a festering boil, dressed to the negative integers in last year's Gap outlet and thrift store "treasures." I adjust my ponytail, as if it'll make a difference. Some of the mothers arrive dressed in Nike running shorts or Puma yoga tights, reminding me that I had better resume my own exercise regime instead of spending every free minute at Barnes & Noble, poring over *Celeb File Weekly* with a self-sabotaging venti mocha frappuccino.

The headache I've been expecting arrives, slam-dancing behind my eyeballs, but my assistant is still in absentia. While the parents and children acclimate to the new environment, I make my move and sneak a phone call to the switchboard, but the operator has not heard anything.

At 9:05, little Zachary Van Buren, who has the unmistakable air of a male figure skater, presses his face to the window and shouts, "Hey, there're two stretch limousines pulling up outside!" The rest of the class, shy one student and one assistant teacher, rushes to the window.

Apart from the jumbo cluster of buildings that is CSA, Eleventh Street between University and Fifth Avenue is an otherwise-typical Village block, lined with stately double-wide brownstones that make the ones in my Brooklyn neighborhood look like dollhouse miniatures. The limos make the quaint tree-lined street look puny, incapable of handling such vast amounts of gleaming metal.

The remaining few parents and I share knowing smiles, as if to say, Aren't the kids cute? and then join the ogling throng.

Down on the street, Nick Seabolt emerges from the first black stretch Lincoln, dressed in "dirty" jeans and an untucked tan button-down shirt, his famously floppy silver hair reflecting the September-morning sun. Behind him, Shelby and Lola emerge from the second limo. Shelby is dressed down today—in black capri pants, black T-shirt, and sandals. Amazingly, I can see how red her toenails are all the way from the sixth floor. If the kids weren't here, I would say something about how ostentatious and vulgar such an overt display of wealth is. I would say it with hostility and venom and glee. If the parents weren't here, I would say, "Oh my God! Oh my God! Wait until my roommate hears about this!" Instead, I remain silent and think of my roommate, Kate, her total disdain for anything "celebrified," and smile. She would absolutely puke from the vanity of it all. I can't wait to tell her that they pulled up in two limos. As if a single shiny stretch limousine doesn't throw the underclass into a frenzy of inadequacy. "The nerve of those cretins," she'd say.

"Who're those people?" asks Rafaela, who, if she isn't already, should be paid hundreds of thousands of dollars for modeling in Gap Kids or Benetton ads.

"That is Lola Magdalena Seabolt," I say. "She's in our class." The hush that ensues is priceless. If I could quiet the kids this effectively all year, I might just enjoy waking up in the mornings. The silence, though, like most things kids touch, breaks easily.

"Is she famous?" asks Mason, chewing his thumbnail casually.

"Her parents are actors," I say with caution.

"What's their names?"

"Are they in the movies?"

"Did they win Oscars?"

"Is it the president?"

"Their names are Nick and Shelby Seabolt. And when Lola gets here, you can ask her all those questions yourselves." I don't want to place any more importance on these people than they deserve. They are human beings, just like me, I think. Just. Like. Me.

God I wish I'd gone to the bathroom when I had the chance.

The nonfamous but very rich parents approach me, one by one, heads down, whispering as if I am a priest whose sole purpose in life is to hear their confessions.

"I just saw them on *Twenty/Twenty*. Have you ever seen anyone age so well?"

"I heard Shelby was suffering from exhaustion. Did you hear about that?"

"Loved the last Soderbergh film Nick was in. Do you think I should tell him?"

But before I can answer any of their urgent questions, the Seabolts arrive, and suddenly all of us wilt under whatever top secret power it is that the famous wield so mightily. All color seems to drain from the classroom, while the Seabolts glow brighter and brighter. My hips widen by an inch. My posture crumbles. My armpits crackle. Even the kids seem lackluster.

While the students welcome a smiling and tangly-haired Lola to the class, Nick and Shelby make their way over to me. I wipe the sweat from my upper lip, urge myself to remember positive things, like the time my best friend, Michelle, told me I could be Sandra Bullock's stunt double, and hold out my hand, praying I am emanating an unfazed, unintimidated attitude.

"Hi," we all say at the same time, and shake hands. So many sensations. So many observations. My system is overloading with celebrity. I can handle such 2-D brilliance in a magazine or on television, but seeing it here in the flesh, I almost feel electrocuted. Does everyone react this way?

"It's a pleasure to meet you," I croak.

"Same here," says Nick. His hand is large and strong, the way it should be. Shelby's is small and papery, immaculately manicured in sheer bloodred. She doesn't look exhausted to me. She looks alert, her famously lusty eyes darting every which way, as if to make sure that this classroom will be acceptable for her royal heiress.

Nick says, "We've heard a lot of good things about you from Art." He's talking about the headmaster in a tone that sounds eerily intimate. I wonder what he would say if he knew we called him the "head molester."

"Oh . . . great!" I chirp, and smile. My brain has crawled into a cave to download this behemoth of sensations, leaving behind a comatose husk.

"Your curriculum sounds fabulous," coos Shelby, a faint twang giving away her Georgian roots. "The gold rush is such a creative idea. Lola's going to love it." She's looking at me so intensely, I can't help but feel there's a subtext that I'm missing in her seemingly innocent words. I hope she thinks I'm good enough to teach her daughter.

"Thanks so much," I say. It is a herculean task for me to talk to these people as if they're not regular fixtures at the Academy Awards. I wish I could tell everyone else to go home, so that I could stay with Nick and Shel until midnight, studying them like lab specimens. When I glance at Nick, I notice that his shirt is suede and that he's wearing black rubber flip-flops. His toes are tan and perfectly shaped, civilized piggies in a meticulously spaced row. I realize with a slight shiver that I could lick all ten of them— for hours. And I don't even have a foot fetish.

"Well, it looks like you have everything under control," Nick says, and I jerk my head up from his toes. His smile melts my insides and I am suddenly mortified. How dare I think of cozying up to his feet at a time like this? What kind of monster am I? To punish myself, I look at Shelby, who, at forty-something, is more beautiful and graceful than I could ever hope to be at thirty, with her compact figure and four-hundred-dollar highlights, which she probably didn't pay a cent for. Here is a woman who's never accidentally left a tampon inside herself for weeks to rot and stink, a woman who's never queefed in yoga class while the instructor adjusted her shoulder stand, a woman who's never vomited on a subway platform at 2:00 A.M. in Brighton Beach. I am furious with myself for wishing Shelby dead. Nick and Shel are clearly made for each other, and I am an evil, evil home wrecker.

Shelby looks at her whisper of a watch, and then she's gone. Nick tells me that she has a meeting uptown.

"That explains the two cars," I say, and Nick touches his nose, nodding.

"Yeah, I'm heading to TriBeCa," he says in that fertile voice of his. I worry that I could sprout offspring if I listen too hard. I stand there like a goon and Nick smiles, reaching into his back pocket. "I know this is probably a little weird for you." *Weird for me?* No. This is my life's dream come true, which, now that I think about it, is a little weird, since I'm so used to being disappointed in my humdrum world of the nonfamous.

Nick pulls a folded piece of paper out of his back pocket and hands it to me. "It's just something we have to do," he says as I unfold the piece of paper. "Confidentiality agreement," he says sheepishly.

I read it over quickly and sign it. "Of course," I say, all the while thinking that this piece of paper has been cradling Nick's ass cheek all morning. I wish I could rub it all over my face before handing it back.

Nick slips it back into his pocket. "Thanks, Maddy. I know it's strange, but, well, you know how the papers are." I nod understandingly as he shakes my hand one more time. Then he walks over to Lola, kisses her on the forehead, and leaves. I curl my hand into a fist around his sexy residual molecules, exhale, and force my mind back on the business at hand.

\*　　\*　　\*

The classroom buzzes with first-day excitement. Nobody seems especially shaken by first-day jitters. Maybe because most of these kids have been at City Select since the twos. Already the block corner is dominated by boys. Another group of kids lie spread-eagled on the rug, surrounded by Uno, Connect Four, chess, Legos, and giant pop-up dinosaur books. A handful of particularly pretty girls huddle at one of the tables, wielding Crayolas like magic wands, designing their own line of tattoos and mend-his. Lola Magdalena Seabolt is among them. Already I can tell she's a leader, with her grubby, chipped glitter-tipped fingernails, leopard-print tank top, and tangle of wavy brown hair, which she keeps pushing out of her eyes.

"I'm putting a dot right in the middle. Like this," she says, and every girl at the table quickly copies her.

"Oh my God, you're such a good drawer!" squeals Eden.

"Yeah," says Lola, not looking up from her Magic Marker masterpiece. She's utterly cool, totally unfazed. A true celeb. I make a mental note, then chide myself for falling under the spell of a six-year-old.

I walk around the room, observing, cradling my chin with a knuckle, grunting my approval, smiling when necessary, lifting my eyebrows at just the right time. This is my first-day performance for the benefit of the few remaining clingy parents, the stragglers who refuse to let their children go. Starting tomorrow, Portuguese and Jamaican nannies will be dropping off the little angels.

When the last parent finally backs out the door, leaving an unmistakable trace of Kiehl's trademark essential oil, I grab four Motrin from my desk, wash them down with the last of my coffee, and turn out the light. All nineteen first graders freeze.

I have relinquished all hope of my assistant's arrival.

"Good job! I can see that you all know what it means when I turn out the light. Who can tell me in words? Reis?" I can't quite tell if Reis is a boy or a girl. He or she has long blond hair but is also wearing slouchy cargo pants and Nike high-tops.

"It means freeze," Reis mumbles, looking at the floor. Okay, I decide. Boy.

"Freeze only your body?"

"Freeze your mouth!" shouts Rafaela, leaping into the air.

"That's right, Rafaela!" Rafaela jumps again, quite pleased with herself.

"It's Raffey!" she shouts, her multitude of braids swinging. I'm sure the class next door can hear her.

"Okay then, Raffey. Thank you," I whisper, hoping to give her a little hint about volume control. I don't want to come out of the gate criticizing, so I take a breath. By this afternoon, the lights will be flicked a thousand times, and we'll have already had the big "rules of the block corner" discussion, its import emphasized with a stern furrowed brow and tightly clasped hands. Even so, I know that, like every school year, these kids will maneuver their way into my tired heart.

I shake my head at these beautiful, spoiled children whose lives I coveted while growing up, the child of clueless nutcases from Cherry Hill, New Jersey. Hell, I still covet them now. And I think to myself, I am going to be these young royals' prisoner/tour guide/baby-sitter/therapist/coat-fastener/shoe-tier for the next nine and a half months. I gear myself for one last big smile, one last second to go before I seriously consider having my assistant fired on the first day of school.

"Okay, let's clean up and then circle up for our first meeting as first graders!"

The class of 2014 is hard at work making room for one another on the edge of the rug. Zachary raises his hand.

"Good hand raising, Zachary. Yes?"

"Our circle is more like a *U* than an *O*," he says, smiling and revealing a gaping black hole where his first adult tooth will be by June.

"You know what? I think you're right. I guess we'll have to 'U' up in the mornings, then," I say, and the class erupts into a fit of giggles. I hope I didn't say anything obscene by accident. I repeat my sentence in my head to make sure.

"Hey, I know!" says Stella, sitting up on her knees. "Let's make an *S*!" Before I can gather my wits, the scrambling begins, and suddenly I've lost all control. And then, as if the devil himself is directing the movie of my life, the door swings open and my assistant arrives. I don't have time to glance in his direction. Why couldn't he have walked in when he was supposed to? When I had a handle on these brats?

"Okay, kids," I say. "I'm extra-specially blessed and pleased that you know your alphabet, but I need a *U* shape. Show me a perfect *U,* please." Please, I pray to the God whose existence I blasphemously believe in only during times of sheer terror. The kids crawl back to their spots obediently. Lord have mercy. I would cross myself if I weren't Jewish.

"You know, guys, I think you may be onto something there. I'm going to think about a way we can use your ideas in here. Would you like that?"

"Yeah!" they say together, looking at one another as if they've scored the deal of the century.

"Okay, I'd like that, too. But in exchange, you need to follow some rules. That means, when it's time for morning meeting, we have to sit where?" Almost all of the hands go up.

"Lola?"

"On the edge of the rug," she says, coquettishly brushing her fingers back and forth on the navy blue carpet nap in front of her knees. I am enthralled, bewitched. I am hooked. That little minx is flirting with me. And I am eating it up.

"That's right," I say.

"That is the most perfect *U* shape I've ever seen," says my new, very tardy assistant from the doorway. We all turn and look. Standing in the doorway is the scruffiest-looking teacher we've had yet at City Select Academy: suede fringed jacket, long, scraggly brown hair, sweaty September residue. He's even leaning on a battered guitar case. If he wasn't an hour late, I might think he was attractive. If he wasn't so relaxed, I might have an ounce of respect for him. If he wasn't my assistant, I might tell him to buzz off, say, "I can teach this class without your help, thank you very much."

"Class, this is James. He's going to be your other teacher. Why don't we all welcome James?"

"Hi, James," says the class in singsong unison with a touch of elite-class jadedness.

"Do you play that guitar?" asks Lola, twirling her hair, cheating on me already, the little slut.

"How did you know it's a guitar?" he asks her. He squints at her hard. "Do you have X-ray vision?" Lola erupts into peals of giggles and falls over.

"No. I can tell what it is by the shape of the case!"

"Oh . . ." he says, nodding, the lightbulb over his head glowing in a contrived eureka moment.

"Why are you late?" demands Raffey, snapping her fingers on every syllable. Most of us wait for his answer, while a few students attempt to snap their own uncooperative fingers.

"Well," James says, taking off his jacket. "I was mugged." The class and I are riveted. A real mugging. This'll kill some time.

James slings his jacket over the guitar case and leaves them in the corner by the teacher's desk. He walks over to us and sits on the edge of a nearby table. "I was on my way over here, crossing Washington Square Park—"

"I know where that is!" shouts Max.

"Me, too!" says Eden, and then the class launches into the first irrelevant conversation of the year.

"My baby-sitter says Washington Square Park is dangerous."

"My baby-sitter says there's drugs there."

"Drugs are so bad."

"When you do drugs, you need a rehab, and rehab is serious. That's what my baby-sitter says."

"What's a rehab?"

As enlightening and socially aware as this is, I feel the need to interrupt. "If you want to hear about James being mugged, I suggest you save the discussion for recess."

James thanks me and continues.

"So I was crossing what park?"

"Washington Square!" the class shouts.

"And I was jumped. Two big guys. Broad daylight."

"Were you scared?" asks Zachary.

"Yes I was," admits James. "I gave them my money, thirty-seven dollars. I figured it was worth my life, right? They tried to take my guitar, but I convinced them that the guitar was a piece of sh— that it wasn't any good."

"He almost said the *S* curse!" pipes up Raffey, arching her back and pointing. She widens her already-huge brown eyes at me. Maybe she wants me to send him to the headmaster's office. Oh, how I wish I could. But how do I explain that the head molester is the one who hired James? That the head molester adores scraggly poet types like James, that Arthur Wilcox doesn't care whether or not they can teach, that he just gets off on *inspiration*?

"I almost said the *S* curse," admits James, "but not quite. I won't say it anymore. It's . . . ah . . . inappropriate, right?"

"Right," says everyone in unison. Moral little brownnosers.

"My grandfather was mugged!" says Reis.

"My daddy says the *S* curse all the time!" announces Lola, and the class veers off on another tangent, like so many yentas sitting shiva, and I reel them back in again. I am way too tired for this.

"Guys, there are nineteen of you. I'm sure that you all have amazing stories to tell, but there is a time and a place. When it's your turn, you'll get to tell your story. For now, let's please listen to James and stop interrupting, or else he'll never get to the end." Beautiful, merciful silence. I've done it. I wipe my palms on my jeans. "James? Would you like to finish your story?"

"That's pretty much it," he says. "So onward with the meeting, I suppose?" he adds, facing his palms to the ceiling and winking conspiratorially.

"Thank you," I say, embarrassed that James has usurped my authority, and more furious than a sane person should be. I hate a guy who winks.

# Chapter Two

Since the kids eat lunch in the classroom, James and I take turns going down to the faculty lunchroom. I go first, weaving my way downstairs through the older kids, fourth and fifth graders shouting at the tops of their lungs, looking like turtles as they hunch under their overfull first-day backpacks. Then there are the anorexic high school girls aching to look like they don't give their appearance a second thought, or their daddy's millions, with their raggedy bell-bottoms, vintage hoodies, and greasy hair.

Once I reach the lunchroom, I give the room a once-over. I'm dying to divulge info about the Seabolts, but Michelle Zucker, my one and only CSA confidante, is still not here. Unfortunately, most of my drunken mistakes from years past are. In one corner, the gym teacher I dry-humped in Prospect Park is reading the "Sports" section of the *Times*. Filling his coffee cup is the language structures teacher, who spent so much time sucking my nipples, I thought I would start lactating. And finally, huddled in deep conversation with the bulimic chorus director, is the English teacher, who's been here forever yet still gets mistaken for a high school senior. We had sex in his bedroom, in the apartment he still shares with his agoraphobic mother. At least the physics teacher, who actually seemed to respect me for a minute, isn't here. Rumor has it he's spending the year trekking in Tibet, studying oxygen.

Unfortunately, none of my flings ever turned into anything more than an awkward morning after, succeeded only by a heated competition to see who could most stealthily avoid eye contact when we returned to school the following morning.

I fill a paper bowl with cottage cheese, tuna salad, and chickpeas from the salad trough. I've been trying to stay on the Bönz diet, because, let's face it, who doesn't want to resemble the one female who managed to get Jordy Hume ($30 million-per-picture megastar, who vowed in 1995 to die a bachelor) to the altar? I don't know how Sofia Lively (sitcom goddess and cosmetic entrepreneur) does it. She obviously doesn't cheat, judging by her wispy arms and hypnotically teeny butt. When I saw her sporting a white lace teddy in *Celeb File Weekly*, I almost died of jealousy on the spot.

I chew my mushy bowlful standing up, one lusty eye on the cookie tray, the other, still twitching eye on the clock. I'm more than a little afraid about leaving the kids alone with James. What with the scraggliness and the mugging, the winking and the cool attitude, they're liable to be passing a bong around the room when I get back. I left him meticulous instructions to make sure the kids finish their lunches in their assigned seats within twenty minutes and then have them clean up their own messes and look at books on the rug.

As I'm finishing up, about to dump my runny remains, Michelle walks in and grabs me by the arm. She leans her pink Revloned mouth into my ear and whispers so close that goose bumps rise.

"Maddy, you'll never guess who I let titty-fuck me last night!"

"Oh my God. Tell me now, 'cause I don't have time to guess," I say, eyeing yet another of Michelle's infamous first-day ensembles: a lime green Lycra miniskirt, sky blue baby T-shirt, and pink foam mules.

Michelle registers me looking at her outfit. "It's from Conway!" she says, making a grand sweeping gesture down the length of her curvy body. "What's a Prada?" she adds, with precision bimbo vacancy and an exaggerated shrug, loudly enough for everyone to hear. Michelle does the trash look scarily well. The sad thing is that not everyone gets that she's making a statement, that her mother is a corporate litigator and her father owns over a dozen high-end antique stores from Nantucket to Boca Raton. As the head of the famous City Select Drama Department, Michelle works hard to look like she couldn't care less what other people think, and to shove it repeatedly in their tastefully dull faces. She worked hard and fucked many to get where she is (or isn't) today. Most people can't stand her, but for some reason, I feel like I can see the other side of her coppery coin, the dog-loyal, so-truthful-it-hurts side. Plus, she's a hell of a lot of fun at a party.

She says, "Did you see that movie with that blond actress who always plays a dopey, watery neurotic, the one whose mother is always meddling?" and gives the room a once-over, locking her eyes briefly on the head molester. Somehow, he looks like he has more hair every year. Maybe because he's shrinking from old age.

"Hope Davis? You did Hope Davis?" I whisper back, looking into my empty oil-soaked bowl. It would almost surprise me.

"No, dearest. I haven't had hairy pits or licked bush since my Bennington days. The man I titty-fucked, the strapping man of almost eleven inches, was a PA on that film!" I think she's bruising my arm.

"Which film? I want to rent it," I say, trying to weasel out of her death grip.

"Sweetie, I don't knoooow," she croons. "Besides. They're all the same. The point is, he's a filmmaker, too. And he's casting his personal project next week, and guess who he has in mind for the lead?"

I force a smile, feeling a little like one of my own students, because Michelle is using a tone that most people reserve for very small children and the mentally challenged.

"Well, mazel tov!" I say, hoping it sounds genuine. I've heard Michelle's stories for six years now, and they're always the same: "I met a guy, he's got a huge dick, he's a great screw, he's connected up the wazoo, and, honey, he's gonna make me a star!" Something always stops me from questioning Michelle's approach, maybe because I am as much of a dreamer as she is, or maybe because, unlike me, she actually tries to make her dreams come true, even if after all this time it still hasn't happened. Maybe I want one of these guys to pull through and rescue her from her life of shameful anonymity. Or maybe it's the overpowering scent of Enjoli working its dark magic on my capillaries.

I stop mulling over the real reason I never object to her formula for success, realizing I'm about to be late getting back upstairs and that the children will surely be mainlining heroin if I don't leave the lunchroom this instant.

But before I can say, "Let's get together this week," she's threading her Pilated ass through the cluster of tables to flirt with the head molester, who, with a fine spray of tortilla chips, is shouting German at the head of the Language Department. I suppress an eye roll and head upstairs.

As I approach my classroom, I don't smell anything funny. Good sign. From the hallway, it looks like the lights are off. Also a good sign. In fact, I hardly hear a peep. Maybe James has stolen them for ransom? I listen at the door and after a couple seconds hear what I can only define as soft, lilting music.

Inside the classroom, with afternoon sunlight just starting to make its appearance on our still-artless walls, all nineteen kids are cozied up on the rug, surrounding James, who is playing his guitar. If the kids weren't transfixed and practically panting with adoration, I would flick the lights.

The kids don't even glance in my direction. I am invisible. I am an intruder. For the previous five years, when I came back from lunch on day one, my assistant was begging for order, flicking the lights so many times that we had to call Buildings and Grounds to replace the bulbs, or ignoring the chaos completely, or, in one case, standing on a chair and holding their lunches hostage until the children "shut the fuck up." (Her words, not mine.) I have corralled, quieted, ruled, and reigned in this room for all these years, practically by myself. My associates have been more hindrance than help. Now for the first time, the crumb-covered Formica-topped tables seem to have turned.

"Hey, you guys, look who's back. Wanna show Maddy what we've been working on?"

"James," I say, "it's your turn to go get something to eat."

But all nineteen heads bob up and down.

James says, "Ah, I'll go right after this song," and gives another wink, this time to the kids. I can't believe how arrogant this guy is, a first-year associate, treating this classroom like it's his own, treating *me* like I am *his* assistant.

My heart starts pounding, but I can't tell if it's from frustration or pure rage. I secretly hope that my supervisor will walk in and witness the children singing Pink Floyd songs about killing teachers and worshiping money, or, worse, maybe James has taught them the latest from Eminem.

"On three, okay? Just like we practiced. A one. A two. A one two three . . .

*"All the leaves are brown/all the leaves are brown . . ."*

I almost well up despite myself. The children are singing harmonies with heart and soul, as if they'd lived in the sixties themselves. Toothless Zachary takes a solo, and I could swear Papa John never did better.

And then the little six-year-olds start to clap and sway in time, like miniature authentic flower children. I can barely believe what I am seeing. Since the door is open, the next thing I know is that Arthur himself is standing there, twitching his prosthetic hand to the beat. Did I mention that the head molester lost his left hand in a childhood farming accident? It's apparently one of his greatest bedroom assets. *Shiver.*

"A stellar job you've done, Braverman," he says to me in his Louisiana drawl, smoothing the back of his thick yellow hair. "Maybe you'll get more than you hoped for this year, eh?" he adds with a deep conspiratorial nod. My face ignites. The head molester is notorious for encouraging romance among his finely hewn flock. But the last thing a head and assistant teacher want to do is team up between the sheets. It's a hell of a lot harder to avoid eye contact the next day, when you share a classroom for six hours. Believe me. It's been attempted.

When Arthur leaves, James and the children fade out, and then James says, "We thought a song about California would go great with your gold rush curriculum."

"Wow," I say. It's all I can think of. I swallow, stand there. When James leaves to get his lunch, I realize that I am marinating in my own jealous juices. Thankfully, the kids seem fine with me when I tell them they can draw quietly at their tables, and suddenly I feel like I'm being silly. James was only doing what he knew best. Whether by instinct or instruction, he obviously knows that the best way to control a classroom is to engage the students. But does he have to be so good at it? What if I don't have what it takes to compete with James's guitar? I don't play a musical instrument. I can't hold a tune in the shower.

While the kids draw and whisper to one another, I get ready for math, and congratulate myself for not thinking about Nick Seabolt. Which reminds me of Nick Seabolt. His smile, his handshake, his toes . . .

"James is so good at guitar."

"Yeah."

"He can sing, too."

"Do you think he'll teach us a song every day?"

"That'd be cool!"

"Yeah!"

I collate photocopies of rudimentary addition exercises and grab a basket of counting bears. I'm wondering what is worse: losing control of my class to my first-year assistant, losing my job for stalking a student's parent, or losing my mind obsessing about the first two possibilities. The kids are just being kids. They like me as much as they like James. And I am just a normal red-blooded American woman. Everything is fine.

When James comes back, the kids jump up from their tables and swarm around him with their drawings.

"James! This is for you!" says Zachary, holding out an imaginative picture of a pink cat playing a purple guitar and singing.

"Here, James!" says Raffey, waving a picture of two guitars, with a third one scribbled out. Some of the quieter kids stare blankly, patiently holding their offerings in their marker-smeared fingers until James graciously collects them. Drawings of guitars, robots, stars, and bunnies dance in front of my new assistant like autograph requests from crazed Oprah fans. He takes it in stride, as if he expects such treatment. The nerve.

I walk over to the light switch, aware that I am accepting the official role of bad guy. Flick, flick. "Okay, kids, give James a chance to breathe. When he collects all your generous gifts, I want to see a perfect *U* on the rug." I give James a look, as if to say, Help me out here, wouldja, buddy?

"Wow, thanks, guys! These are great," he says, and shrugs at me. No wink this time, thank God. He walks over to the rug like the Pied Piper, all the little muskrats and weasels following in his patchouli-scented wake, and instructs them to sit down in an orderly fashion, which, despite their unbridled energy, they do. I have never seen anything like it. I may as well pack up and go back to my cramped floor-through, skulk into my bedroom, and crawl under the covers with a pint of Chubby Hubby and a spoon—a big spoon.

The tiniest girl in the class, Nina, walks over to me with a drawing. On the piece of white paper is a dime-size flower and, surrounding it, a ring of hearts. She doesn't say anything. Just holds it out and looks at me. My heart melts on the spot. It's as if she can see right into my lonely soul.

"Nina, thank you! It's beautiful! Would you sign it for me?" Nina takes the drawing back to her seat and struggles to sign her name in the corner, a series of veering lines in alternating blue and purple. It takes about a minute and fills most of the page.

She hands it to me again. "Nina, it's beautiful," I say again, and hang it on the wall, the first piece of art to go up in our classroom.

\* \* \*

After the students demonstrate their knowledge of numbers, it's time to head to the roof for recess. I "U up" the class and explain the concept of "safety" and "partners." It's a big roof, even if it is netted and fenced and reinforced like a maximum-security prison.

I decide that on this first school day, I will decide who pairs with whom. Lola and Nina are the first pair I choose. They will walk in the front of the line with me. James will be the "caboose," with comatose Nico and prim Kylie. That should keep him out of my hair for a few minutes.

Since it's still warm, there are no coats to deal with, which will give us an added few minutes of outside time, an extra few minutes to zone out. I pack a column of Keebler graham crackers into my bag for snack time.

Within a minute of being outside, before the line has broken up, the class is singing again. It starts in the back of the line and works its way forward to Lola and Nina and me like summer BO on the F train. As long as they don't start screaming the lyrics, I will be okay. I am not a witch, after all. I am a supportive and patient teacher, a warm and bighearted woman. I smile at the cashmere-cozy brownstones across the street, and then at the dazzling sun-drenched cityscape, first north, and then south to the bittersweet but still breathtaking view of lower Manhattan and Brooklyn beyond, where I will finally escape to at the end of the school day.

I join in on the chorus of "California Dreamin'" and swing my partners' hands.

Once I park myself on one of the wooden benches that border the rooftop playground, I unwrap the graham crackers and distribute them, two entire rectangles per customer. Raffey eats both at once. Nina shares most of her allotment with an imaginary dog. It's a good thing pigeons can't get in here, or else she'd be surrounded by flying rats. The girl is a giver. Lola breaks hers apart on the perforations, exactly the way I would if I ate carbs. I offer one to James, who gladly accepts.

"Aren't you going to have one?" he asks.

I shake my head. "Too much sugar," I say, as if I hate the stuff.
"Don't tell me you're on a diet."

"What?" I look at James, who seems exasperated with me.

"You look great," he says, gesturing at my body.

I start to grin despite myself. I look great? Really? I want to ask
him *how* I look great. What part of my body looks particularly
great? Or is it more of a vague, generalized great?

James continues: "I mean, how much more weight could you
lose? I'm telling you, the media is evil. I don't know what it is with
women these days. Don't tell me you think anorexic is beautiful,
Maddy."

"I'm not trying to look like Calista Flockhart, if that's what you
mean. But maybe I want to look . . . Oh, I don't know. And anyway, it's not a diet. It's Bönz." I still want to know how I look
great.

"Bones? What, do they make you gnaw on rawhide all day?"

I ponder this idea and wonder if there are women out there
who would do this, and if I am one of them.

"That's so funny. But no, it's named after a very prestigious
nutritionist. Josef Bönz. From the Swiss Alps. Who spent years
perfecting his plan."

"So what do they make you eat?"

If he knew I was never allowed to eat any starch other than a
grape-size boiled potato ever again, he'd probably fall off the
bench laughing. Avoiding the question, I say, "Jennifer Aniston
did the diet for like a year, and look at her. She looks great."

"I like Jennifer Aniston. She's . . ."

"Hot?"

"Hot. Yeah." James nods his head with enthusiasm, like he's
already in bed with her, the lech. Who knew that all it took to distract a guy was the mention of everyone's favorite Friend?

"You need a napkin?" I ask.

"What for?"

"To wipe the drool off your chin."

"Nah." He grins, mimes scooping drool from his chin, and
points the graham crackers at me again. "Sure you don't want just

a tiny bit?" He waggles the package in front of my face like a loaded gun.

I turn my head away. "No thank you," I say with dignity.

"Okay," he says in a singsong voice, as if I don't know what I'm missing, and then he begins moaning with pleasure as he munches away. I roll my eyes at his immaturity.

At the doorway, Rachel Tepper's third-grade class is arriving. Rachel Tepper is somewhat of a City Select celeb herself. Her younger sister Felicia is the latest indie queen since Parker Posey stole the crown from Eric Stoltz.

Every once in awhile, Rachel shows up in the pages of *Celeb File* or at a premiere party, charity event, or restaurant opening, her arms thrown around her sister's neck, smiling like a lunatic, wearing way too much makeup and a low-cut designer dress. Everybody knows that Felicia Tepper completely outfits her big sister, from her Jimmy Choo heels to her Gucci tote bags, from her La Perla panties to her Burberry trench coats. Somehow, the fact that I pay for my own secondhand shoes doesn't make me feel any nobler.

Rachel's assistant hands out pretzel rods to their class while Rachel heads toward James and me, sporting a sassy new razored haircut and showing off her tiny figure in low-slung Habitual jeans and a buttery soft leather jacket. I suppress a green-eyed growl.

Zachary is conducting Lola, Eden, and Stella through a rousing rendition of "Oops! . . . I Did It Again." They are all frighteningly good at mimicking Britney Spears, whom I secretly adore. I try not to bob my head to the beat, since to CSA faculty, Britney Spears represents everything that's wrong with American culture today.

"So, that must have been awful this morning," I say to James, hoping to change the subject to something a little more civil.

"What was awful?" asks Rachel, squeezing into the six inches between us on the bench and turning to face James, leaving me a view of her leather-jacketed back.

"I'm Rachel Tepper," she says.

"James Watkins."

I assume that they shake hands.

"So what was awful?" she says.

"James got mugged this morning," I say, making a concerted effort to be a part of this conversation.

"Oh my God, how terrible. Are you okay?" Rachel asks, show-ing more concern in these five seconds than I have in an entire school day. Her timing is impeccable.

"Yeah, I'm okay. Thanks," he says.

Rachel leans forward and shouts to Zachary, "Hey, don't you know anything by Joni Mitchell?" Then she shoots me a look and asks, "Maddy, what are you teaching them?" James looks at me, his eyebrows knotted into a question mark, and I answer him with a gesture that says, I have nothing to do with this.

"Wow. So, like, what *happened*?" Rachel asks, returning her full attention to James.

"He was crossing the park and a couple guys jumped him," I say with more hostility than I would like to betray.

"You must have been so scared," says Rachel.

I can only imagine the look on her face, since all I can see is the back of her head.

"Uh, yeah . . . it was pretty shitty," he says. It's a good thing the kids are twenty yards away and screaming their heads off, or else they might arrest James for using the *S* curse again.

"What was it like? I mean, I would have just frozen," she says.

"Well, yeah—"

"Did they hurt you, James?" she interrupts, and I take this opportunity to roll my eyes so hard that my head flies backward.

"They took thirty-seven dollars," I say.

James says, "Yeah, it really wasn't—"

"You're so brave," says Rachel. "I can't believe you came to work after such a traumatic experience. I wouldn't have."

As I press my fingers into my eye sockets, I believe I have heard everything now.

James says, "Uh, thanks, but really—"

"Were there no police anywhere, James?"

"We have to go now," I say, putting an end to this charade. I stand up to emphasize my point. Then I shout, "Maddy and James's class, time to line up!"

"Well, bye," James says to Rachel. "Nice meeting you."

"Bye, James. It was really nice to meet you," she says, and smiles like they're in on something together.

# Chapter Three

——

*I* stifle a yawn while we sit on a stone bench in the courtyard with the last couple of kids, waiting for their parents to pick them up. I crack my knuckles.

Lola was picked up by her driver. I've never met an actual employed limo driver before. I'm used to dealing in cryptic wordplay with foreign baby-sitters and older siblings. This is the first time I've ever dealt with a Frank Caruso from Queens. It's refreshing.

Raffey's baby-sitter approaches us. "Bye, Raffey—oh, wait, did you shake my hand?" The rule is that the kids aren't officially dismissed until they shake one of our hands. Raffey bounces over and pumps my hand twice, then sprints off, leaving her sitter in frenzied pursuit. I catch James's eye and we share a grin over the fact that we're not the ones doing the chasing.

"So what kind of music do you play?" I ask him. Now that Rachel's not around, maybe I can gain some sort of civility with this guy.

"Americana, mostly. A little bluegrass. And some Hank Williams covers."

"Americana? Is that country?"

"Yeah, but not like Garth Brooks or Dwight Yoakam. More like Lyle Lovett or k.d. lang."

"I love that song about the cheeseburger," I say.

"Jimmy Buffet?"

"No, Lyle Lovett."

"Yeah, it's a good one," James says, and smiles. "Hey, since you know so much about Americana, you should come check us out sometime." He reaches into his back pocket, pulls out a slightly curved postcard, and hands it to me. I guess this makes me a collector of ass-shaped paper.

"Thanks." The postcard is flimsy, printed on Kinko's quality neon orange card stock, and has a photocopy of a cowboy boot on the front. On the back is the name of James's band, Spur. They're playing in October at a place on the West Side called Finally Fred's. "I'll try to come," I say, folding the card.

"So how'd you get into teaching?" I ask.

"I heard this was a good gig for struggling artists. I tried bartending but hated the hours, and the smoke. But this is a great gig."

I nod in agreement. There are tons of aspiring actors, writers, painters, and musicians here. It beats waiting tables, you can wear what you want, and you get health coverage.

As Max and his mom walk to their sage green Ford Expedition, I realize that James is completely penniless. "Look," I say. "If you need to borrow any money, like for the subway or dinner—"

"I wasn't mugged," he says slowly.

I stare at him. "You *what?*"

"I'm sorry. I lied. I was not mugged. There were no thugs. I have enough money to get home. But thanks for asking. I appreciate it."

"You *lied?* To me? To the kids? On the first day?" This is too much. "What are you, a drug lord?"

"Drug lord . . . Maybe that'll be my next career. . . ." James pretends to ponder his potential for a life of crime.

"Well?" I ask, getting impatient. "Can you not joke?"

"I'm sorry, no. You're right. The truth is that I was running so late, on the first *day.* You know how it is."

"I do not know 'how it is,'" I say, holding up two very angry sets of bunny quotes. "In case you didn't notice, I was at school since eight-freaking-thirty. Oh, but that's right. You wouldn't have known. You didn't walk in until—when was it, nine-thirty?"

"Jeez, it's not like I'm taking your money. I'm coming clean here. I thought you'd have a little empathy."

"Oh, I'm supposed to reward you now?"

"No, I mean—"

"James, how old are you?"

"What does that have to do with anything?"

"Twenty-three? Twenty-four?"

"Twenty-five. But why—"

"Because that's exactly the twisted, immature logic a cocky twentysomething would use." I shake my head in disbelief. Arthur really screwed up this time. "You know I could tell the headmaster about this. He'd probably fire you." I am talking out of my ass. In the five years I've been here, not even my foulmouthed assistant was fired. They just switched her into the library and gave me a floater. I have no idea if James would be fired for this, and I'm not sure I want to find out. Arthur'd probably call me a party pooper and treat James to the finest Cubans at an uptown cigar bar. And the kids would never forgive me. I could cry from the injustice.

"Look," James says. "Would it make you feel any better if I told you I had a really late gig last night and I didn't get home until five and I was locked out of my apartment and had to sleep in the hallway?"

"Is it the truth?"

"Yes. It's the total, honest truth, cross my heart and hope to die."

"Do people still say that?"

"I just did."

"That is so irresponsible! It is so . . . so . . . *undergrad*. Meanwhile, how do I know you're not lying about this, too?"

"Smell," he says, and holds out a fringed jacket sleeve. It reeks of smoke and dive bar.

"Don't you have a roommate to let you in? Or a girlfriend?" Why did I add that last bit? What am I, snooping?

"No, I have a mouse hole of a studio in Brooklyn. And that's the other thing. The subway takes forever to get here."

"Is this where I'm supposed to be sympathetic?"

"No, you're right. You are totally right and I am totally wrong. Look, Mad, I'm *really* sorry."

I don't know why, but when he said my name like that, my thighs tingled, the way they used to when I worshiped Scott Baio. I rub my legs.

"So, how are you going to get into your building tonight?" I ask.

"I got a buddy who works at a bar in Chelsea. He's got an extra set."

"That's lucky," I say.

"Yeah, he feeds my cat when I tour."

A pathologically lying Americana musician with a cat? This guy is an enigma.

"Wait a minute," I say, alarm bells ringing. "You're not planning on going on any tours while you're working, are you?"

"Nah. It's slow right now anyway. I might do a week in France over Christmas, but I won't let my music get in the way of work again, I promise. Anyway, I love the kids."

I groan despite myself. This feels like an arranged marriage of the worst kind.

"Maddy," he says, "look me in the eyes." I turn my head and look at him, his twenty-five-year-old greenish eyes, his twenty-five-year-old stubble-covered cheeks, his twenty-five-year-old scraggly brown hair. I do not like what I am seeing. It is all way too young and reckless. His twenty-five-year-old mouth starts to move and he says slowly, "I am not going to let this happen again. Tomorrow morning, you will see this face at eight-thirty, and every morning after that. I came clean because I can tell you're a really cool person, that deep down you know where I'm coming from, and lying is a crap-assed way to begin the year, for all of us, so . . ."

James's mouth makes one more move, this time into an annoyingly endearing smile. I look away and exhale. "Maybe you can start wearing your keys around your neck?" I suggest.

James laughs.

"I'm serious," I say.

"I can tell," he says.

When I get off the N train in Brooklyn, I stop at the health-food store and buy a packet of spicy wasabi peas. I need to decompress. The walk home to my apartment takes ten minutes. Usually, I take Court Street, past McDonalds, Blockbuster, multiple Starbucks, and the brand-new, hugely protested multiplex/Barnes & Noble, where you can also purchase a Starbucks beverage in case you missed it the first three times.

Beyond the evil corporate chains are smaller, quirkier stores and bakeries, which have stood in Cobble Hill and Carroll Gardens since I don't know when. These struggling businesses represent the Brooklyn I moved to six years ago, and I hope they stick it out, even though I indulge in more than the occasional grande skim, half-caff, no-whip mocha.

My roommate, Kate, is still at work in midtown, where she works as a charity fund-raiser. We met at Ithaca, in a class called Insanity in the Arts, and have been roommates ever since.

There are two messages on the voice mail. One from Casey, Kate's boyfriend, and one from my stepmom, calling to remind me to call my dad and wish him a happy birthday, something she does every September, so that my dad doesn't have a temper tantrum. I call right away and, mercifully, get their machine. After singing the birthday song, I pad into my room, taking advantage of this window of time alone. I hurl myself into bed for some serious fantasizing, conjuring up the image of Nick Seabolt's toes, and thank God that a school like City Select can help me support my celeb habit.

"Maddy!" shouts Kate, and I open my eyes. It's 8:30 and not totally dark out yet. I have been dead asleep.

"Oh, I'm sorry! I didn't know you were asleep!" she says, and backs out of my bedroom.

"It's okay," I say into the pillow, but I don't move.

"Wow, was it that bad today?"

"I can't believe I'm still there," I say, forcing myself to sit up. While I rub my eyes, the buzzer sounds. Kate shrugs and smiles an apology.

"Is it okay that Casey's here?" she asks, hopeful.

"Yeah, sure," I say, lying.

Casey is Kate's latest Mr. Right, the shining example of what a boyfriend should be. Casey is the one who shows up on time, the one who compliments her looks, who calls her at work just to hear her voice. Casey has a respectable job as a writer and editor at *Brooklyn's Own* magazine. And although I am thrilled for her, I'd be lying if I said I wasn't jealous and a tiny bit resentful at the same time. Since she's the type who always has a boyfriend, our relationship is never as intimate as I'd like it to be. Still, after ten years, she's like family. She's seen my moods and doesn't run away screaming, and I will always be grateful for that.

She says, "Thanks, Mad. I really wanna hear about your day, though. Maybe tomorrow night we can have girls' night in? Just us two?"

"Okay, yeah," I say, and swallow, looking away from her. Usually, I find myself wishing I were more like Kate McGurran, the sensible girl who stopped buying trendy clothes in 1992 and started her career straight out of college. The only magazines she subscribes to are *Newsweek* and *Brooklyn's Own*. She doesn't wear makeup, diet, or highlight her hair, but somehow she still looks great next to a high-maintenance primper like Rachel Tepper. The only things Kate stresses about are stretching the dollar and doing event-planning for her job, unlike me, who nearly has a coronary if the Brita filter is overdue for a change.

I hear Kate greet Casey at the door. They're already kissing and giggling, so I duck out of my bedroom to grab the cordless before it becomes totally uncomfortable.

"Hey, Maddy, how was your first day?" Casey asks, removing his lips from Kate's, conscientious as ever. Kate tousles his hair, a halo of sand-colored ringlets.

"My new assistant's a total asshole," I say, trying to sound flippant and casual, and speed it up to my room. I am having one of those moments where as soon as I speak, I will start to cry uncontrollably.

"Why, what happened?" he asks.

"Oh, I don't know. It just—" Why am I starting to cry? Oy vey. Kate and Casey both stretch their lovey-dovey heads at me and lift their eyebrows so high, it looks like they might fly off their foreheads. Before I know it, I'm sitting between them on the sofa in the living room, cradling a roll of toilet paper and spilling my guts—about the Nick and Shel anxiety, about James, about being back at CSA, when I swore to myself last June that I'd quit, about being single and thirty. It doesn't take much for my problems to assume global proportions.

"It'll be okay, Mad," says Kate, optimism shining. "You'll figure it out."

"I hope so," I whimper.

"You totally will," she says. "I know you."

I think about the fact that I've barely come close to having a real boyfriend, that most of the romance I've experienced in my life has been inside my head, or for one drunken night only, that my fantasy boyfriends are all movie stars. The closest I ever came to having a real boyfriend was in college, when I had a semester-long fling with a film grad. His name was Harrison. He was twenty-five; I was twenty. Since I was majoring in creative writing, I helped him write his screenplay, and he was the subject of most of my poetry, when I wasn't writing about drunken one-night stands and smoky pool halls. But then, just as things were getting serious, just as I was starting to orgasm consistently, he told me about his fiancée. I found out through mutual friends that he rewrote some of my poems and gave them to her. I think he even quoted some of them at their wedding.

Instead of seeking revenge, like a person with a spine, or even going on a serious booze bender, I burrowed even deeper into my own head and dreamed up affairs with everyone from Johnny

Depp to Tommy Lee Jones. In my fantasies, Harrison was always there, too, pathetically crying on the sidelines, his mangled heart rotting in his hands. I cracked a smile over that every once in awhile, but it never made the pain disappear.

"Do you want me to order a pizza?" asks Casey. "My treat."

"Okay," I squeak, and blow my nose.

We stay up until 1:00 A.M., munching pizza and watching Letterman, even though Kate hates talk shows, especially when the guest is Julia Roberts, who is laughing like a mental patient tonight, swearing up and down that she's really in love this time, and plugging her latest role as a haughty criminal in a "risky" indie, produced by her dear friend George Clooney. But I'm having a crisis, so Kate's being generous.

"You know, Maddy, my company's planning celebrity events now."

"Really?" I say, perking up.

"I knew you'd like that," she says, rolling her eyes.

"What—I mean, how did you get involved—"

"What can I say? Charities are cutting edge for celebrities nowadays. Everybody's got one. I'm planning a Halloween party for Dylan Hover's extreme sports injuries charity. Do you want to come?"

"Oh my God. Yes!" I say, and finally feel like there's something to look forward to before Thanksgiving break. Dylan Hover's a little young for me, more *American Pie* than *Chocolat*, but beggars can't be choosers, and there's sure to be other, older celebs there.

When I finally fall asleep at 2:00 A.M. I feel comforted by the fact that I am finally connected to the celebrity universe by a thread that has nothing to do with City Select Academy.

At 8:30 the next morning, I am too tired to stifle my yawns, although relieved to see James's face, just like he promised.

"Hey," he says, bright-eyed and bushy-tailed. "See?" He gestures down at his body, still rumpled, but definitely cleaner than it was yesterday.

"Somebody gets a gold star," I say as I take the chairs down from the tables. James takes this as the cue it is intended to be and assists me. Things are looking up.

During reading group, the classroom phone rings.

"Maddy, I have to tell you about Jacob Neshkowitz," Michelle says when I answer.

"Michelle, I'm in the middle of reading," I say, even though I am more curious about Michelle's latest conquest than I am about sounding out three-letter words.

"Just tell me you're free tonight?" she begs.

"Uh, yeah, I'm free," I say. I am pretty much always free.

"Thai Pad at six?" she says.

"Yeah, cool," I say, and get back to my group.

After school, I stop in at Barnes & Noble. At the Starbucks counter, armed with a stack of magazines, I buy a tall skim decaf cappuccino, then snag a much-coveted table by the window. Before I meet Michelle, I want to get a head start on my costume ideas for Dylan Hover's charity bash. As I skim through the pages of *Vogue* and *Harper's Bazaar,* I grieve for the millions I lack. I grieve for the hips I do have and wish there was a way to trade cellulite for dollars, the way Ren and Stimpy bartered hair balls for gold.

While I'm lamenting the latest trend in pointy death-defying stilettos and asymmetrical bias-cut silk minidresses, a flash of suede fringe passes before my eyes. I look up in time, to see James and Rachel walking down Court Street, gabbing away like the best of friends. What is she doing in Brooklyn? What could she possibly have so much to talk about with a twenty-five-year-old musician? I could have sworn that British novelists with trust funds and graduate degrees in medieval history were much more her type. At least she's not making a beeline for a guy I actually like, I think as I turn yet another glossy Michael Kors-scented page.

*     *     *

I arrive at Thai Pad on Smith Street at 6:05. Michelle isn't here yet, so I take a seat at the bar and order a Pinot Grigio from the T-shirted bartender, who's far more interested in her conversation with the hostess than she is with me. I take a look at the latest group of oversize, overly bright paintings to grace the concrete walls of this trendy restaurant, and try to look comfortable teetering on my cube-shaped steel bar stool. Thank God I bought a magazine, so I don't have to stare into space while I wait for Michelle. Just when I'm starting to relish the article about Botox injections gone horribly wrong, she arrives.

"Maddy!" she squeals, and kisses my cheek.

"Hi, honey!" I say, and close the magazine. Michelle's fuchsia satin jacket puts the gigantic paintings to shame.

"Did you read the Sandra Bullock article?" Michelle asks, pointing at my *Celeb File Weekly*. Michelle and I have a special fondness for all things Sandra. We are big *Miss Congeniality* fans. Sandra Bullock's snorting laugh liberates us.

"Not yet. I'm saving it for later," I admit, but Michelle doesn't hear; she's already air-kissing the hostess, and before I know it, we're seated at a cozy table for two by the sliding doors that lead to the patio in the backyard.

"So tell me," I say, getting right down to business.

"Oh my *God*, Maddy, Jacob Neshkowitz. Does it get any better than that?"

"I guess not," I say, not quite following. I break my chopsticks apart and scrape them together to remove the splinters.

"My father will be so proud of me. A real Jew. With a real job."

"So everything's going great?"

"Maddy, you have to see this guy. He is huge—everywhere. Last night, he said he could not wait until he sees me nail the audition. And then he nailed me." She leans back and smiles with satisfaction. Then she says, "He told me that I am 'ripe with fuckability.' Isn't that sweet?"

"That's great!" I say, cheering her on. I really hope it works out for her, though I can't ignore the panic button this news pushes. I have this fear that I will be the last single woman left standing in Brooklyn. When Michelle finally settles down with someone, who will I spend girls' night with?

"Oh no, Michelle, I totally forgot. Kate and I were supposed to do something together tonight. Can I use your cell for a second?" I have decided to wait until the last-possible second before I surrender to the cell phone phenomenon. Although I appreciate the look of importance a cell phone gives a person, I can't deny the reality that I don't actually need to be reached very urgently, ever. Michelle hands me her leopard-print Nokia with the Hello Kitty spangles and I dial Kate at work. Turns out she already made plans, too. She's getting together with Casey for dinner and a movie. I hang up, feeling abandoned by my roommate, even though I bailed on her first.

"Hey, at least you usually have someone to go home to," says Michelle, reading my mind. "What do I have? A dead plant? A surly cat who hates my guts? Maybe when Casey moves in, you can come live with me?"

"Uh, maybe," I say, and change the subject. Michelle might be a lot of things, but roommate material is not one of them. I've seen Michelle's apartment, and let's just say that crusty silverware and broken window shades are not my idea of home. Not that I'm an anal-retentive freak, but, well, compared to Michelle Zucker, maybe I am. Clean, aesthetically pleasing surroundings make me feel like I have the tiniest bit of control over my life. A vase of fresh flowers on a clean countertop comforts me, sometimes profoundly.

I tell Michelle about Rachel and James walking together in the neighborhood after school. Michelle has hated Rachel with a passion ever since Rachel spent an entire year flirting with Michelle's yearlong fling, the only muscle-bound poetry teacher anyone had ever known. If ever there was a time to take advantage of Michelle's ire, it is now.

"Ugh, please, any guy who falls for that brownnosing bitch has ass for brains," Michelle says, spearing a slice of spring roll with a single chopstick. "Meanwhile, she's interested in a child with a guitar? Could anything be worse than that?"

I nod my head, egging Michelle on. There's nothing like a little Rachel bashing to lift my sagging spirits.

"It's not that I even like James," I say. "It's just that she's so obvious about being such a bitch."

"The next time she turns her back on you like that, you should tape a sign to her jacket that says 'Kick me. I'm a cunt.'"

"Arthur'd love that!"

"Arthur's already had Rachel."

"Really?" I say, my eyes widening. "Why don't I know this already?"

"He told me one night in his Nietzsche Nook," she says casually.

"He never told me about it in his Nietzsche Nook," I say, somewhat resentful. Arthur has an enclosed widow's walk at the top of his brownstone, custom-built. He has every syllable ever written by or about Nietzsche in there, so everyone calls it his Nietzsche Nook, even Arthur.

"Maddy, is there something you'd like to tell me?" Michelle asks, cocking an expertly waxed eyebrow, swirling her rosé.

I sigh and tuck a stray hair behind my ear. "Arthur invited me over last year," I admit sheepishly.

"Maddy! Why didn't you tell me?"

"Because nothing happened. I chickened out." I don't know which is worse: having sex with the head molester or passing up the opportunity.

Michelle gives me a pitiful look and pats my hand. "You are stronger than you know, sweetie. Believe me. Arty Smarty might be a great party, but the hangovers are the worst."

"Huh?"

"You see the way I practically fall over myself for his attention. Once he's had you, he forgets you exist. And you know me. If I'm not the center of attention, it's a nightmare!"

"Wow, I didn't know he did that."

"Yeah, he's an expert at making you feel like a whore. So see? You're lucky. You escaped having sex with an elderly one-armed misogynist." We toast to that. Then Michelle lowers her voice and says, "And Maddy, honestly, if I could take back that night, I would. It's not worth it. Now *that's* a secret. But if I ever told, I'd probably have to find another job."

"Wow," I say again. From what I'd heard over the years, not counting his stump, Arthur is supposed to be some kind of tantric guru, a cunnilingus aficionado. The joke around school is that he even knows the perfect accompanying wine. "But then how come he doesn't ignore Rachel? Is she, like, gifted?"

"*Gifted?* Ha! It's because she's a leech. Every time I see her, she's practically spelunking up his—holy shit, Maddy. Speak of the fucking devil," Michelle says, and I snap out of my reverie. I know what she's seeing before I see it myself.

"Is she heading this way?" I ask, staring straight at her. Michelle prompts me like a good friend should.

"Nine o'clock. You can look . . . now."

I turn my head just in time to see James push Rachel's chair in for her. They're both beaming, chatting it up like best friends, or like . . . lovers. As I slump into the booth, I count this as yet one more reason not to trust James. I am suddenly exhausted and starving all at once. I stuff a huge bite of veggie pad Thai into my mouth.

"Well, he's not exactly my type, but . . ." Michelle licks her lips à la Kim Catrall, but when I shoot her a dirty look, she resumes trying to make me feel better. "Ugh, don't worry for a second about her, Maddy. She can't do anything to you. And if he likes her and is in any way influenced by her, all you need to do is think of June. It's not a life sentence, you know." I nod sadly and then force myself to look only at Michelle for the rest of our meal. When we leave, Rachel and James are so engrossed in their conversation that they don't even see Michelle's fuchsia jacket when we pass by. I am forced to conclude that it must be one hell of a date.

*     *     *

It starts to drizzle on my walk home, which complements my lonely mood perfectly. It occurs to me as I watch the pattern of falling water in the glow of the streetlights that I never got to tell Michelle about Nick and Shelby Seabolt. We were too busy *not* watching Rachel Tepper work her dark magic on my not-so-innocent assistant.

At home, Kate's bedroom door is closed and I can smell her gardenia-scented votives. The line of light under her door flickers, and every now and then a giggle escapes, making its way to my damp and lonely ears. As I curl up with the Sandra Bullock article, I wonder if James and Rachel are still together, but by the time I'm done with the horoscopes, I'm lost in my fantasies, imagining Nick Seabolt spooning me, nuzzling my neck, telling me that I'm the most beautiful woman he's ever laid eyes on, while he presses his sizable erection into the small of my back to prove it.

I put the magazine on top of a perilous pile of celebrity rags and pull out a porn DVD, my favorite way to get myself off ever since I read that the cast of *Gal Pals* takes turns hosting porn parties. As I watch a randy, silicone-pumped, bleached, and Brazilian-waxed babe get it on with a well-muscled, neatly shaven, yet sweaty "construction worker," I imagine the duo is Nick and me, that we're holed up in an anonymous motel room somewhere far north, and that we just couldn't bear to be apart.

# Chapter
# Four

—

$L$ook at the clock," I say to James the moment I see him in the morning. It's 9:05 and the kids are enjoying the last few precious moments of free play before I "U" them up for morning meeting. James is more than a half hour late. I could kill him.

"I know, I know, I'm late," James says. "It is unacceptable, and I have no excuse." He winks at me then, a little too cocky for my taste, and I start shaking my head.

"Have you no shame?" I ask as he pulls a loaf of bread from his dirty army bag.

"Here, you gotta try this. Truce bread. It's pumpkin spice." I reach out instinctively to take a piece, but then he yanks it away from me. "Ah, Maddy, is this acceptable food on the Bönz plan?"

I take a step closer and tear off a chunk just to spite him. Chewing, I manage to say, "I haven't even had coffee yet, so don't start with me."

Raffey and Zachary approach us then with puppy-dog eyes and salivating little toothless mouths. "Can we have some?" they ask, hopeful.

"Sorry guys, nice try," I say, and glare at James in case he tries to undermine my authority again.

"You heard Maddy. Now git," he says, and they groan melodramatically, shuffling away, plans foiled.

"Have you been to the farmer's market?" James asks.

"Is that why you're late?"

"Well, Rachel told me about it and—"

"James," I say, interrupting him. "You promised me you'd be on time." I stifle the overwhelming urge to tell James that Rachel's a total bitch, but of course I know he sees a side of her that I will never know, all because he has a dick between his legs.

"You know," he says, cocking his head to the side like he's looking at me in a new light, "you remind me of my mom."

"And you're telling me this because?"

"My mom rocks," he says, nodding his head to a beat only he can hear. This makes me wonder. Does he think of Rachel like a mother, too? She and I are the same age, after all.

"Look, it's time for meeting. Would you mind putting your magic bread away now?" I say, heading for the light switch.

"No problem," James says, grinning, and I can almost swear he's stifling an urge to say "Yes, ma'am."

When James goes to get his lunch, it's my turn to keep the kids quiet for twenty minutes. I don't know if it's my foul mood or if it's the kids, but no matter what I do, they refuse to cooperate. Eden and Stella won't stop singing the same Nelly verse over and over. Or is it Shaggy? Or Scooby-Doo? Lola keeps getting up to switch books. Zach and Raffey are in hysterics over some private joke. If only I were James, I'd whip out my guitar and teach them a song. Instead, when I feel like I've reached the end of my rope, I take another cue from Mr. James Watkins: I lie.

"I guess you've never heard the story of the City Select Phantom," I say, and suddenly, I have their attention.

"Ooh, this place is haunted?" asks Raffey, wide-eyed.

"Well," I say, thinking fast. If I don't keep them engaged, I'll lose them for the rest of quiet time, and the last thing I want is for James to think he's got the edge. "Well, remember the year of the gold rush? If you were paying attention yesterday, I told you, it was eighteen—"

"Eighteen forty-nine!" shouts Tyler.

"Yes. Good job. In 1849, a little baby girl was born in what is now Mendocino, California, the only daughter of a poor miner and his sick wife. . . ."

For the remainder of quiet time, I spin this yarn, a story about a little girl whose mother dies in childbirth and whose father raises her with the help of his miner friends. The kids listen, enthralled. They know that at some point I'll get to the part that has to do with CSA being haunted, but I don't quite know how that's going to happen. But as long as I keep talking, the story keeps coming. And that's the other thing; I'm having as much fun telling this story as the kids are listening to it. It's wild, like maybe we can all feel a little magic working its way into the classroom.

When James comes back, I'm nowhere near the part where Amanda makes her way to New York. "Well, I guess it's time to stop," I say, and all nineteen kids sigh with disappointment.

"Will you please finish the story, Maddy?" begs Lola, and I can hardly resist this little raggedy beauty, but I force myself to stop.

"I will later. Or tomorrow. But I will. I promise."

The kids seem satisfied with that, and they go about the business of getting ready for gym.

"What were you guys doing?" asks James once the kids have gone. We're preparing for an art project—the kids are going to make their own mining pans.

"Oh, I was just telling them this story," I say, but I am so pleased with myself, I tell James that I made up a story about the school being haunted.

"You lied to the kids?" he says, and gives me an exaggerated look of disapproval.

"I learned from you," I say, smiling, and hand him a batch of cardboard to cut.

Before I know it, October has arrived. As we work on the gold rush curriculum, adding paintings, new vocabulary words, and more of James's songs to the repertoire, the room starts to feel like a cozy home away from home. Everybody seems to have forgotten that Lola is Hollywood royalty, and she and Zach and Raffey are inseparable.

The class gets into a groove, and going to work actually feels fun again. The kids beg me to continue telling them the story about Amanda Porter, the little orphan girl from 1849, and James even skips lunch a couple of times to listen in, which I admit is flattering, until he starts nagging me to write it down.

"You know what you are?" I ask him when the kids are at gym one day.

"What?"

"A nudge."

James tilts his head, considering this. "That's cool." He shrugs and winks at me. "You should still write it down, Maddy."

The only time things get dicey is when we go to the roof for recess and Rachel fawns over James, ignoring me completely. I handle the situation by paying more attention to the kids, and after awhile, I've formed a bond with every one of them, especially Lola.

"Maddy, look at me!" Lola shouts, from the monkey bars, which she's straddling while raising her arms above her head.

"Way to go!" I shout, and she's so happy that she waves her body back and forth, her tangled hair shimmying behind her. As usual, I'm charmed. I give Lola a lot of credit for not being the stereotypical movie star's kid, with overly coifed tresses and a snooty "My dad can buy you ten times over" attitude. Here, Lola fits right in with the rest of the gang. By the end of lunch, she's got just as many crumbs clinging to her cheeks, her fingers are just as sticky, and she couldn't give a hoot.

I'm watching her daring performance on the monkey bars, and just as she reaches down to disengage herself, two of Rachel's third-grade boys come tearing through the narrow area and collide with Lola, sending her crashing to the ground. The blood-curdling howl that ensues sends me bolting from my seat.

"Okay, Lola, let me look at you," I say, trying to sound calm and doctorlike. Nothing looks out of the ordinary until I see her right wrist. Her fingers are turning an ashy gray color and they are pointing in an unusual angle. The line of her wrist is no longer straight, and I can tell I need to get Lola to the school nurse ASAP.

"It hurts!" Lola wails as Rachel and James come rushing over.

"Wow," James says, and looks like he's going to lose his lunch.

"Maddy, you really should keep a better eye on your kids," says Rachel, who has her arms wrapped around the two reckless maniacs who maimed my student.

"Excuse me?" I say incredulously, then look at James to back me up, but he's doubled over, trying not to hurl.

Rachel walks her two boys over to the benches for what I assume is a time-out, but as I lift Lola into my arms, I see them munching on pretzel rods, looking like they don't have a care in the world.

"James, you're in charge of dismissal!" I shout over my shoulder, and Lola and I are off.

"Sweetie, it is going to be okay," I say. "Try to keep it raised so it doesn't swell up." I cannot imagine what it must be like to have children. So many possibilities for disaster. I feel so sorry for this kid, my heart is actually breaking with worry.

"Maddy, it hurts!" she wails again, and I croon to her. "I know, sweetie, and you are so brave. The nurse is going to fix you up like new." I try not to huff and puff, but six-year-old girls are heavier than I thought they would be.

One look at Lola's broken wrist and Barb, the nurse, immediately reaches for the school phone book. "We gotta get this munchkin to the hospital," she says in a calm voice, though I can tell she thinks this is serious, because she's not as patronizing as she usually is. I tell Barb Lola's last name as she cradles the phone between her shoulder and her ear and begins flipping the pages of the phone book. "Well, well, Seabolt," she says, raising her barely discernible eyebrows. "Sweetheart, are your parents home?"

"I don't know," says Lola. "It really hurts, though."

"Is Mr. or Mrs. Seabolt there? This is the City Select Academy nurse calling. . . . Uh-huh, uh-huh . . ."

Lola and I wait under the fluorescent lights in this tiny office, both of us in agony. Finally, one of her parents must have come to the phone, because the nurse's face lights up and she starts gushing to whichever Seabolt she has on the line, alternately shooting Lola looks of syrupy concern. Barb says something about getting Lola to the hospital STAT. "Okay, great!" says Barb. "We'll see you soon." She hangs up and says, "Sweetie pie, your daddy's on his way." Then she turns to me and whispers, "Nick said he'd rather take Lola to the ER *himself.*"

Barb produces an ice pack and a small pillow. "It's important to keep this elevated," she says, propping the pillow under Lola's arm. Then she rests the ice pack on top, and gently ruffles Lola's hair.

My heart thunders into action despite my worry, because I can't stop thinking about Nick.

After all the sex fantasies I've been indulging in my self-pitying state, I am incredibly nervous about seeing him again. Will he be able to tell what I've been thinking? Hopefully, my concern for his daughter will keep me from going over the edge. In a few moments, out of pain and fear, I presume, Lola closes her eyes and falls asleep. I sneak a whiff of her head and my heart flutters with affection for this wounded little trouper.

When Nick finally arrives almost an hour later, he looks exactly the way a totally concerned and frantic dad would about his ailing daughter, except that he is famous around the world. Although his expression is genuine, it strikes me as strange, because I've seen him exactly like this before—in *Bluebell,* the epic film, where his mistress dies giving birth to their secret love child.

Lola's still asleep, though now she's been moved to a paper-covered examining table. Her wrist is wrapped in ice and propped on her chest like an injured bird.

"I got here as fast as I could. The traffic on Broadway—" he begins, then stops abruptly at the sight of his daughter.

"Lolo," he whispers. He lifts his amazing eyes away from his daughter, looks at me and then at the nurse. "How's her wrist?" he asks both of us.

Barb holds out her hand for an introduction before launching into a speech about getting Lola to the hospital. "If they give you any hassle about waiting, just tell them who you are," she says slyly, and I blink rapidly at this grossly inappropriate flirting.

"Maddy," says Nick. "How did this happen?"

"She was on the monkey bars, and a couple older kids were running and, well, they just collided," I say, clapping my hands loudly as a demonstration. Nick looks more than a little horrified, so I quickly add, "Kids will be kids," but it comes out sounding sheepish and weak. I shrug and force a smile, hoping he doesn't decide to sue me for negligence. Not that he needs my money. Not that I have any money.

Barb cuts in, saying, "Mr. Seabolt, Nick? Lola's not going to be able to use her arm for about six weeks. She'll need someone to help her write, to take her schoolwork home, to—"

"I'd be happy to do that, Mr. Seabolt," I say, interrupting Barb. I'm eager to make him relax and thus calm my anxiety. I don't know how I would face life if I knew I'd already made an enemy of a parent, no matter who he was. "May I call you tonight to work out the details?"

"Uh, yeah, okay," Nick says, still flustered. He brushes his hand over Lola's forehead, looking sadder than I've ever seen him in a movie. His hand makes Lola look even smaller and softer than she already is. "Lo? Sweetie?" He leans over her head and whispers, "Lolo, my brave little angel," and hoists her gently into his arms without waking her. Barb and I both hold our breath, watching this display of affection, our own private Seabolt screening. And, as real and terrible as this situation is, I can't help but crave popcorn.

"Mr. Seabolt, Lola's going to be fine," I say.

Nick looks at his daughter and nods, then heads toward the door. Then he stops and turns to face us. "Thank you. Both of you." Then to me, he says, "I'll talk to you tonight."

I smile at them, thank Barb, and head back to the class-room.

"Is she okay?" James says when I get back. He's standing on a chair, hanging the kids' artwork. I'm surprised to see him here. It's almost four o'clock.

"Her wrist's broken. Mr. Seabolt looked like someone died or something," I say, slouching on the edge of a table. I realize that I'm exhausted, that my jaw is clenched from anxiety, and that my eyelid is going mad. As I rub my cheeks and stretch my mouth, I look around the room. James is hanging the kids' mining pans from pipes that crisscross the ceiling, attaching them on neon strands of yarn.

"James, thanks for doing that. They look great," I say.

"Well, it was the least I could do."

"That's true," I concede.

"See that? We agree on something," he says, and smiles that annoying smile.

"I'm going to start taking Lola her work at home. I have no idea how long she'll be out for," I say, my mind returning to the nurse's office.

"She'll be fine. Kids break bones every day. I broke my leg, my arm, and knocked out a tooth all before I was ten," he says.

"Yeah, but you're not the son of two of the biggest movie stars in the world."

"Yeah, but she's still *human*," he says, reaching toward the ceil-ing to tie a piece of yarn. "You know, like flesh and blood?"

"I guess. I just hope they don't sue me."

"Oh, I'm sure they look at you and just sniff money."

"What is that supposed to mean?"

"Maddy, if they're going to sue anyone, it'll be the school. Maybe Arthur. You'll just lose your job. Not your net worth." I look at him, speechless, and he winks at me.

"Thank you. I feel so much better now," I say sarcastically. I think I will tear his eyelids off if he keeps winking at me like that.

While I sit on the edge of a table, absently fraying yarn scraps, I realize that celebrity does not faze James in the slightest. Whereas Lola is practically surrounded by blinking neon lights when I look at her, she's like any other student to James.

"Hey, why the long face, Maddy? You need some cheering up?"

I look at him mutely, as if to challenge him, and he launches into a tale of childhood hockey games, I guess to commiserate, or to show me that he comes from abject poverty. The thought of James coming from squalor does have a certain cheering effect.

"So the one kid in the neighborhood whose parents actually had money shows up in full goalie regalia," he says, sweeping his hand across his lap, "and here I am with these plaid *sofa* cushions *duct-taped* around my legs."

"That is funny," I admit, smiling.

"Ha, see? I knew I could make you laugh."

The door opens then.

"James, are you still here? Aren't you ready yet?" Rachel says in her nasal drone, completely ignoring my existence, as usual. Now's my chance to let Rachel know how little I appreciated the way she handled the situation during recess. My heart starts pounding in my ears. I'll just take a breath and then launch right into it.

"Yeah, sure," he says brightly. Then he turns to me and says, "Maddy, I gotta go."

For the first time all year, Rachel Tepper looks at me. "Maddy, how's Lola?" she asks, her voice syrupy sweet, eyebrows like twin ski slopes. It's like she won't even give me the chance to hate her completely. She has to go and be nice, just when I get into the groove of despising her, just when I'm about to tell her off once and for all.

"Her wrist is broken. Her dad came to take her to the hospital," I say, defeated.

"Poor thing."

"Yeah, well."

"Hugo and Thor are so sorry," she says. "They just feel terrible." They didn't look too sorry, nibbling pretzel rods, I think.

"Thanks," I say, and pick up another piece of yarn to destroy.

"So, you're okay?" James interjects, standing up.

"Yeah, great!" I chirp, lying.

"All right then, see you tomorrow at eight-thirty," he says, and winks, slinging his fringed suede jacket over his shoulder and disappearing with Rachel.

# Chapter
# Five

—

*I* plant myself in the center of our olive green sofa from Jennifer Convertibles and dial the number while my heart trumpets in my ears. "Hello, is Mr. Seabolt there?" I ask. If I had a phone with a cord, I'd be wrapping it around my fingers with nervous energy.

"May I ask who eeth calling pleathe?" a woman says in a Castillian accent, then puts me on hold for so long that my heart slows to a mere tango.

"Seabolt," says the voice, in a clipped tone that sounds hugely important and hugely successful. And hugely fuckable.

"Hi, it's Maddy," I say, hoping I sound like a normal teacher talking to a typical parent of an injured first grader.

"Maddy!" Nick says jovially, and suddenly he does sound suspiciously typical, like a regular guy who's happy to hear from me. He tells me that the doctors took good care of his little girl, that Lola's bravery impressed everyone around, and that she should be good as new in a couple of months. "So why don't you come by tomorrow with whatever work you have? Unless you have something for tonight? I know Lola would love to see you."

"Well, I don't have much for tonight, but I would love to see her, poor thing." He certainly doesn't need to twist my arm, no pun intended. I am more than curious to see how the other half lives, and I promise I am concerned, truly concerned, about Lola, as well.

"Ah, she's fine now. Thrilled with her cast. You have to sign it. Why don't you come on by tonight? Have you eaten? We could feed you while you're here."

"Okay," I say, feeling more excited than I should. Nick is a married man, after all, with a daughter and a busy career.

"Where do you live?" I ask.

"Where do *you* live?" he counters. "I'll send Frank to pick you up."

Now all I'm missing are the glass slippers, I think. "That sounds great."

Hanging up, I can't help but wonder if he realizes just how unusual this all is. Me, plain old Maddy Braverman from Cherry Hill, New Jersey, being picked up by Nick Seabolt's personal driver, being taken to Nick Seabolt's very own sure-to-be dazzling home. If ever there was a time to pinch myself, it is now.

All of a sudden, every stitch of clothing I own looks like Salvation Army rejects, which, let's face it, they are. I can only imagine how effortlessly amazing Shelby will look, probably lounging on some obscenely expensive sofa, curled up with a script. No doubt her bras cost more than my best winter coat.

With my body vibrating from nerves, I change into a pair of faded Levi's, a tight black T-shirt, and pointy black ankle boots. The jeans and T-shirt say, I am casual and fun! I may or may not be rich, but you never can tell with Levi's and a T-shirt! And the boots give me what I call "ass-esteem," because they elongate the leg, and right now I could use all the esteem I can lay my shaking hands on. Plus, they were $130, not $39.99, like the usual Nike sneakers I buy at the outlet.

I wish I were more like Kate at times like these, and that I didn't give a shit about looking a certain way for a certain kind of person, but I do give a shit. I give a million shits. Of course, Nick Seabolt probably realizes that he makes my entire salary as soon as he's on the set for a single minute.

Looking in the dinky, cloudy bathroom mirror, I try for the thousandth time to get my hair into a ponytail that I can live with. The first 999 attempts leave me unacceptably lumpy-headed, and

I'm *this close* to throwing my brush at the medicine cabinet. I fling my head down toward the floor to freshen my uncooperative hair and try one more time before I burst into tears from sheer frustration, and miraculously, it works. When the rubber band is fastened, I detect no bulges, stray hairs, or unsightly spaces where my hair parted unattractively, making me look like I need Rogaine. That's the trouble with hair as dark as mine. Any space between my hairs glows blindingly white. My arms are positively spent, as if I've done fifty push-ups. Maybe next time, I'll try to put my hair up using my legs, instead of jogging.

I take one last look at myself in the mirror and feel satisfied. Like Michelle says, I could be Sandra Bullock's sister. Sandra's a little taller and richer, though. And even though she's not known for having big boobs, Miss Congeniality still puts my barely B's to shame. And Kate always tells me that I look great, no matter what I wear, like I imagine my husband will someday. I turn away from the mirror before I find a million flaws with my outfit and have to start all over from scratch.

Finally, after pacing a dent into the living room floor, the buzzer sounds. I grab my three-year-old secondhand leather jacket and scram, nearly breaking my own bones in the process. By the time I reach the first-floor landing, I've started to give myself a little speech about grace, elegance, and nonchalance—three virtues that are never used to describe me.

Idling on the corner is a gleaming black Lincoln Town Car, and standing next to the rear door is Frank Caruso from Queens. As we greet each other, I reach to open the door, but he does it for me. He seals me into the plush leather cocoon, smoked windows protecting me from the oh-so pedestrian masses (yawn!), and we're off.

Once we're on the Brooklyn Bridge, I crack my window and enjoy the view. The wind whipping at my ponytail feels somehow more expensive than the everyday wind I am used to. But after a few seconds, I start to panic about the hair, so I push the lever to close the window again. Thankfully, I can still enjoy the glittering

river and South Street Seaport below me, which look more cine-
matic than usual. Go figure.

I'm expecting SoHo or the Upper East Side, but Frank heads up
the West Side Highway, past SoHo, past the West Village, and
into the Meat Packing District, the most cutting-edge neighborhood in Manhattan. The Meat Packing District is home to clubs
that are so trendy and popular that they change their phone numbers every three days to keep people out. Not that you could even
find them without someone in the know. The slew of French
bistros in this newly elite ZIP code all boast tiles and fixtures
imported from Paris, along with their award-winning chefs.
Unfortunately, I've never sampled the food in any of them. I read
in *Time Out* that a simple onion tartlet appetizer costs twelve dollars at one of these places, so until I am a millionaire, I'm stuck
with Fresco Tortilla. Also, I have to admit, I'm more than a little
intimidated by a restaurant that hosts the party to celebrate
Julianne Moore's *Vanity Fair* cover story.

Along the Hudson River are brand-new apartment buildings
with huge concrete patios and angular modular units cantilevered
on top of one another. We pull up to such a building with trailing
vines spilling over the roof, and Frank gets out to open my door.

The massive industrial lobby, with its immaculate concrete
floor and exposed copper pipes, uniformed doorman, and massive
steel-lined elevator still do not prepare me for the sight of the
Seabolt residence.

The Castillian maid answers the door and tells me to wait
"jutht a moment pleathe," while she scuttles off to get one of the
Seabolts. I am relieved to have even a moment to take it all in
without having to shut my gaping jaw.

*Gigantic* is not the right word for the penthouse. The phrase
"dripping with money" doesn't begin to describe the furniture, let
alone the architectural design of this space. I have perused enough
copies of *Elle Décor* and *The World of Interiors* to know that this is
a seriously designed abode. From where I stand in the foyer, I can
see that the industrial theme from the lobby continues throughout

the apartment in the form of rough patches of concrete and distressed wooden beams. Mostly the wide-planked dark wooden floors are bare, but scattered around are Turkish kilims and zebra skins, as if a giant genie dropped them carelessly on his way home to Arabia. Halogen spotlights twist down from the ceiling on silvery cords and wires, highlighting a collection of abstract oil paintings so big that they wouldn't even fit in my front door. A tan leather sofa and a couple of oversize leather armchairs occupy the area by the floor-to-ceiling glass doors, which seem to lead out to a private terraced patio. In another corner of the loftlike space, a gargantuan stone fireplace is flanked by a tangle of iron tools, sumptuous cushions, and fur remnants. As I pry my jaw from the floor, Nick appears, already enticing me with his bare feet and threadbare T-shirt.

"Maddy," he says, closing his cell phone. "Ride okay?"

"Yeah, it was great!" I say, smiling like a goon. I wish Michelle or Kate were with me now, if only to assure me that I am really here. I could kick myself for fantasizing so recklessly about Nick. I'm sure the guilt must show on my face, but either he is being gracious or he is just plain used to it.

"Good, good. Come in, then. Are you hungry? Do you eat trout?" he asks, leading the way into the apartment.

"I'm not kosher, if that's what you mean. But I don't eat chicken or pork or beef. . . ." I stop myself from babbling like a complete idiot, but Nick's already in the kitchen, rummaging around in the industrial-size stainless-steel refrigerator. I stand by the massive center island and muse over how, despite luxurious surroundings, Nick seems so normal. So . . . human. I decide that there are probably scads of personal assistants, college-age nannies, yoga gurus, nutritionists, and publicists lurking in the apartment, just beyond my field of vision.

"Where's Mrs. Seabolt?" I ask, looking out the arched doorway at the bottom of a stairway whose banister seems to be made of the same copper plumbing pipes I saw crisscrossing the ceiling in the lobby.

"Uh . . . on location," he says, inserting a white container into a silvery microwave. I don't know whether I should press on and ask what kind of film she's working on, or if it would be inappropriate. Maybe there's some rule where people like me aren't supposed to know the inside scoop. Instead, I say, "That must be difficult, being separated like that," to which he responds by shrugging.

"We choose our lives, I suppose," he says philosophically, and I stifle a shudder. It's all well and good that he chose to be a hugely successful movie star, but does that mean I chose to be a poor dreamer who wishes she knew what her true passion is? If I chose to be a famous celebrity, would I magically transform on the spot?

"I guess," I say.

Nick transfers the contents of the container to a plate and sets it in front of me while I perch on a stool. Beside the fist-size portion of muesli-encrusted fish is a teeny boiled potato and two cubes of cheese.

"Is this—"

"A Bönz meal? Yeah," he says almost apologetically.

Now I feel privileged. The Bönz plan has a service, where for something like three hundred dollars a week, they'll deliver to your door perfectly balanced high-protein, low-carb meals, plus snacks. I could order the plan, but then I'd be so broke, I'd have no address for the delivery. Private schools in New York City pay notoriously low salaries to lower-school teachers, and City Select pays the lowest of the low.

"Thank you," I say, as if he's just handed me a tureen of Nobu sushi, which wouldn't be bad, either, not that I've tried it. "Aren't you going to have any?"

"Oh, I ate before." He smiles. "Let me go see if Lolo's awake. Be right back," and he disappears through yet another doorway. As I munch my Bönz treat, I still cannot get over the fact that I am here in Nick and Shelby Seabolt's house. The trout is too salty, the potato tastes like dirt, and the cheese reminds me of Velveeta. No wonder people lose so much weight on this diet. The food sucks.

There's a collection of vintage salt and pepper shakers on a shelf to my right, and they're so cute that I have to get a closer look. One of them is in the form of a lavender poodle with a wobbly tin head. As I pick it up, the head flies off and pepper scatters everywhere. My heart starts pounding at my mishap and I bend down, manically sweeping pepper into a pile with my hands just as a pair of pint-size feet shuffle into the kitchen. I look up with what must be a pained expression, to see Lola's in her pj's: a dad-size heather gray T-shirt. Her legs and feet are bare and she has a perpetually charming tousled look.

"Hey, you," I say, swallowing, trying to appear normal and teacherly. "Nice cast!" Lola's cast covers almost her entire arm and is deep violet. She holds it up like a trophy, which, I guess, it kind of is.

"Will you sign it, Maddy?" She's completely unfazed by the fact that I am on her kitchen floor with a broken collectible that probably cost hundreds of dollars. Just then, Nick appears in the doorway with a silver paint pen, and I grimace from shame.

"I'm so sorry. I just saw the collection, and the poodle was so cute, and I—"

"It's okay," he says, grabbing paper towels and wetting them in the sink. He doesn't even call for Consuela, or whatever the maid's name is. He just walks over and bends down with the wad of paper towels, our heads almost touching. I can smell his aftershave. "Happens to the best of us," he says mercifully, and smiles, less than a foot from my face. I think I am going to die of excitement or embarrassment. I can't tell which yet. He lowers his head back to the task at hand, and I can't help but stare for a second at his beautiful floppy hair, his strong arms, his whole luscious body dedicated to cleaning up the pepper I spilled. The pepper that—

I sneeze and bolt to my feet, more than sure that I've shot a booger halfway out of my nose. I desperately grab for a paper towel and wipe away the offending snot, probably until my nose turns bright red. And then I sneeze again, and again, and it's unstoppable—it's never going to end—and Lola starts giggling hysterically. To her, I am hilarious. A clown. A cartoon character. To myself, I'm shameful. Of course, her father, the perfect celebrity, is immune to fits of pepper-induced sneezing. Nick stands up, probably staring at me as if I have fifty heads (I'm afraid to look at him), Lola shouts, "Gesundheit!" for every one of my sneezes, and Nick walks over to me with a box of tissues, retrieved from God knows where.

"Thanks!" I say, muffled behind gobs of tissue, looking at the floor, already berating myself for ever leaving my seat in the first place. Damn those lavender poodles and their wobbly heads.

When it looks like I've finally reached the end of my hilarity, I throw the tissues and paper towels in the garbage and smile sheepishly.

"Ta da!" I say, as if I don't give a damn that I just spewed snot all over Nick Seabolt and his million-dollar professional kitchen. Then I concentrate on the paint pen. I shake it up, pop the cap, and sign my name and the date: "Maddy Braverman, October 2002. (AH-CHOO!)" A moment to remember.

"Daddy, look!" she says excitedly when I'm done, and Nick and I smile at each other, which sends my stomach lurching. His smile is so drop-dead gorgeous, all the more so for being directed right at me.

For a moment, I lose my ability to speak. When I recover, I launch into full business mode, I am so embarrassed. "Did the doctor say when Lola could return to school? I was thinking that I could bring Lola's work on Friday. There's really not an extraordinary amount, but the consistency will be good for all of us."

"She'll be back at school on Monday, and Friday sounds great," Nick says, smiling at me curiously. God, I am so insecure around this guy, I could sink into the floor. I almost wish he'd stop looking at me.

"Thanks so much for the food," I venture, "and I'm so sorry about the . . ." I trail off, pointing at the poodle. Then I turn to Lola. "I'm glad to see you're feeling better." There. I can do this. I can be professional and grown-up.

"It's not that bad. I think I was more scared before." I look at Nick, and we shrug at Lola's premature wisdom. I realize that it's kind of a shame that Shelby's not here to take care of Lola, to have taken her to the hospital and held her hand through all this. And it's rather striking that Lola doesn't seem the least bit unhappy about not having her mom here, but then I remind myself that this is a lifestyle I know nothing about. I set about wiping the image of Nick Seabolt out of my mind.

"So, how are you liking New York?" I ask, standing up with my empty plate.

"Oh, here, let me take that," he says, and puts my dish in the sink. "I grew up in the Bronx, so I couldn't wait to move back. Shelby prefers L.A., but she's there practically every week anyway. I'm about to start rehearsals on a film here in the spring, and we wanted Lola to have a New York education with some, uh, real people." He smiles apologetically, and my heart flips out all over again. "I mean, all the schools out there are—" He shrugs. I imagine a double-processed sea of designer brats toting solid gold pagers and Palm Pilots instead of pencils and books.

"Yeah." I nod sympathetically. "So, um, what movie, uh, film will you be working on?"

"It's an indie, new director. Brilliant woman from Iceland. It's a . . . small picture about an ex-CIA operative who gets into hot water with some Czechoslovakian terrorists in Tokyo."

"And the CIA operative is played by you?"

"*Ex*-CIA operative," he says, correcting me with a wily grin.

"You must love your job."

"Yeah." He shrugs again. "I really do. I guess I'm pretty lucky."

"I think so!" I say, sounding a little too much like a teenager and not a whole lot like a teacher.

"Well, what about you?"

"What?"

"You must love your job, too."

Oh boy, now I've done it. I've trapped myself into a lie. I don't love my job. I tolerate my job because I don't know what I truly want to do. I fell into teaching after grad school. When I realized I wasn't going to be a poet, teaching children just sort of happened. Everyone says teaching is so noble, but teaching children of obscene privilege is not noble. They're all going to Yale or Vassar or whatever Ivy League school, whether I'm the one flicking the lights or not. If I were noble, I'd quit and get a job teaching in East New York or Harlem. But I am not noble. Talk about choosing your life. Meanwhile, if I don't make it look like teaching first grade is my absolute calling, Nick'll probably pull Lola out of my class. At the very least, he'll be disappointed.

"Oh yes. I love teaching. It's . . . the life I chose," I say, and hope it sounds like a positive spin.

When panic sets in that I am overstaying my welcome, I look over at Lola, who's tracing her cast in wistful circles on the polished granite countertop. I say very professionally, "Well, Lola, I guess I'll see you on Friday with some math and reading work." I tell Nick I must be going, not that I have anywhere to be. I could literally stay here all night, ogling and asking him questions about his life, but I don't want to seem like a deranged stalker, when I should be impressing him as a capable, respectable professional. At the door, he smiles warmly and I smile awkwardly. As soon as the door closes behind me, I could swear I dreamed the whole thing.

# Chapter Six

―――

*H*oly motherfucking shit, you guys," I say when I walk in the door. "Guess where I just was." Kate and Casey are planted on the sofa, drinking red wine and eating from wide bowls of pasta, which I used to eat all the time when I wasn't trying to stay on the Bönz. Right now, however, my stomach is growling for some real food, after sampling a bona fide Bönz meal, so I help myself to whatever's left in the kitchen. The TV is on, as usual. Kate reaches for the remote as Casey takes a guess. "Blind date?"

"Ha, no," I say. "That's hilarious. Guess who broke her wrist today?" I hold up my arms and twirl them around so they won't think it's me.

"Rachel Tepper?" asks Casey, because, of course, they've heard all about her.

"Ennnhhh. Wrong again," I say, imitating a game-show buzzer. "I'll give you a hint. It's one of my students."

After a brief and thoughtful pause, Kate picks up on my agenda. "You were just at Nick and Shelby's house?"

I nod my head victoriously, as if I've just been accidentally undercharged at Barneys.

"Ugh, the other half." Kate sighs resignedly. "You know what you call a thousand celebrities at the bottom of the ocean?"

"Dinner?" Casey says with contrived dopiness.

"Yeah, well, still. Oh my God, their apartment is *so* unfair. I might go blind from seeing it. But Nick was soooo nice." I sigh and smile at the memory despite myself, sitting on the arm of the sofa with my bowl of "bad" food.

"What about Shelby?" Kate asks.

"On location," I say, stuffing a forkful of rotini in my mouth.

"Lucky for you," Casey says, and wiggles his eyebrows.

"Yeah right, he was all over me," I say sarcastically.

"Maddy, Nick Seabolt is a Hollywood Frankenstein, just like the rest of them," says Kate, not picking up on my sarcasm. "You can do so much better, and meanwhile—*hello*—he is married." Then she adds quickly, "Not that that means anything by celebrity standards." I roll my eyes, which makes Kate go on, even though I'm not sure I want her to.

"Maddy, the only reason you don't have real, normal, available guys falling at your feet is because you never give them a chance."

"That is so not true. Alex went all the way to Tibet to get away from me."

"Screw him, then!" says Casey. "The dick!" I love when Casey is one of the girls. He does it so well, especially when Kate refuses to play along.

"Maddy," Kate says seriously. "Nick is a married celebrity android. He is not human. But there are plenty of available, good-looking, hardworking real men out there who would die for a girl like you."

"Okay, okay," I concede. "I am a goddess." And with that, I stuff in another mouthful. "But Nick Seabolt looked really real to me," I say, chewing.

"Home wrecker!" Casey scolds playfully, and I strike a pose of mock innocence, because I know that there is no way in hell that a guy like Nick Seabolt would ever be into a girl like me, and I also know that there is no way I would ever jeopardize anyone's marriage, let alone his family.

I decide to be generous tonight and let Kate and Casey monop-olize the living room, partly because Kate's in one of her righteous, humorless moods. I pour myself a glass of Pinot Grigio from the fridge and head to my room to attempt some poetry. "Later, guys. I've got some work to do," I say, shutting my bedroom door behind me.

As I turn on my laptop, I think about what Kate said. As much as I want to believe her, my self-esteem where men are concerned feels permanently damaged after Harrison, and all the other fish that swam away. I mean, let's face facts. I am the girl who pines but never possesses. I lust after guys like Nick Seabolt precisely because I can't have them. I am totally in the dark about what makes a girl couple-worthy for longer than a season of *Sex and the City*. I know it has something to do with starting out as friends instead of starting with blow jobs—and liking each other while sober—but beyond that, I'm mystified. I look at Casey and Kate like they're a different species. The thing is, Kate must know what she's talking about. It's not like the advice is coming from Michelle, who's as single as I am.

For starters, forgetting about Nick Seabolt is absolutely a good idea. God knows, my conscience could use the break. Between the desire and the guilt, I'm ready to explode. But what could possibly take his place in my imagination? I've developed strict rules for my fantasy life, and the most important is, my fantasies have to be somehow plausible. The fact that I actually know Nick makes it so much easier, but I'm kept so busy because there are still so many details to be smoothed out.

In other words, I can't just close my eyes and see us humping like lunatics. First, I have to make sure that Shelby is out of the picture, in a humane way, something that won't traumatize Lola any more than it needs to. Basically, Shelby needs to die suddenly of a rare form of cancer. Then, Lola needs time to grieve and get used to me taking her mother's place. Nick needs to lean on me for support through his loss, and slowly realize that he's been in love with me from the first moment he saw me. And on top of all this, I need to be wearing the perfect outfit, and nothing I own comes even close, so I need to figure out a plausible way to get the money for the outfit. So much to take care of . . . What could possibly replace this obsession?

I look at my glowing computer screen, and it dawns on me.

Taking James's advice is not a habit I'm particularly proud of. But it's not poetry that's going to take my mind off of Nick. Instead of rhyming couplets about scattered rose petals and kisses stolen in the night, I write about Amanda Porter. I write down everything I've told the kids—about Amanda frolicking in crystal-clear streams while her father pans beside her, about how quickly she grows and the mischief she finds herself in with the other miners' children, about the town the miners are building, and about the telegram that arrives from New York via the Pony Express from Amanda's maternal grandmother after Amanda's dad was arrested for stealing another man's gold. It doesn't take long before I realize that this is more than a picture book, that it's quite possibly a novel in progress. As I reach the bottom of my twentieth page, I lean back on my bed and smile. After all these years, my degree in creative writing is finally coming in handy.

I spend all day Thursday immersed in work. Not even Rachel Tepper can break my concentration. Of course, the fact that she sends her two goons in with apology letters helps immensely. I put them in a folder set aside for Lola, barely thinking of where this folder will take me tomorrow.

Thursday night, I head straight to the computer, and on Friday during quiet time, I tentatively pull a thick stack of paper from my bag and begin, for the first time, to read the Amanda Porter story to the kids.

"You wrote it down!" shouts Raffey, pointing. James, who is halfway out the door, on his way to lunch, turns around and comes back in.

"All right, Maddy!" he says, and perches on the edge of a table to listen.

When Amanda was old enough to understand, the miners told her it was time. Amanda's granny was too old to attempt the journey west, so the girl, eleven years old, would travel east, to meet her mother's mother for the first time. Amanda cried and cried. She had grown to love the scruffy miners. They were as much her family as her pa was, and she would miss them terribly. Because she was crying so hard, none of the miners had the heart to tell Amanda that she would be leaving California for good, that Margaret Granite had ordered the little girl back to New York City, and away from her crook of a father.

When Zachary volunteers to illustrate the story chapter by chapter, the rest of the students are eager to contribute. I can't help but agree, even though, technically, they're supposed to be resting.

Nina raises her hand and I go over to help her transcribe the title for her drawing. Together, we sound out the words, *golden ghost,* and a chill runs down my spine.

"Nina, are you thinking what I'm thinking?" Nina looks up from her drawing, her puzzled expression making her mouth into a bent pink line.

I squat beside her so that we are face-to-face. "What do you think about this for a title?" I say, touching the words on her drawing.

"For the whole story?" she asks, and I smile in answer. Nina's eyes light up. "Really?" she asks, as if I've just told her we're taking a field trip to FAO Schwarz.

"I kid you not," I say, and she nods.

We shake hands, sealing the deal.

By Friday, I've worked myself so ragged writing, prepping, and teaching that I can barely stand up, let alone think about Nick Seabolt. For the finishing touch, I force myself to go to his apartment wearing a bulky sweater, overalls, and sneakers. I don't even powder my nose, I'm so determined to break my celebrity habit. I do brush my teeth, though—for hygiene.

Lola seems more sluggish today, maybe from lack of company. She's sitting on the floor in the huge living room, lazily flipping through the pages of the latest *Vogue*. I wish I could tear it out of her hand to save her from the self-esteem-sapping destruction fashion mags wield, but then I realize that to Lola, *Vogue* magazine is probably like the family photo album. Still, when she sees me, she leaps up and runs to hug me with her good arm. While she plants a kiss on my stomach, Nick walks in, and despite all my careful preparations, my mind-bending strategies, my horribly unflattering outfit, I turn to swill on the spot. Great.

"Hey!" he says brightly, and I turn to open my bag so I don't have to look at him. I find the folder and pull it out.

"Let's see. We've got, um, Reading. You remember the rule, 'When two vowels go walking, the first one does the talking and says its name'?"

She nods. "Like the *o* in *boat* says, 'I'm an *o*!'"

"Exactly," I say, smiling. "So you'll underline those. . . . And here's the math. Circle all the tens, okay? Oh, and a couple apology letters from Hugo and Thor." I turn to Nick, but only briefly. "They're the kids who, uh, well, who . . ." Nick is giving me that curious smile again. God, why does he have to look so *interested* in me? And I haven't even broken anything. "Do you think you'll have some time to read with her?" I ask, sticking to the subject.

"I think I can arrange that," he says, stuffing his hands into his back pockets.

"Oh, I almost forgot!" I say, and reach into my bag, thanking my lucky stars for a diversion from Nick's horrible beautiful smile. I pull out another pile of paper and hand it to Lola. "From your classmates."

Lola takes the pile from me and eagerly investigates on the floor, using her left hand and her right elbow to separate the stack. When I told the class I was visiting Lola at home, we decided to make her "Get Well" cards, something of a City Select tradition, not that the kids don't unanimously adore her. I stare at her, never taking my eyes off her, not for a second. She's pretty good with that left hand of hers, but I hope that her writing and fine motor skills won't be seriously affected because of all this. I remember what James said, that kids break bones every day and heal just fine. Of course I'll do anything I can to help her catch up to the other kids when the cast comes off, but I wish it didn't mean having to spend time with Nick. I am failing miserably at not being into him.

"They love her," I say, staying focused.

"She's a lovable kid," Nick says. "Right, Lolo?" Lola looks up at Nick and nods quickly, smiling and panting, which infects us all, and soon, despite myself, we're all laughing together. Oh God, that smile! Why did I have to look?

"So what film is Shelby working on?" I ask, fixing my eyes on the glass doors ahead of me in order to nip this shame in the bud. And there I am, reflected in Nick Seabolt's very own penthouse doors, a schlumpy, insecure lower-school teacher who's hopelessly infatuated with a world-famous married man. I look at the floor in utter defeat.

Nick says, "Uh, some uh—oh, it's a studio picture. You know . . ." He trails off, but I need to hear about Shelby. I decide that she is the key to releasing my mental hold on Nick.

"What's it about?" I ask, continuing to prod.

"Ah, same old, same old. You know those studio pictures."

Is it some James Cameron top secret epic? Or a Woody Allen picture, where not even the cast gets to read the entire script? Is he evading my question? Is he annoyed? Suddenly, I feel ashamed for pressing him on the subject. I was only serving my own selfish motive.

"Sorry," I say, still looking at the floor. "I just—oh, I don't know—it's just interesting."

"No, it's okay, really." We look at each other then, and I don't know if it's me or what, but our eyes seem to lock for just a moment longer than what should be necessary.

"Okay, so I guess I'll be seeing you on Monday," I blurt to Lola, feeling the heat rise in my face. "The kids can't wait to have you back." I turn to Nick and say good-bye, trying to look anywhere but into his eyes.

I start heading for the door, full of determination, but Lola slides across the wooden floor toward me and yanks on my sleeve.

"Maddy! Come see my room!" she pleads. I look at Nick.

"Cool idea, kiddo," he says, and then I'm being tugged along through the living room, past the mammoth paintings, and then I'm in a hallway I couldn't have guessed would exist, a whole additional wing, and at the end of the hallway is a bathroom, mosaicked in Chiclet-size rainbow tiles. Rubber and sponge animals litter the floor, and Lola kicks them out of our way as we traverse the entryway to her bedroom, a room that I can only describe as a child's wet dream. One entire wall boasts a poster of Andy Warhol–inspired wallpaper, multiple multicolored Lolas in a grid. Her bed is done in fake zebra skin and hot-pink gingham, and her carpet is hot-orange shag. Beanbag chairs in a fabric that glitters like silver prisms sit in a corner by a huge window, and piled on a hammock in the corner are about fifty stuffed animals, which Lola proceeds to introduce me to one by one. I shake each of their hands, paws, flippers, tentacles, and while I'm having a particularly intellectual conversation with the donkey from *Shrek,* I hear a giggle behind me, and it isn't Lola.

"I see you've met the rest of the family," Nick says, and as I turn around, I can feel the color rise up my throat, into my face, as hot as the carpet on which I stand.

"Yeah, Lola was acquainting me. The, uh, donkey is particularly . . ."

"Verbose!" Lola shouts, and falls over in a peal of giggles.

"Yes," I say. "Very verbose. We couldn't get him to pipe down, could we?"

Lola shakes her head no, but she can't seem to find her way to speech through her laughter.

"You're a funny woman," Nick says, tilting his head, as if he's seeing me for the first time just now.

"Maddy," he says. "Thanks again for doing all this. It means the world to us."

"It means the world to us!" Lola mimics before losing her composure again.

"Well, I love being able to help," I say, hardly believing the possibility that I have just impressed one of the most famous stars on the planet with my wit.

Nick walks me to the door. I float to the door, actually. I'm almost there, almost free from this death grip of lust.

"Lola loves you, Maddy."

I freeze in my tracks. "Thanks," I mumble, turning around. "Really, it's no big—"

"No, I get the feeling you don't realize how much you mean to her." He's so close, I can smell him, expensive aftershave mixed with a hint of musky body odor. Smelling this on anyone else, I might be repelled, but on Nick Seabolt, it is so comfortingly human and carnal that I can feel the moisture percolate in my panties.

"Well, the feeling is certainly mutual, Mr. Seabolt," I say carefully.

"Call me Nick."

"Okay. Nick." I give his first name a verbal test-drive and it rolls around in my mouth like a frozen dark chocolate pastille. We shake hands good-bye. Nothing out of the ordinary there. Then he places his left hand on top of mine, and suddenly I have the luckiest hand in the world, suspended in a cloud of dreamy Nick Seabolt. Does he feel the same storm brewing in his stomach that I do? Does he realize how much power he holds over me?

When he finally releases me, I stand there motionless. I don't even replace my hand at my side. He sees what a love-struck puppy I must be, and I think he must absolutely have lost all respect for me. I jerk my hand into my pocket and grimace. Nick smiles and squeezes my shoulder. "Is being beautiful a job requirement at City Select?"

I don't say anything. My faculties have shut down. No sound will escape from my mouth.

"Uh . . ." I manage to say, suddenly thirteen years old again.

"All right, kiddo. I will see you soon," he says casually, as if he hasn't just turned my entire universe upside down.

I blurt out "Thanks!" and practically slam my face into the front door as I make my escape.

# Chapter Seven

Michelle, I think I've lost my mind!" I wail over drinks at Tahiti Tiki, this cozy bar on Smith Street, one of our Brooklyn faves. I poke at my Frozen Flamingo with a straw between gulps and slump into the raffia-trimmed banquette.

She smiles. "Girlfriend, I should have your problems."

"I know. I just . . . I don't know. I'm probably making a huge dramatic deal over nothing. . . . But he is so . . ."

"Ripe with fuckability?"

"Yes! Oh my God, Michelle. I could really do some damage, not that he even thinks of me that way. I mean, he did say I was beautiful, but—"

"Sweetie, people like that think of *everyone* that way. Because everybody thinks of *them* that way."

I ponder this and decide that she's right. The whole world is Nick Seabolt's sex toy. What an animal. Still, I want him so badly, it makes my whole body vibrate like a . . . like a vibrator. I analyze this phenomenon with Michelle for over an hour, when she finally interrupts me.

"Meanwhile, in my teeny life—" she begins.

"I'm sorry, Michelle. I'm just consumed."

"Apparently."

"How's . . . Jake? Nesh . . ."

"Jacob Neshkowitz. He hasn't called me in a week," she announces with an ironic flourish of her arm, as if she's one of the girls from *The Price Is Right,* presenting a fabulous washer-dryer unit. Her smile is huge, but it doesn't hide her hurt feelings.

"Oh Michelle." I shake my head. "I'm so sorry."

"It's okay, he got a piece of me. A piece of this." She clutches her huge breasts, and I welcome the invitation to ogle. "And he decided he didn't want it." I open my mouth to say something encouraging, but Michelle is on a roll. "So, when am I going to stop giving free samples? I mean, why *should* he call me back? He already had his dick in my pussy!" At this last comment, a couple of prim-looking blondes in yawn-inducing Ann Taylor outfits turn to stare. Michelle catches their eyes and practically shouts, "Great! Now the whole WASPy world can know that I'm not only a slut but a pathetic slut reject!" The blondes turn back to their vodka gimlets, and I finally get a word in.

"First of all, Michelle, you are beautiful," I whisper, hoping maybe she'll keep her voice down. And she really is, with her liquid brown eyes and mane of frosted blond hair, let alone the infamous natural rack. "If I were a guy, I'd be all over you."

"Really?" she mewls, all ears. "Go on, Maddy."

"It's true. Way prettier than Fairuza." Fairuza Balk is the celebrity Michelle looks like the most, if Fairuza had blond hair. They even competed as children for the role of Dorothy in *Return to Oz,* which Michelle contends is the defining moment of what she calls her "epic downfall." She was twelve. "You're not only a total knockout but talented as hell, too!" I add for emphasis.

"That's right! I am!" she says, victorious. "So what if I flubbed my audition! So what if Jacob doesn't know what he's giving up. What he's throwing away. . . . Oh Maddy, I feel like such a schmuck!"

"Michelle! The audition! I'm so sorry! It was that bad?" Now *I* feel like a schmuck.

"Maddy, you would never know I'd ever stepped foot in Juilliard," she says with another giant smile, on the verge of maniacal laughter now.

"Was the script any good?"

"My tampon could write a better script than that Neanderthal," she says, and I realize why I love Michelle. There's simply no one else like her. Except maybe a drag queen. But they don't use tampons.

I wish I could help Michelle, introduce her to an agent or someone important who could help her. I'd introduce her to a single guy if I weren't so desperate for my own. Then I remember Kate's new job, planning celebrity benefits. "Hey, Michelle, what're you doing for Halloween?" I ask.

"Overdosing on Xanax?"

"How about joining me for Dylan Hover's extreme sports injury charity costume party?"

"Extreme sports injury *charity*?" Michelle says in total disbelief. "People actually give money to paralyzed bungee jumpers? It figures. I should be so lucky."

I smile triumphantly, for it isn't every day that I have the ability to impress the girl who invented shock value.

"So?"

"Sure I'll come. How'd you hear about it?" I explain Kate's new position, and before I know it, we're ordering our third round, our fourth round, and furiously scribbling shopping lists on bar napkins in preparation for our costumes.

Oh, my head. My head. My stomach. The light. Somebody please turn off the light.

Michelle and I parted ways on Smith Street at about 3:00 A.M. and I stumbled home, bloated with bourbon. We were so drunk, we actually left the bar singing (well, it was more like bleating) the theme from *The Main Event,* and if I had the ability to cringe, I would, because I think we even serenaded anyone who stopped long enough to gawk. And even though my head is throbbing, the lyrics are relentless: "I'd always dreamed I'd find the perfect lover . . ." If only I could turn off my mind, which is jackhammering me with guilt-laced images: making faces at the Ann Taylor girls, forgetting to feather the nest when I peed, announcing to

Michelle that I want to be Lola Magdalena Seabolt's new mommy. . . . Oh God. I close my eyes, try a new position. Nothing works. I am doomed. I'm trying desperately to turn off my head, but thoughts of Nick won't stop swirling around all the other crap like empty plastic bags in a storm. As I pull the pillow over my head, I wonder, Did Michelle and I sing to anyone we knew? Did anyone else hear me going on about my death-defying and embarrassingly pathetic crush on a movie star? Can I ever show my face in the neighborhood again? I'll have to call Michelle when I wake up, which hopefully won't be until sundown. Ohh . . .

I never call Michelle. I never call anyone. It's a rainy Sunday, which is perfect, since I have no plans to change out of my flannel pajamas. I spend the day inside, hunched over my laptop.

Writing *Golden Ghost* takes my mind off of Saturday night's antics, and of course it doesn't hurt to have a break from thinking about you know who. It's no coincidence that little orphan Amanda isn't feeling too well. Of course, for her it's typhoid. This doesn't bode well for her cross-country stagecoach ride, but little Miss Porter is a feisty heroine, fueled by the prospect of meeting her granny, who lives in New York and is worth more than her weight in gold.

By Monday, I feel like my old self again. Everyone's excited to have Lola back, and her cast is brimming with good wishes from students and teachers alike. James and I take turns transcribing her work during writing time, as does Raffey, who is quite advanced in the motor skills department. Zachary draws hearts and stars with his glitter gel rollers in the margins.

I get to the lunchroom and Michelle's there, heaping some Caesar salad onto a paper plate. When we see each other, we share a meaningful nod, acknowledging the insanity of our Saturday-night antics. I've barely filled my Bönz bowl when the head molester stands up, hoisting his clear plastic cup of pink lemonade in his prosthesis.

"Ah'd always dreamed Ah'd find the perfect lover . . ." he croons in a scary falsetto, staring at us. Everyone in the lunchroom, which includes Rachel and about ten other teachers, most of whom I don't know very well (thank God), turns to watch the show. Michelle and I freeze, of course, but not before I have a chance to drop my bowl of cottage cheese all over the floor. If ever there was a time to define Michelle's and my personalities, it is now. While I scrape white goo from the floor, mortified, Michelle sticks out her chest and joins Arthur, becoming Donna Summer to his frightening Babs. Of course, Michelle wishes she lived in a Broadway musical.

Hazy bits and pieces from Saturday night reveal themselves to me. Michelle and I arm in arm, screaming to the sky. "Enough is enough is enough . . ." Spotting Arthur across the street. Was he alone? I think so. Did we call him the head molester to his face? Please, God, no. I think we called him Arty. Smarty Arty? Arty Farty? Oh God. He whistled for us. He came over to us. He . . . I think he stuck a dollar in the waistband of Michelle's skirt. I brushed my Banana Republic sale scarf across his cheeks? Please no. Michelle . . . gave him a thank-you kiss. A peck on the cheek? I don't want to remember. Oh God. It was on the *lips*.

Finally, the madness ends and Michelle runs over to give Arthur a hug and bow to her audience. This looks like a good time to make my exit.

"Maddy, mah deah," Arthur booms, stopping me in my tracks. "You are a veritable nightingale, illuminating the New Amsterdam autumn with your unique brand of joie de vivre." He continues on in Cajun-spiced French, and I take it as a blessing that I have no idea what he's saying. I look at the ceiling, as if maybe it will open up and an alien spaceship will drop a ladder for me. I wouldn't care if they took me to a whole other galaxy and sautéed my ovaries. I just want to get out of here. I toss my bowl in the trash and scram.

When I get back to the classroom, it isn't much better. James, for the first time, has lost control. I should be happy about this, given my propensity for domination in the classroom, but I'm not. I'm too drained. The eyelid—it's twitching. James looks at me and shrugs, helpless, while Zachary leads the class around the room, bunny hop–style. I bolt over to the light switch. Flick.

"Freeze!" I shout with venom, and they do. "Everybody go to your tables and sit in your assigned seat. Now." The children follow my directions, having the common sense not to try my patience by running.

I hand each child a photocopied math sheet and a pencil, thus ending their quiet time twenty minutes early. On his way out the door to get lunch, James shrugs apologetically. "I guess I lost my magic touch," he says, and then hands me another crumpled invitation for his band, his look of concern morphing into a carefree grin. "You're still coming tonight, right?" Before I have a chance to make an excuse, he's gone.

"Maddy? Can you help me?" Tyler asks. I walk over to his table and teach him to cross out the pigs he's already counted, so he doesn't get confused, and then make my way around the room to check on the other kids' progress.

"Maddy, are you going to read *Golden Ghost* to us today?" Raffey begs.

"Sorry, you blew it when you guys started a conga line," I snap. With that, she slumps in her seat and sighs like a soap star. An audible collective moan ensues, and with smug satisfaction, I feel I've found the perfect bargaining tool. Plus, the kids' enthusiasm may be just the motivation I need to sequester myself in the computer lab after school to write and stay out of trouble.

Finally Fred's is a dive in the West Village, and when I get there, I am already full of regret. The stale smoke is enough to make me yearn for my bedroom. I order a Bud, since I don't want to stand out, and look at my watch, thankful that Kate said she'd meet me here. The people here mystify me, as they appear to have missed the progression of fashion beyond 1987. Mostly, the clientele includes burly biker types with long ponytails and leather vests.

The women are mostly older than I am and look like they've seen hard times. Maybe their lovers left them alone in their trailers, or maybe their lovers died in hunting accidents. Whatever the case may be, practically all the women have cigarette lines around their mouths and raucous laughs that seem to dare anyone to shush them. Also scattered around this hole-in-the-wall are Stetson-topped cowboys. At least they look like cowboys in their hats, jeans, and boots. One of them sidles up to me and I see that the person under the hat is James.

"Howdy," he says, tipping his hat and grinning that smile. "Thanks for coming! We go on in about five minutes downstairs." I've seen James in fringed suede and denim in the classroom, but somehow the addition of the hat and the bar setting bring out his sex appeal in a way I wish I could deny.

"Great," I say, hoping he can't read my mind. I start to ask him if he's played here before, but then I see Rachel snaking her way through the crowd, and I don't want to give her a chance to interrupt, so I stop in midsentence, leaving James to adopt a puzzled expression. Rachel wraps her arm around James's elbow, which is all the proof I need that they're now officially an item.

"Hi, Maddy! It's so nice of you to come!" she squeals condescendingly, as if I am a guest in her home, and I realize that she is a monster. In her free hand, she holds what looks like a cosmopolitan, which further illustrates my theory. Whereas I am trying to be respectful of the obvious beer-drinking vibe, Rachel has to go and make a personal statement by ordering a hoity-toity cocktail. She probably had to walk the poor bartender through the entire process. "Isn't this place the best?" She smiles, her face straining under the pressure. I take a slug of my beer and look at my watch. Of course by "the best," she means, "Isn't it camp?" It's just like the way rainbow-striped platforms and Graceland are "the best," but you'd hate to make either one a regular part of your life.

"Yeah, it's, uh, pretty cool," I manage to say, trying to sound blasé. I start making my way to the bar for a second beer and

James says he'll meet me downstairs. Rachel opts to remain glued to James. Go figure.

And then, bless her heart, Kate arrives. "Hey, Mad, sorry I'm late. Meeting ran a little long. Dylan can't decide what costume to wear to the party." She shakes her head at the obscenity of it all and takes off her jacket, slinging it casually over her arm. After I get us drinks, two very inconspicuous and respectable Budweisers, we head down the narrow stairway.

"Casey wanted to come, but they have him working late on a new column about Brooklyn writers," she says.

"That's okay," I reply, secretly pleased that I'll have Kate all to myself.

The basement space is as narrow as the room upstairs, and the seats are all miles above the floor and against the wall. It takes me about five minutes to get comfortable, since in addition to the seats being so high up, there is no place to rest your feet, so you always have the feeling of being about to slide to the floor. Of course Rachel and even Kate master this difficult task, while I finally chuck the whole civilized routine and sit in the lotus position, formerly known in the un-PC days as Indian-style. I pray I don't have to get up until we leave, so that I don't have to untangle and rearrange myself. I'm already practically schvitzing from the effort.

"Kate, this is Rachel Tepper," I say as innocently as I can muster, considering Kate knows everything about evil Rachel and her man-stealing ways. Kate, of course, plays it like a champ, as if she's never heard the name before in her life. Rachel, true to form, is oozing with molasses sweetness, and before I know it, they're ensconced in conversation, leaving me to my bottle.

"Maddy was so funny this afternoon in the faculty lounge," says Rachel, who proceeds to tell Kate about how I spilled my lunch all over the floor.

"Oh God," I say, as in "Oh God, please let's forget the whole embarrassing event."

Kate listens intently, laughing in all the right places and shrugging at me as if I'm a cherished puppy who peed on the floor, when I'd much rather she sock Rachel in the jaw for patronizing me in such an insidious way. I regrettably unfold myself and go to order a third Bud, vaguely considering turning to a life of alcoholism. But then I realize that alcohol is what got me into trouble in the first place.

When I get back downstairs, Rachel and Kate are still talking about me. I know this because Rachel looks at me and says, "Maddy, you're so crazy." Then, stroking her glass, she says, "I so rarely drink anymore. This is it for the week, you know? It ages you like *crazy.*" There's that word again, I think, and look at Kate, who's nodding with knitted brow to show that she totally agrees, even though she's a harder drinker than I am. I guess I'll be the only wrinkly crone serenading strangers tonight. I lift the bottle to my lips in giddy anticipation.

James is onstage—if you can call the dirty sheet of plywood a stage—tuning his guitar and asking the soundman for more volume in his monitor. He strums a couple of chords and my heart does a little somersault. For the first time, I wish him well. At least I think I do. I take a big swallow of my Bud, as if that will calm me down.

"Thanks, y'all, for coming out on a school night," he says, and winks at me. At least I think he's winking at me, but then Rachel turns to Kate and says, "Did you see him wink at me? Isn't that sweet?" I look at Kate for some assurance, but she's too busy agreeing with Rachel. Figures.

As I continue my descent into drunkenness, James launches into his first number, a fast-paced song about a guy who is lamenting over ever going out with an actress. His voice is pitch-perfect, which I knew, but I had no idea he had such . . . presence. Something about the way he holds his guitar, or the way he leans into the microphone and touches his lips to it while he sings. The other three members of the band are pretty good, too. One of the guys sits on a bucket at the foot of the stage, sliding his fingers back and forth on some sort of guitar on his lap. His jet black hair is pulled back in a ponytail and the stage lights reflect off of his chunky black Elvis Costello glasses. The bassist looks more like a punk rocker, with his woolen ski hat and pierced eyebrow, but the drummer, who's wearing a plain blue T-shirt and black jeans, looks like he just rolled out of bed.

I look around the room and see that all the trailer-park widows are bobbing their heads, jutting their acid-washed hips, and flicking their eyes up and down James's body as they greedily suck on their Merits.

The rest of the set flies by, with a lot of hooting and hollering, mostly from our group. James introduces the band. It turns out the laptop guitar is actually a laptop *steel* guitar. I feel really good about my decision to come tonight, even if means spending time with Rachel. I figure if I can survive her, I can do anything.

Rachel turns to me then. "You're so lucky, Maddy. James is such an amazing guy. I'll bet he's a fabulous assistant," she shouts into my ear.

"Yeah, the kids love him!" I shout back.

"Who doesn't?"

"I don't know!" And it's true. Who doesn't love James? I must be really drunk.

"So what's going on with you two?" I ask, filled with courage and optimism.

"What do you mean?"

"You know, like, are you guys an item?"

She laughs then and gives me a playful shove.

"What?" I ask.

"You're so funny!" she says, as if I am a child. But I feel like a child, and she's an adult who's keeping important information from me, as if it might be detrimental to my development. I shake my head with frustration.

"What?" I ask. "How am I funny?"

"No offense, Maddy, but it's really none of your business," she says, and takes a sip of her cosmopolitan.

I am crestfallen, humiliated. Weren't we just smiling and laughing like buddies not less than a minute ago? Why does she always pull the rug out from under me like that? And why am I always right where she wants me to be? I guess it's time to go back to hating her.

When the set is over, James comes over and we bombard him with praise. We're all so genuinely impressed, and, I have to admit, relieved. There's nothing like seeing a friend perform, only to hate it and have to lie to his face.

"I was telling Maddy how lucky she is to have you," Rachel says.

"Nah, I'm the lucky one," he says, tipping his hat to me and winking. I want to say, See? He winked at me that time! *At me!*

What I really say is, "You're damn right." Then I give James a giant wink right back. Rachel stares at me, horrified. I shrug at her and then fall off my seat. So much for perfect poise.

# Chapter
# Eight

*D*ylan Hover's extreme sports charity Halloween bash is being held at Planet Hollywood in Times Square, home of the Midwest tourist brigade, who notoriously infuriate pedestrian traffic with their gawking, picture snapping, and general cluelessness. In this case, the Jenny Craiged, sweatpants-wearing masses are pressed up against the glass of the restaurant, hoping to catch a glimpse of Dylan Hover, Hollywood's latest cookie-cutter actor, who has more triceps than talent. There are a lot of screaming teenage girls, some wearing cat-ear headbands and eyeliner whiskers, and a few dressed like poor imitations of Britney Spears, which does not bode well for Michelle and me. When we raided Ricky's beauty-supply store in SoHo, we'd planned to go as Morticia and the Bride of Frankenstein, but when we saw the array of blond wigs, we changed our minds on the spot and decided on Britney and Christina. In an ironic, satirical way, I swear. Michelle looks sexy but hilarious in her black rubber short shorts, platform boots, grease-streaked wife-beater tank top, and cornrowed silvery streaked wig. And I feel pretty darn sassy in Michelle's super-low-slung Brazilian jeans and baby-doll Pepsi T-shirt, even if my cleavage is subpar.

As our feet touch the ground on the corner of Forty-fourth and Broadway, someone bellows, "Oh my God, it's Britney Spears and

Christina Aguilera!" Everyone in the mob turns to look at us, squints, and then mutters a collective groan of disappointment as they turn back toward Planet Hollywood. But the woman who has allegedly spotted the megastars waddles toward us, Coke-bottle glasses askew, jelly rolls a-jiggling, a flesh-and-blood female version of Hans Moleman from *The Simpsons*. I wince in pain for this poor creature and wonder why she's not home in Cleveland listening to Celine Dion.

Michelle, who's been waiting for the star treatment since she could walk, immediately starts signing Christina Aguilera's name in big loopy letters, hearts dotting all the *i*'s. I try to tell the woman that I'm in costume, but she's sweating up a storm and wheezing, and suddenly it seems like more trouble than it's worth, so I start signing, too. The smile on her optically challenged face could light an entire department store. All for a scrap of paper with Britney Spears's name on it. The fear and fascination I feel is the same sensation that people usually experience when witnessing a car crash.

"I have all your CDs!" she calls after us, clutching the paper to her massive heaving bosom as we scurry toward the door.

We tell the dreadlocked person at the entrance that we're on the guest list. I look around for Kate but don't see her anywhere. She never told me what she'd be wearing.

It feels really good to be escorted inside, leaving the pedestrian masses to their pedestrian lives, poor saps. At a folding table, a young woman checks to see that our names are on the guest list and then hands us two giant passes strung on neon orange shoelaces and emblazoned with the word FRIEND. We carefully slip them on over our wigs and ascend the staircase like the pop-music divas we are. I can practically smell the celebs.

Planet Hollywood is shaped like a doughnut. There's a circular sunken dining room in the center, like a doughnut hole, and a ring of a dining area around it, the actual calorie-packed doughnut. Between the two areas is a Plexiglas display case, loaded with outfits from various movies, like *Legends of the Fall* and *The Witches of*

*Eastwick.* The circular display cordons off the doughnut from the hole, but here and there are spaces where you can pass between the two dining areas. And those passageways are manned by uniformed security guards. Michelle and I find out the hard way that our passes do not grant us entry into the inner sanctum, that the doughnut hole is reserved for real celebrities, who have passes that say FAMILY. We stare through the Plexi, peering between Arnold Schwarzenegger's leather jacket from *T2* and Johnny Depp's scissorhand, and sigh with disappointment. Justin Timberlake's music swells like a bad case of hives.

"How're we going to meet celebrities now?" I groan.

"Don't worry, Britney. We'll think of a way," Michelle says, adjusting her shorts.

I can just make out Dylan Hover, relaxing on a banquette, dressed as an old-time Yankee baseball player. I wonder how long it took for Kate's committee to agree on that decision. I have to admit that Dylan is cuter in person than he is in the movies, but he's so very young. Like twenty-one, I think. In costume, interestingly enough, he looks like a normal, nonfamous person, as if the Yankee uniform equalizes his status. There are a couple of real NBA players here, towering around with Coronas, very much not in costume. I'm sure there are a lot of people out there who'd love to hang out with the Knicks, but I am not one of them, never having been a sports fan. But they certainly are huge. Then I see something that sends my heart skittering.

"Michelle, oh my God, isn't that Billy Hawk?" Michelle looks over to where I'm pointing and nods. Billy Hawk is on *Yo New Yawk,* the new *SNL* rival late-night comedy show. He is the cutest comedian I've ever seen. When I saw the skit where he played an android Mark Wahlberg, I realized that I never gave guys in comedy a second thought as far as crush material. And now there he is, dressed like a pirate, with striped tights and an eye patch and everything. He even has a plastic parrot on his shoulder. Unfortunately, he's talking to someone who looks like the *Alias* girl, but I can't tell if it's Jennifer Garner or someone unknown. Fortunately, however, I read in *Celeb File* that he is twenty-eight and single. Ka-ching! Move over Nick Seabolt; there's a new man in town.

A woman in a Gypsy getup walks by with a tray of smoking test tubes, and Michelle and I each take one. We toast to the tune of "Lady Marmalade" and down our sweet neon green potion.

We manage to position ourselves near the bar, so that whenever a fresh tray of test tubes comes out, we can get our grubby mitts on them first. After we start getting dirty looks from the bartender (dressed as an alien vampire), we teeter over to the buffet table and load plates with salmon and skull-shaped pasta drowning in vodka sauce. Hello drunken debauchery and cellulite, good-bye Bönz! We squeeze into a booth as another cocktail waitress (Playboy bunny) comes over with a trayful of tall icy orange cocktails.

"Would either one of y'all like a Hurricane?" she booms, and we each gleefully take one and toast again. Even if we don't get laid, this is still an amazing spread, and you can't ask for much more than free fish and complimentary cocktails.

"I wish I'd brought Ziplocs!" I say between mouthfuls. "And a camera!"

"I wish I'd brought a thermos!" Michelle says, and it's so true.

"So how're we gonna get in there?" I ask, gesturing over to the Doughnut Hole of Fame.

"Leave it to me. I have a way with security," Michelle says, sticking out her chest.

When we're good and stuffed, we make our way to one of the guarded passageways. The security guard looks us up and down and stifles a giggle.

"What?" asks Michelle. "Haven't you ever seen Britney Spears and Christina Aguilera in the same room before?" The security guard takes his hand away from his mouth and guffaws.

"Naw, it ain't like that," he says. "You look fine and all, but on Britney and Christina, it looks, like, normal. On you ladies, it takes on a somewhat humorous effect."

"What's your name?" asks Michelle.

"Lawrence."

"Well, Lawrence, do you think a girl can be funny and sexy at the same time?"

"I prefer that, actually. A lady who isn't humorous puts me to sleep."

"Well then, Lawrence, this is your lucky day."

I stand by and watch this friendship bear us fruit. Before long, Michelle is writing her phone number on a slip of paper and Lawrence is directing us to the table directly in front of him, where he can keep an eye on us. This will be just close enough to let Billy Hawk become aware of my existence. I watch him intently, honing my radar for any bodily contact between my prized pirate and the *Alias* girl. Thankfully, she seems much more into a hulking guy dressed as Frankenstein's monster.

"You take Billy," Michelle says, making herself comfortable in a booth. "I'm going for the gold."

"Dylan?" I ask, impressed with her balls, as usual.

"*C'est soi!*" she says triumphantly.

We toast the remaining sips of our Hurricanes just as Kate heads over to our table. She's obviously forgotten it's Halloween, as she's wearing boring black jeans and a sweater. She's not even wearing makeup. Her FAMILY tag swings back and forth as she hurries toward us.

"Kate!" I say, standing up. I go to give her a hug, but she stops me with her glare. "What's wrong?" I ask.

"Maddy, how'd you guys get in here?"

"Um, are we not supposed to be here?" I ask innocently. Kate reaches into a fanny pack and pulls out two FAMILY passes.

"Here. Give me your passes. I don't want you guys getting me in trouble. You should've come to me first."

"Oh my God, Kate. Thank you so much!" I go to hug her again, but she gives me the Glare. "Thanks so much," I repeat as soberly as I can muster. "Don't worry, we won't get you in trouble. Right, Michelle?"

"Abso-fucking-lutely," says Michelle, slurping loudly.

"Okay I gotta go. But remember. No antics, okay?" Kate doesn't seem to have a smile to spare.

"Okay!" we shout after her, and then she's gone, all business as usual.

"Doesn't her boyfriend ever fuck her?" Michelle asks, shaking her head, cornrows rustling.

I start to answer, but she cuts me off. "Maddy," she says, jutting her chin toward the doughnut hole's core. "Look who's coming this way."

I follow Michelle's gaze, and, holy shit, Billy the Pirate and Dylan the Yankee are getting up from their table. I'm dreaming, I'm dreaming, and then they're passing us, walking away, walking out of the inner sanctum, and into the "Friends" section, heading toward . . . toward a video game? What are they, twelve? I roll my eyes. "Michelle, they're playing Ms. Pac-Man?!" But she's already up and running. "Maddy, we have to get to them before they start! Come on!" We practically break our legs running after them in our platforms but get there just in time to wheeze a challenge.

"Betcha we can kick your ass!" declares Michelle, panting and pointing at the machine. Billy and Dylan give us the once-over. I dig a finger underneath my wig to scratch a spot on my scalp while Michelle stares them down, waiting for their answer. Then they crack up.

"Oh, like you guys look any cooler?" I say, indignant, careful to treat them like anybody else. Like shit.

"No. You girls look fantastic," says Billy, his gaze lingering on my exposed midriff. I suck it in, as if on cue.

"So you wanna play or not?" I say. Just think! Ms. Pac-Man with Billy Hawk! Could life get any better than this?

"You got a quarter?" Billy asks, and I start fishing around in my jeans, but I can barely get a finger into one of the pockets. "Hey, Britney, I'm kidding!" he says, waving a coin in front of my face. Hmph.

"You ladies need another drink?" asks Dylan, and suddenly I think Michelle's chosen the winner tonight, at least in terms of gentlemanliness. Michelle and I order Hurricanes and Dylan goes to get them.

"So which one of you sexy ladies wants to go first?" asks Billy, inserting quarters into the machine. His overuse of the word *ladies* makes him seem more Las Vegas than New York, but hey, who am I to complain?

"She does!" Michelle says, shoving me forward so hard that I step on Billy's foot.

"Oh man, sorry!" I say, and smile sheepishly. We are not starting off too well, and suddenly I feel as if my costume is literally sucking brain cells out of my head. But then it could be the river of free booze. Maybe I'll never know.

I am better at Ms. Pac-Man than Billy, and he seems genuinely impressed when I make it to the board with the banana. In fact, he's so impressed that I feel his hand stroking the exposed small of my back as he chants, "Eat that banana. Eat that banana," and it makes me so giddy and nervous that I run my Pac-Man right into Blinky.

"Fuck!" I say with more anger than I'd like to betray, and Billy laughs.

"See that? Now watch as I kick *your ass.*" He cracks his knuckles and gets to work, but he dies before he even makes it to the strawberry. Even though he's hopelessly pathetic at Ms. Pac-Man, I am hooked on this salty seaman. I remind myself not to stare at him too intently, or sigh too audibly, lest he think I am a deranged fan.

Michelle is even worse at the game than Billy, but Dylan practically doubles my score. At first, I think this is somehow going to mean that we have to switch conquests, but after Dylan finally loses, like an hour later, he and Michelle start dancing their butts off to "Music," by Madonna.

Billy and I join the dancing, and soon Michelle and I are taking turns pretending to be Madonna. They hoot and clap, and I think in my drunken state that this is how life should be. That there should be a national holiday where the nonfamous people get treated like celebrities and the famous people have to gawk and clap and ask for *their* autographs.

I'm just about to launch into a vintage Madonna high kick when Kate rushes by, shouting into a walkie-talkie. She steps over to me and whispers in my ear, "Maddy, be careful. These guys are players."

"I know, Katie-watie! So am I!" I wink at her and try to plant a kiss on her cheek, but she's off already to do damage control in another part of Planet Hollywood. As I watch her disappear into the crowd, I can suddenly feel every ounce of alcohol I've imbibed. I think I'll just sit this next one out.

Billy comes over to the bar, where I'm sitting on a stool, and starts rubbing my shoulders. How can these magical fingers be attached to the body of an evil, sleazy player?

"That feels so good," I say.

"Plenty more where that came from," he whispers into my ear, then starts rubbing the back of my neck, just under the wig. A shiver runs down my spine and I can feel my nipples harden under the bippy shirt. I hope he sees, I think brazenly. He hands me his beer and I take a grateful sip, willing myself back into the spirit of the evening.

Before I know it, we're hailing a cab, on our way to Dylan's hotel suite. *Yo New Yawk* is putting him up at the Midtown Marriott, because he's the celebrity guest this week on the show. It's amazing what a few cocktails and a blond wig will do for a girl's sense of adventure. If I were sober and brunette, I'd probably be sitting alone in my bedroom.

Dylan takes out a flask, Billy produces a tiny silver pipe, and we continue the party for the duration of the ride across town. Occasionally, I look over at Michelle, who's perched on Dylan's lap, inhaling the pot smoke from his mouth. Billy takes a hit and looks at me questioningly, and I open my mouth, answering him. Between tokes and sips and kisses, I hope Billy will like what he sees under the wig. I still can barely believe that I'm in a taxicab with two authentic celebrities, let alone kissing one of them. Billy's lips are fantastic, too, thin but strong. And he keeps kneading the back of my neck, which makes me want to rip his billowy blouse off right here in the backseat.

The great thing about being a celebrity guest on *Yo New Yawk* is that you get a suite of rooms. So while Dylan leads Michelle to one bedroom, Billy and I get another one all to ourselves. I can't believe I'm about to sleep with a real live superstar. I would call Michelle and squeal with delight about it if she weren't right down the hall, doing the same thing. I can hear her screaming the lyrics to "Genie in a Bottle."

Billy starts licking my neck, guiding me to the king-size bed. His hands are everywhere, fumbling with the snap on my jeans, reaching up under my T-shirt, then all over my ass. We flop on the bed, and within a minute I'm completely naked, while he still has a plastic parrot on his jacketed shoulder.

"Hey, sailor, what about you?" I slur.

"What about me?" he asks, coming up for air.

"What about your clothes?"

"What about them? You like my sense of style?" He wiggles his eyebrows and starts kissing my belly again.

"I'd like it more if you were naked. But you can leave the eye patch on if you really want," I coo.

Billy stands up on the bed and starts bouncing and weaving around, yanking at his clothes, all the while keeping his eye patch on. He even reaches over to the dresser and replaces his giant black felt hat. I feel like I'm on a boat caught in the perfect storm.

"Arr, matey! That's more like it!" I shout as he whips off his ruffled shirt and striped tights. I decide that I am still Britney as long as I am wearing the wig. In fact, I decide that I don't want to take it off, ever.

"Well?" he says, once he's down to his hat and hard-on.

"Get over here, Silly Billy," I say, and he does. Arrr, matey!

Maybe it's the wig, or the drinks and the pot, or maybe even the eye patch, but I think it's the fame. Billy makes me come at least three times, three different ways. Having sex with a celeb is like no other sex. Harrison couldn't come close to the excitement I feel with Billy Hawk. And Billy is zany, too. Like switching positions and sticking his finger in my ass and all sorts of stuff I probably shouldn't mention. And his kissing is sublime. I don't think he neglected a square centimeter of my body. In fact, I can't think of the last time a guy was this attentive. Maybe he really likes me. As I finally drift off to a blissful sleep, images of paparazzi-hounded Billy Hawk and Maddy Braverman—hottest celebrity couple— swim like angelfish in my blond head.

"Britney! Hey, Britney!" Someone jostles me, and when I open my eyes, all I see is white. Oh my God, where am I? And why does a strange man keep shouting "Britney"? Then I realize that the white stuff is my hair, my wig. And that I am Britney and that the man is . . . Oh my God.

"Britney, you up?" he says again, and I brush the hair out of my eyes, look up at Billy Hawk's face, and break out into a huge smile, despite my throbbing head, despite the fact that I am so unprepared for morning-time intimacy in this headachy, woozy, bad-breathy, makeup-smeared state. But Silly Billy's such a sweetie. Maybe he won't hold it against me.

"Good morning," I purr, reaching out a hand to touch his back.

"Look, I hate to be a dick, but I gotta be at rehearsal in like twenty minutes, so . . ."

"No, that's cool. Of course. I mean . . ." Okay, so it's going to be like this. I should have known. I get out of bed and start maniacally leaping into Michelle's borrowed jeans. The magic is gone. The spell is broken. The genie is back in the bottle. "Oops! . . . I did it again" is right.

Where in the night does it happen? I wonder. What time exactly does everything go from being the best night of my life to being officially weird? Four A.M.? Five? And why is it always like this? Awkward, humiliating. Like, are there girls out there who have celeb shagging down to a science? Or just regular shagging, for that matter? And why am I talking like Gwyneth Paltrow in *Sliding Doors*?

I glance over at him, and he's already showered and is wearing a very respectable, very sober bowling shirt and Seven jeans. Halloween is already a distant and foggy memory to him, while I'm still dressed like Britney fucking Spears! Now I have to take the cab of shame. At least Michelle will be there. I feel like such a piece of shit.

"Okay, well, um, I had—it was, like . . . fun!" I say. "I'm just gonna go get my friend."

"She's gone," Billy says, tying his sneakers.

"Gone?" She left me here alone? At a time like this?

"Yup."

"Oh. Uhm. Cool! Well, it was, uh, nice, uhm . . . meeting you!" Somebody please put me out of my misery.

"Later," he says, not looking up. "Later"? *Later?* That's all I get is a "Later"? Fuck this asshole, I think. I am going to give him a piece of my mind! I am not a tramp! I am not a girl you can just say "Later" to without even looking at her after fucking her ten different ways since Tuesday. Whatever that means. I look down at my outfit—my 9:00 A.M. Hurricane-stained T-shirt, painted-on jeans, and grimy platform boots—and realize with horror that I am exactly that girl.

"Later," I mumble, and disappear.

# Chapter
# Nine

—

*C*elebrities suck! The whole world sucks! Who the hell ever made celebrities so damn important? All they do is make people laugh, or cry. Or sit there looking pretty. I mean, what does Billy Hawk really have to offer the world? Or Tom Cruise, for that matter? Well, not Tom Cruise. But what about—oh, forget it. Meanwhile, here I am, acting like a complete lunatic over a celebrity who is such a player. I could die of shame.

I'm sitting in the bathtub with a raging headache and a green tea, trying like crazy to detoxify, to shed last night's humiliating misadventures. Okay, so the sex was the best I've ever had. And the only sex I've had in a year. Okay, so Billy Hawk has no idea who I am, let alone my name. I mean, let's just face facts. I fucked a stuck-up celebrity who called me Britney and probably wouldn't have cared if I had gotten hit by a bus on my way home.

Kate was right: Billy and Dylan are players. I was fairly warned and took no heed. Granted, I was tanked, and well into the game by the time Kate whispered in my ear. And the player bit wouldn't have been so bad if I hadn't gone off and started naming our children and picking out our china pattern. Billy probably saw the crystal goblets in my eyes. Why can't I be a player? Why do I always have to take it to the altar? Or, in my case, the chuppah?

I take a sip of tea and wince. No wonder I'm a first-grade teacher. I have the mind of a six-year-old. I still believe in Prince

Charming and happy endings and being swept away from my humdrum existence to a mansion in Beverly Hills.

The phone rings, and soon Kate's knocking on the door, which doesn't make my head feel any better. She sticks an arm through the door and hands me the cordless.

"Thanks," I say, hoping the single syllable will convey the heartfelt apology I know I owe her for my childish behavior last night. "Hello?"

"Maddy? Hey! It's Nick. Have a good Halloween?" I snap to attention, water splashing out of the tub.

"Um, yeah. You?" Holy Moses, there is a God. Even if Nick hangs up right now, this phone call more than makes up for the Billy Hawk travesty. If only Billy could be here to witness it. Ooh, that'd show him.

Nick and I speak at the same time, then insist that the other speak first. Since I have nothing intelligible to say, he finally speaks.

"So, Maddy, Shel and I were making some plans. I know it's only November, but if you're not doing anything over winter break, we could use your help. Come with us to the Hamptons, help Lola with her writing. Her cast comes off right before we leave." I start to stammer an incoherent reply, when he adds, "Unless you have plans, which of course I'd understand."

"No, I don't think I do," I find myself saying too quickly. Of course I don't have plans, unless you call renting DVDs and getting free makeovers at Sephora with Michelle plans. I rarely see my parents anymore, even for the major holidays. I notice that my heart is pounding so hard, it's sending ripples across the surface of the water.

"So we can count you in?"

"Yes," I say, my head clouding with disbelief. It's almost as if I'm watching the scene play out from somewhere else. The neighborhood multiplex perhaps. This is truly a Shirley MacLaine moment.

After I towel off and wrap a bathrobe around me, I float into the kitchen area, which is more like a hallway in the living room, albeit one with a sink, stove, and cabinets. Kate's brewing a second pot of coffee and separating the *Times* into neat, digestible sections. I have major apologizing and groveling to do before I can crack any kind of celebratory smile. I try to summon my headache back for effect, but it's nowhere to be found.

"You want to go to the park with me and read the paper?" she asks, as if she hadn't bored holes into my head with that glare of hers last night.

"Kate, I am so sorry about last night. I was such a nutcase." I think I sound sincere. I actually am sorry. Just because I'm spending winter break in the Hamptons with the hottest actor this side of George Clooney doesn't mean I'm not filled with remorse for embarrassing my roommate.

"Totally all right," she says, not looking up. "Believe me, there was far worse going on than your little love party." Kate tells me about Frankenstein's monster slapping a camera out of a photographer's hand when he zoomed in for a close-up of the *Alias* girl. And then there were the basketball players who harassed the Gypsy, and the vampire bartender who got caught doing lines in the men's room, and the Playboy bunny who walked out in the middle of her shift after being squeezed on the cotton tail one too many times. My stomach lurches a little as I realize that Michelle and I were two of the tail squeezers. I am such a lech sometimes.

"So you're not mad at me?"

"Not at all. Did you have a good time?" Kate never ceases to mystify me. She's so good at not holding grudges. At not analyzing every interaction to death. She just gets mad, gets over it, and gets on with her life, while I fester in a pool of my own suspicions and unspoken grievances.

I tell Kate bits and pieces about my night with Billy Hawk. I tell her about the kissing and the neck rubbing but leave out the part where he was a total dick and the raunchier details of the sex. Not that it's any of her business. But she's used to getting a play-by-play. She calls me the queen of TMI (too much information). And it's true. Well, there's one thing I can change about myself. I can become secretive. Mysterious. An enigma. I think I'll start now, and not tell her about my new vacation plans. Also, that way, she won't be able to warn me.

As if on cue, she asks, "Who was that on the phone? He sounded sexy."

I tread carefully, tentatively. "That was Nick." I clear my throat from nerves then, hoping I sound nonchalant.

Kate doesn't say anything at first. She doesn't even look at me. Just continues sectioning out the *Times*. Finally she says, "What did he want?"

The question I dreaded. Kate's intense disapproval of anything celeb leaves me no choice. I'm cornered. "He just wanted to tell me that Lola's cast is coming off in six weeks or so." She doesn't respond. "He told me she's doing great, though. No pain or anything." Kate nods, apparently not buying my casual act.

"Promise me you'll be careful, Maddy. I'd just hate to see you get hurt over somebody like . . ." She shakes her head, not finishing the sentence.

"Like what?" I ask, prodding like some self-sabotaging first-grade teacher. It's times like these that my roommate's intimate knowledge of my brain's celebrified goings-on irks me no end.

"You know like what, Maddy. A celebrity. A self-involved, self-inflated, self-important, self—"

"Yeah, yeah. Self-centered," I say, playing along like the sub-servient, confrontation-fearing wuss that I am around people who have their act together.

"Self-aggrandizing," Kate offers, stumping me.

"Um, self-hating disguised as self-loving."

"What?"

"Was I reaching?"

"Mm . . . maybe," she says, scrunching her nose.

We laugh then, thank God.

"So you wanna go to the park with an unfamous chick or not?"

"Oh Kate, I have to get some work done. Thanks, though."

Even though she vehemently disapproves of my crush, I know I'd spill my guts as soon as our asses hit the bench, and there's no way I'm going to put myself in the crosshairs of temptation.

When Kate leaves, I open my laptop, but I can't concentrate on anything except Nick and the Hamptons. I have no idea what to pack. I can handle one night, a weekend maybe, but two weeks' worth of cute outfits? And just how am I going to keep my mouth shut for the entire month and a half until I leave? I'll have to tell her sometime. I'll just tell her the week before, when it's too late to make other arrangements. It won't be a lie, exactly, just a withholding of a truth she doesn't even know exists yet. Meanwhile, Shelby will be there, and the whole point of this excursion is Lola. I am a teacher, for God's sake, and my job, my mission in life, is to teach, come hell or high water, and, God as my witness, I will get that little girl up to speed with her fine motor skills.

I feel so much better now. So . . . noble. I can almost concentrate long enough to write a syllable of *Golden Ghost*.

Oh fuck it. I reach for the phone and go to dial Michelle, but there's no dial tone. Just empty space.

"Uh, hello?" I say.

"Maddy?"

"Michelle? I was just calling you!"

"I called you! Listen, Maddy, get your ass over here now. They're filming right outside my window. It's Sandy baby, and she's so close, I could spit in her hair."

I throw the phone down and nearly kill myself getting dressed. The things I do for Miss Congeniality, I swear. Thank God Michelle lives four blocks away. Otherwise, I'd be taking the subway on a Sunday, which I loathe, especially since the trains run like sludge on the weekends.

I'm practically hyperventilating by the time I turn the corner onto Michelle's block. The sidewalk is mobbed with oglers and production people. I wish my job was this exciting. I can see it now, hordes of strangers from every walk of life, pressed up against the window outside my classroom door, all just to catch a glimpse of me holding morning meeting. As if.

As I make my way through the crowd, a ponytailed production assistant barks at me to use the other side of the street.

"But I live here!" I say, lying.

He looks at me suspiciously then. I can tell, even though he's wearing mirrored Bolle sunglasses. What an entitled asshole. He thinks he's so great, keeping New Yorkers off their own sidewalks. The lowest form of life, besides the paparazzi. Please God, let him let me through.

"All right, but hurry up. They're about to shoot."

I pant my thanks over my shoulder and bolt for Michelle's door, all the while darting my head around for a glimpse of Sandra Bullock.

Michelle pulls me inside her second-floor apartment and we run over to the window, screenless and open, a crisp prewinter breeze tickling the broken blinds. She's already set up camp. There's a bowl of Veggie Booty, a bowl of steamed edamame, and two bottles of diet Snapple on the windowsill, all of which I find myself salivating for, since I haven't eaten or drunk anything except for my cup of green tea.

I start to ask her about her night with Dylan, and why she left me behind, but Michelle is preoccupied. She points toward a black canvas tentlike structure out on the sidewalk. "They're under there."

"Who's they?" I ask, popping a soybean into my mouth.

"Sandy B. and Shelby of the Sea."

"Shelby Seabolt? That can't be right. Nick told me she's in L.A."

"See for yourself."

We stare at the black canvas for what seems like an eternity, until it looks like they're actually about to shoot. Shelby and Sandra emerge from their makeshift hut and head toward the Martucci Bakery, two doors down from Michelle's apartment. Sandra's dressed as a baker: flour-smattered houndstooth baggie pants, a white shirt, and a paper hat perched on her perfectly mussed brown hair. Shelby, on the other hand, is decked out in what looks like a Chanel suit, complete with cap-toed pumps, an endless rope of pearls, and the largest sunglasses I have ever seen. Her hair is shellacked and sculpted into a glossy dome, and if I were to take a guess, I'd say she's playing the Bitch from Hell and that Sandy is the lovable underdog scamp.

They start shooting the scene as we munch our snacks, and I am overcome with our good fortune, but Michelle sighs about once every minute or so. I know she's just beside herself with jealousy that she's not down there starring in a movie, instead of Sandra Bullock.

"So what happened with Dylan?" I ask. Maybe changing the subject will cheer her up.

"It was okay."

"Really? Just okay?" I can barely believe my ears. I thought that Michelle would at least be psyched she nabbed an actual celeb.

"Well, he is only twenty-one."

"Oh yeah." I nod, reminding myself that Dylan Hover is an actual human as well as being a movie star.

"So I sucked his dick, he came in like two seconds, and then fell asleep. I left before the sun came up. That's why I didn't come get you."

"Oh," I say, thankful to have an explanation.

"Yeah. Never, ever spend the night," she continues. I stare at her, nodding. I guess that's the player secret to avoiding morning weirdness. Don't hang around. I want to ask her why she didn't warn me, but what does it matter now? The damage is done.

Shelby pulls up to the corner in a cab and walks into the bakery. She does this about seventeen times. One would think I'd be bored by then, but, in fact, it's just the opposite. The more takes they do, the bitchier Shelby becomes and the goofier Sandra gets. At around the tenth take, while she's getting into the car, Shelby screams, "I'm ready when I say I'm ready!" For take thirteen, she threatens never to get out of the car, saying she'll have the driver take her all the way to White Plains. I am riveted.

Someone, maybe the director, shouts from beneath the canopy, "Take five, everyone!" Shelby says, "Thank God," and when she's under the canopy, an argument ensues. We can't see her, but we can hear bits and pieces. I stare at the black canvas, willing my every cell to hone in on the conversation. The only voice I can hear is Shelby's, maybe because she's practically bellowing. "Nobody said anything about that to me. . . . can't do a scene if I'm not fully prepared. . . . takes as long as it goddamned takes. . . . suffering from exhaustion. . . . Fuck you, too. . . ."

"Wow, what do you think is happening?" I ask Michelle. She's an actress after all.

"They probably have a tight shooting schedule and she's fucking it up with her diva crap. Imagine having the clout to yell at your director like that. It's like a dream come true." She sighs. I smile to myself as I imagine Michelle giving Arthur an earful.

Sandra walks out from the bakery and stands right below us, where a makeup artist starts doing maintenance—powdering her nose and redistributing her hair while checking it against a batch of Polaroids. When the wardrobe girl starts adjusting her costume, Sandra looks up, right at us, and sees us standing there in Michelle's window. We wave to her like the freaks we are and Sandy gives us this huge Hollywood smile and waves right back. I didn't think Michelle and I were the type to high-five, but there we are, smacking each other's hands in the air and howling with delight. Sandy leans over to the canvas hut and points up at us, and just when I see a cap-toed shoe emerge, I run for cover, lest Shelby see me acting like a starstruck goon. Michelle stays at the window, brazen as ever.

"It's okay, Maddy. Shelby just came out to have her makeup reapplied. She probably wouldn't look up here if we were covered in killer bees."

I inch back over to the window, shaking a little, and take a tentative glance outside. Shelby is muttering as the makeup girl pats powder on her forehead. Then Shelby shouts, "What are you, retarded?" She grabs the powder from the makeup girl's hand and does it herself.

"God, I hope she's not like that in real life," I say.

Michelle looks at me. "Maddy, there's no such thing as real life to people like Shelby Seabolt. Obviously, the entire universe was created for her personal use."

"Well, I guess I'll find out for myself soon enough," I say, baiting her. All of a sudden, I am itching to tell her about Nick's phone call.

"Ugh, I know. Parent-teacher conferences. *Night of the Living Assholes.*" Michelle not only misses my agenda but reminds me like a smack in the kisser that in all my celebrity bingeing, I never once thought about the fact that parent-teacher conferences are this week, which means that reports are due in one week. If I don't start writing them this minute, I'll never be done on time and Arty Farty will have my pussy on a platter.

I look out the window and fret, my headache worming its way back into my life like a long-lost evil twin. Gazing down upon Sandra Bullock, I realize how jealous I am that she doesn't have to write exhaustive progress reports for nineteen children during an already activity-packed week. Suddenly, I don't feel so much like stargazing anymore.

Without telling Michelle my news, I stuff another handful of Veggie Booty in my mouth and brave the crowd to make my way back home.

City Select Academy does not give letter grades. Instead, we pride ourselves on lengthy, meticulous (often poetic) written reports, which cover every aspect of the precious student's development, from social conduct and artistic ability to reading comprehension and scientific reasoning. And everything in between—anything you can think of to fill two single-spaced pages. Winter and spring reports are the main reason tuition starts at fifteen thousand dollars, and the main source of commiseration among all the faculty members.

I spend the remaining precious weekend hours racking my brains for things to say about the students. I begin with Raffey, who "bounds into the classroom every Monday morning, huge smile in place for everyone, eager to share the adventures of her weekend." Kids like Raffey are easy to write reports about because they are a real joy to teach—plus, they make you aware of their existence every minute of the day. The ones who prove to be a struggle are boys like Max and Duncan, who obsess about Game Boy and use sticks as guns in the park, and kids like Mason and Fiona, who are so achingly mediocre in every area that I have a hard time gathering any good adjectives for them.

I look in my files and note who is a sight reader, who plods methodically along, who uses his fingers to count, who can't wait to settle down on the rug with a book, who has an eye for composition and color, and who makes a great mediator should she see classmates disagreeing. I remind myself how important it is to paint plausible pictures of the students as future Harvard-educated lawyers, Pulitzer Prize–winning novelists, and world-renowned artists. My job, as I pack each report with enough euphemisms to sink a Disney cruise ship, is to reassure City Select parents that their dreams can come true, and to keep them reaching for their leather-bound checkbooks year after year.

As I flip through the kids' watercolor paintings of stagecoaches lurching through the plains and across streams lined with glittering gold, I make more notes about curriculum enthusiasm and participation, and make sure I include how "thrilled the entire class was" when Zachary brought his mother's gold Cartier wedding band in for "afternoon sharing."

# Chapter
## Ten

—

*W*ith the entire week completely booked with parent-teacher conferences, I barely have time to lament my pathetic existence before my head hits the pillow at night, let alone time to continue my work on *Golden Ghost*. Poor Amanda Porter will never get to New York City at this rate.

I'm seated with a folder in front of me at Nina's round table when Mr. and Dr. Berman walk in the door, dressed as if they're on their way to the office: drab gray but expertly tailored his and her wool suits. I'm used to James being late by now, so I'm more exhausted out of futility than actually angry. Still, Nina is in James's reading group, and we decided that James would cover that area of her progress when it was time. And now it is time.

"Good afternoon, Dr. Berman, Mr. Berman," I say, smiling my conference-ready smile. I motion for them to sit down. "This is where your daughter sits, so you get a chance to see the class from her perspective." The Bermans gaze around the room, looking at the "silly sentences" lining the chair rail, the mining pans hanging from the ceiling, the life-size self-portraits done on brown roll paper with tempera paints, the illustrations of Amanda Porter from *Golden Ghost*. Then they look at me suspiciously, waiting for me to begin, to lead them. If parents don't start by telling me how much their little one loves school, then I start for them, before they have a chance to be a nudge.

"Nina just loves school," I say. They nod. They are mute. This should be a breeze. I open the folder in front of me and get to work, methodically explaining how Nina excels at math, works independently, and is never any trouble. They say nothing. I tell them about the drawing she gave to me on the first day of school, how much it meant to me, how perceptive she is, and they nod again, not uttering a single word.

"She is so imaginative, too," I say, and tell them about her habit of feeding her leftover snack to the pigeons in the courtyard during dismissal. I do not tell them that she also holds lengthy discussions with the pigeons, and the squirrels, the starlings, the sparrows, and the ants, to the point of alienating herself from the rest of the class. I do not tell Mr. and Dr. Berman that Max and Daniel call Nina "Pigeon Person," or "PP" for short, and that every time they say it, Nina inspects the dirt under her fingernails while Daniel and Max turn beet red from laughing so hard. But, come to think of it, if I did tell the Bermans, they might simply nod mutely and glare at me. The mystery of Nina's habitual introversion is unraveling at an alarming rate. I almost want to suggest that they conceive a sibling for Nina, someone who might actually talk to her.

I point out Nina's artwork, show them her math work sheets. Just when I've stretched this meeting to the thinnest-possible point, James arrives, bounding through the door, shattering our monasterylike quiet.

"Hey, guys!" He waves and pulls a clear plastic bag out of his army-regulation backpack. "You gotta try these." James plops the bag on the table, obscuring the view of Nina's personalized seat label. "Cranberry muffins with white-chocolate chips. Man, you've never tasted anything like this. Care for a muffin, Mrs. Berman? Mr. Berman? Maddy?" Before any of us can answer, he makes himself comfortable on the edge of the table and opens the bag.

"Um, James, I'm not sure if this is the time," I say, attempting to apologize for James's unorthodox behavior. I also point out that she's Dr. Berman, not Mrs.

"Oh please, just call me Pam. And I would love a muffin, James." I lift an eyebrow as Nina's mom reaches an unmanicured, almost Amish-looking hand into the bag and extracts a muffin the size of a wrestler's fist. She peels a chunk from the muffin top and places it into her mouth, which curves into a huge smile, almost orgasmic. Can no one resist James's charm?

"Pamela loves these," explains Mr. Berman to James, placing an arm around his wife. "She'd eat them every day if she could."

James heartily agrees, and before I know it, the three of them are reaching into the bag at regular intervals, cramming their faces with gourmet starch, spilling crumbs every which way, oohing and ahhing as if they were on a safari. A minute ago, this place was deader than a Winona Ryder performance, I realize, looking wistfully at the quickly emptying bag.

Pamela Berman beams at James while she presses her finger into the remaining crumbs on the table, and Mr. Berman starts pointing out every painting and drawing he sees of Nina's on the walls. Still chewing, James gets up from his casual slouch on the table's edge and walks over to the wall, where he starts to deconstruct Nina's drawing of Amanda Porter.

"See, now this is Amanda Porter. She's a poor orphan girl, but she's also this feisty heroine. Now in this picture that Nina expertly rendered, Amanda is crying over the loss of her parents. Nina handles these complicated emotions like a pro. Wise beyond her years, if you know what I mean." The Bermans nod vigorously. "See how she painted every tear a different color? And if you look real close, you can see that she placed a gold sparkle—a single piece of glitter—in the center of each tear." James gazes intently at the painting while the Bermans practically knock me out of my seat as they clamor to get a close-up view of their little Frida Kahlo's masterpiece. While their backs are turned, I mouth the words *oy vey* at the ceiling and shake my head.

"What a beautiful piece of artwork," Pamela whispers, as if she were viewing Millais's *Ophelia* at the Tate Gallery.

"And," James continues, "it's a beautiful story. Maddy's actually writing it. It's called *Golden Ghost.* And guess who came up with that title?" Mr. and Dr. Berman almost swoon with joy when they hear that their little sensation is responsible. Somehow, I don't think the news would have quite the same effect had they heard it from me, but still, I scribble a note to myself to include this tidbit in the next draft of Nina's progress report.

The last meeting of the evening is with the Seabolts, and James, for the first time this year, is finally on the other end of the waiting game. Unfortunately, it doesn't seem to affect him. He just sits on the edge of a table, strumming his guitar. When glaring at the clock doesn't prove to be helpful, I begin to reread and edit my pile of progress reports.

The door opens at 8:15, a half hour after the Seabolts are supposed to arrive, and my heart leaps into action. Sherman, the custodian, pops his head in the door.

"Maddy? You about finished in here? Time to lock up."

"My last appointment is running late," I say, sagging into my chair, and pray Sherman won't say something that will make me feel guilty for keeping him late. "Do you want me to lock up?" I add weakly.

Sherman thinks for a minute, smiles, revealing his gold tooth, and tells me not to worry. I thank him profusely and look at James, hoping he'll see how much pull I have at this place after six years.

"James!" Sherman says, noticing him for the first time. "Where you playing at next?"

"Two Boots, man." James gives his guitar strings a few fast licks for emphasis.

"All right! I'm bringing my woman this time. I keep telling her she got to hear you play. Won't never believe you're a white boy." James gets up and the two shake hands with vigor. "Stay here as long as it takes," Sherman adds, nodding and grinning at James as if he invented the blues.

"Thanks again, Sherman!" I wave, but he's already out the door, humming a tune. James's no doubt.

By 8:45, we're admitting defeat. James and I start putting the chairs up.

"I just don't get it," I say.

"Maybe they're with their lawyer," James says, wiggling his eyebrows at me and zipping his guitar case.

"What? Oh, yeah. They're suing me for negligence. Very funny," I say, gathering my things.

Just as I'm turning out the lights, Shelby walks in with Lola. The fact that they're wearing matching red patent-leather jeans and black fur jackets is not even enough to distract me from my frustration.

"Hi, uh, Maddy." Shelby is flustered enough not to give me a second glance, but not so much that she doesn't have time to ogle James from the bottom of his pointy cowboy boots to the top of his ponytailed head. "Um, James, is it?" she drawls, and then resumes being flustered as she looks around the room frantically, thick, glossy shopping bags swaying every which way, colored tissue paper rustling in the breeze she's creating. "I'm not late, am I?"

"Well, we were supposed to meet an hour ago," I say, hopefully striking a tone between patience and assertiveness, not resentment and hostility. I touch the space between my eyebrows to unfurrow my brow.

James puts his hands together and smiles widely, the way he always does when he's about to soothe a person with his unfailing charm, but Shelby piles her shopping bags into his arms, as if he's her private caddie. It takes a tremendous amount of effort not to laugh, despite how rude she's being. James looks at me and mouths the word *psycho,* then shuffles mutely over to the door and piles the bags on the floor.

I decide it wouldn't be wise to mention to Shelby that there are explicit instructions for parents not to bring their children to the conferences, and that that is why they're called parent-teacher conferences. I force myself to remember that some nonfamous parents have made the same mistake in the past, but it doesn't help me see Shelby as anything less than an overgrown spoiled brat with no regard for rules or other people. How could Nick, sensitive, caring, responsible, beautiful, sexy Nick, be with such a prima donna?

I pick up a stack of books, walk Lola over to the rug, and ask her not to interrupt unless it's to let us know that she's going to the bathroom.

"I have to go now," she says, crossing her legs.

"James?" I say. "Will you take her?"

Lola grabs James's hand and the two shuffle out of the classroom. Shelby and I are alone in the room, sitting across from each other at a midget of a round table.

"So, Nick—Mr. Seabolt, I mean—couldn't make it?" I ask, hoping I sound casual and not like I am obsessed with her husband.

Shelby rolls her eyes. "He puts on a good show, doesn't he?" she asks me conspiratorially. "Got you going, huh? He's not an Academy Award winner for nothing."

I open my mouth to ask for some clarification, but nothing comes out. I'm bewildered. Finally, changing the subject, I say, "A friend of mine saw you filming in the neighborhood recently." I am squeaking like a lab rat.

Shelby tosses her hand next to her ear. "Honey, work is work is work. Just because autograph signing comes with the territory doesn't mean the job is any better than yours. Or a prostitute's." She sighs. I twitch.

"Mr. Seabolt had mentioned that you were in L.A.?" Now I'm digging.

Shelby shoots me a glare and I immediately regret ever opening my mouth. It's none of my business. Why am I meddling? Why?

She stretches her head toward me. "Nick's bloated head, if you must know, resides permanently up his ass." Then she leans back in her seat and gazes at the ceiling, almost smiling. "It's the only place he feels at home."

I try not to look quizzical. I try not to stare, but *who are these people*? And what planet are they from?

I realize I am frightened of this woman. "Are you"—I gulp—"going to be in the Hamptons over break?"

"I most certainly am not. Nick's idea of fun is wintering in East Hampton when no one's around. He gets off on the whole recluse thing." She stabs at the air with two sets of immaculately mani-cured bunny quotes. "I, on the other hand, will be doing post-production work in Hollywood. You may want to tell him that while you're there. He'll need reminding."

"Hm," I say, and shuffle some papers, relieved and yet not.

James and Lola finally return and Lola settles on the rug with an *I Spy* book. The cast on her arm has faded to a dusty lavender and threads hang off both ends like fringe on a pair of cutoffs.

James joins us and Shelby turns to him.

"Damn that Fernanda," Shelby says, fluffing her hair. Is she actually batting her eyelashes at my assistant? Her voice softens to a purr as she continues, looking into James's eyes. "I asked her three times when the meeting was. I've got in my book that it was for eight-thirty." James and I nod at Shelby carefully as she roots through her Tod's "hobo" handbag, then flips furiously through her Louis Vuitton day planner, and then shoves the page with today's date under our noses. She looks at us almost pleadingly, her wet brown eyes straining in their sockets, as if she's begging us not to hold her responsible. My eyelid does the samba.

"Huh," I say, and shake my head. "Well, let's get started, shall we?"

James lets out a long whistle and says, "Man, she's a piece of work."

We're sitting at a dark wooden table in the back of Cousin's bar on Court Street in Brooklyn, celebrating the last of our parent-teacher conferences. It's after ten o'clock and I'm completely wiped out, but it is mandatory to decompress before heading home. A basketball game plays on the television above the bar, and the place is mercifully devoid of rowdy patrons.

Shelby, we agree, couldn't care less about Lola's work. She sat there fidgeting during the entire conference. Every time I thought we'd reeled her in and captured her attention, her cell phone rang, or her hair needed fluffing, or she'd just remembered an important appointment that she had to write in her planner before she for-got. It was as if she hadn't heard a thing we'd said the entire time.

Lola could barely stand by the time they left, and James carried her out to the limo, since Shelby couldn't carry her and all the shopping bags. Afterward, James and I sat there, silent and dumbfounded, suffocating in the lingering scent of Shelby's French perfume, face cream, hairspray, and six-thousand-dollar leather bag.

James takes long pulls from his pint of Guinness while I stab at my Jack and soda with a straw between gulps.

"So you still think the rich and famous are where it's at?" he asks, cocking an eyebrow. Not waiting for my answer, he plows on. "What could those people possibly possess that you don't already have?"

"Oh, I don't know, money . . . the adoration of millions . . . personal stylists."

Then he points at his heart and says, "No. I mean in here."

"You didn't tell me you watched Oprah," I reply, teasing him.

"Only on Wednesdays," he says, lifting his eyebrows. "But I'm serious, Maddy. You build these people into deities, and they are not."

"What about Rachel?" I blurt out, immediately regretting it.

"What about her?" I can feel my cheeks heat up. I shrink into my chair and gesture into the air in front of me as if it holds the tidy answer.

"I don't know. Just that. Well, she's kind of famous. By association anyway."

James gives this some thought. "Yeah, I guess," he says. "But I don't really think about it. I don't judge people on how well they're known by the public or—"

I interrupt him, bolting upright. "Neither do I! That's not what I mean at all. It's just—she's, like, part of that whole world."

"And that 'whole world' is like a giant lollipop and you're a sugar-starved kid."

"Thanks, Freud," I groan, swallowing the last of my drink.

"Ze problem, zen," James says with that infuriating wink, "eez een here." He leans across the table and places a finger in the center of my forehead. When he touches me, I can smell the old suede of his jacket and a hint of patchouli oil. He surprises me by brushing a stray hair out of my eyes, and my heart speeds up. He's sitting there, leaning his crossed arms on the table, grinning at me. I look away, hold my breath and think, I refuse to be one of James's adoring minions. When I glance back at him, he winks.

"Why do you have to wink all the time?" I ask, growing ornery.

"What? I don't wink."

"You do so. All the time. It's really patronizing. And what makes it even more annoying is that you're younger, with less life experience. If anything, I should be winking at you."

"First of all, I do not wink," he says, and leans back in his chair and folds his hands behind his head. "But let's say, for the sake of argument, which we're both fond of, I do wink. I'll give up my habit if you give up yours."

"What habit?"

"Celebrity, baby. You're a junkie. You're . . . star craving mad!" James cracks up at his own joke, his eyes twinkling with delight.

"You're hilarious," I deadpan, annoyed, and yet, at the same time, I notice that his eyes are the clearest shade of green, not swampy-mucky like I thought. They're nice, those winking eyes. It's almost too bad they belong to Rachel Tepper.

"Well, that's going to be difficult," I say, darting my gaze at my empty glass.

"Why?"

"They asked me to spend winter break with them."

"Who, the Seabolts?"

I nod.

"And you're going?"

I nod again.

"Well then, you've got your work cut out for you." He gets up and orders us another round.

"It'll be a lot easier to break my habit than it will be to break yours," I say, following him.

"How so?"

"Mine's emotional. Yours is physiological." I put my hand on my hip triumphantly. It sounds like it might even be true.

"Well, Miss Emotional, what do you want if you're right?"

"Huh?"

"The bet. The winner has to win something."

"Oh, yeah. And the loser has to lose something."

The bartender places the drinks in front of us. We don't touch them.

"Okay," James agrees. Then he tilts his head, thinking. "If I win, you . . . dedicate *Golden Ghost* to me: 'To my dear friend James Watkins . . . who made this all possible. Without you, I'd never—'"

"Oh, like that will keep me motivated to finish it," I say sarcastically. "Okay, I agree," and then I think for a minute. I want to get him in the same place. His creativity. "If I win . . . you have to . . . write a song about me. A *nice* song. And you have to perform it in public."

James considers this. He holds out his glass and we clink, sealing the bet. Then we chug.

# Chapter
# Eleven

*I* am a terrible roommate, a terrible friend, a horrible, despicable excuse for a human being. I haven't told Kate a thing about my vacation plans, and here I am, at 9:00 A.M., the Saturday before Christmas, sneaking around like Julia Roberts in *Sleeping with the Enemy*.

As I unlock the column of dead bolts, Kate steps out of her bedroom. I turn toward her, shame and guilt suffocating me like an overheated subway platform. In Casey's flannel pajamas, Kate looks like a confused child who can't tell if she's awake or dreaming. Concern shadows her sleepy face, and I want to run over to her and smooth her crumpled hair, beg her forgiveness. But then I know I'd regret not going to the Hamptons, and resent my roommate for the rest of my life.

"What's going on?" she asks, adjusting her eyes to the light.

"Kate," I say, apologetically, dropping my bag to the floor. She waits for my answer. I pull out my Filofax, copy the number in the Hamptons, and place it on the coffee table. "Lola needs help with her writing," I explain feebly. "The Seabolts asked me—they invited me to— I'm really sorry, Kate. For not telling you. I just thought—" My sentences crash into one another.

"It's okay," she says, putting me out of my misery. She doesn't say it bitterly, but I can tell she's hurt. She rubs her eyes. "Call me if you need to."

"Okay." Then I run over and hug her. "I'm sorry."

"It's okay. Have fun." I can tell by the smile she's attempting that she's trying to be supportive of my decision.

"Thanks," I say.

And then, as I run down the stairs, schlepping my stuff, I hear, "Be careful, Maddy!" I shut my eyes for a second and whisper, "I'll try."

From the moment I step off my stoop and hand my old Crate & Barrel duffel bag to Frank Caruso, I know I am a goner. Climbing into the plush leather interior of the idling limo, I take a moment to imagine the dedication page of my novel, bursting with acknowledgments for a certain smoke-reeking Americana musician.

And then, deeply sighing, I fully succumb to this alternate reality, a place I've only accessed secondhand through movies like *Notting Hill* and *America's Sweetheart.* Julia Roberts is haunting me, I decide. Nonetheless, I am leaving my black-and-white life behind for a brand-new digital, Technicolor, surround-sound life, if only for a couple weeks. I intend to enjoy every star-studded second, even if my roommate wouldn't approve. She has Casey, after all. What does she know about loneliness?

For a minute, I pretend I'm fabulous, pretend I'm Julia Roberts, watching the highway whiz by, sniffing the pristine smell of fresh Cadillac. What would she be doing right now? Reading a script? Arranging to visit a terminally ill child somewhere in the Midwest, or to star in a documentary about endangered jungle animals? Talking to Marc or Calvin or Ralph on her sleek silver cell, planning her outfit for the Golden Globes? I am stumped as to a plausible answer. One thing is certain: She wouldn't be doing it in a pair of seven-dollar corduroys from the Goodwill.

As the limo glides through Long Island, the grass is higher, the road bleaches from black to white, and the sky opens to a blinding winter white. Nick and Lola will be meeting me via helicopter at the "cottage," as Nick affectionately referred to it on the phone this morning before Frank arrived. Shelby, he confirmed for me, is in L.A. So Shelby was wrong when she said Nick had his head up his ass all the time.

I am dying to ask Frank what the deal is between Nick and Shelby. Are they headed toward splitsville? I lean forward to ask, but then I'm afraid he'll think I'm going to sell the story to the *National Enquirer.* And I'd hate to put him in an awkward position. As thorny as Shelby was, I have to admit that a part of me is fluttering with the hope that Nick and Shelby won't make it. If Nick were single, I could have my cake and eat it, too. I could . . . Oh, who am I kidding? If Nick and Shelby got divorced, Nick would probably hook up with Charlize Theron.

When Frank pulls into the long driveway and passes through a tunnel of perfectly pruned hedges, the "cottage" appears, and I have to say, *castle* is the word that comes to my mind. The house is more like ten cottages. It's a mansion of a cottage, and why wouldn't it be, with owners like these? At least it has shingles and a pointy roof, not turrets and a drawbridge.

Frank stops at a wrought-iron gate and punches a series of numbers into a security panel. After we park inside, he takes my duffel bag and leads me along a flagstone path that winds through a brown crew cut of a lawn to the front door. I clutch at the strap of my Manhattan Portage bag in anticipation.

Frank's cell phone rings then. I step a few feet away to give him some privacy. It must be ten degrees outside; I shiver and put my fleece hat on, making sure to cover my ears.

He snaps his phone back into his hip holster. "Miss Braverman, it looks like you will have the place to yourself until eight o'clock. Mr. Seabolt called to say he has a last-minute meeting. The kitchen is fully stocked, and there's a screening room in the basement. Make yourself at home."

Frank opens the door and gestures for me to enter. I stand in the doorway, wishing Frank could join me, so I wouldn't have to spend seven hours alone. "Thanks, Frank."

He tips his hat and then is gone.

I turn around and gaze at the huge room before me, the biggest, most austere living room I have ever seen, complete with giant white concrete orbs balancing on steel pedestals. I drag my duffel bag across the gleaming ebony floor and leave it at the foot of the wide, curving wooden staircase.

The huge kitchen is dark. The stone floor, the rows and rows of distressed pine cabinets, the brushed-nickel hardware, and gleaming granite countertops all sit quietly in the darkness. I wander outside again to look at the backyard, a phenomenon I rarely get to experience in Brooklyn. After crossing through a grand dining room (table for sixteen, anyone?), I see that the backyard is not a yard at all. It is the Atlantic Ocean, a private beach, strewn with yet more concrete spheres resting on the sand, as if they landed there from outer space. I stand outside, mesmerized by the crashing waves, the utter lack of human beings, heaven on a New Yorker's earth. Then I realize I'm freezing my ass off again.

Back in the kitchen, I begin to root around for a snack. I settle on a mug of Ghirardelli hot white chocolate, four chocolate-dipped strawberries, and a gigantic croissant. I know, I'm going to explode overnight. After I polish off the croissant, I refill my mug and head downstairs.

The screening room is covered in white shag carpeting, floors, walls, ceiling. I feel like I've been swallowed by the abominable snowman. Huge matching white cushions line a sunken pit in the floor. Inside the pit is a center console, with a stereo, DVD and VCR, cleverly concealed beneath a thick glass tabletop. On one side of the room, after I figure out the remote control, a giant screen descends from the ceiling. Opposite that is a projection room, which I am not even going to try to mess with. I set the room's lighting scheme to a hot-pink shade and then understand why white is the color of choice. Then, after about twenty minutes, I locate the DVD library, hidden behind a panel in one of the walls. After some careful rummaging, I settle on an appropriate classic, *Pretty in Pink,* and sink into the plush cushions to be entertained by the heartthrobs of yore.

At seven o'clock, after a John Hughes double feature, I make my way upstairs and enter what must be the master bedroom. Sisal carpet spans the massive space framed by floor-to-ceiling windows loosely strewn with layers of silvery organza. On a zebra-skin rug, a white love seat and chair reside under one of the windows. Three steel cubes serve as a coffee table. At least I think that's what it is. In another corner, a life-size marble bust, nude, poses on a steel pedestal. Inspecting it, I get the distinct feeling that I'm looking at the likeness of Shelby. Even so, the sculpture pales in comparison to the room's main attraction. Freestanding in the center of the room sits a king-size bed, outfitted with a brushed-steel canopy and draped with loads of organza and beaded silk.

I sit on the edge of the bed, running my hands over sheets so smooth and soft, they should be outlawed. I imagine Nick sitting here beside me—no, lying beside me—with no clothes on. I imagine Shelby locked up somewhere, Bellevue perhaps. Lola is . . . with some nanny, and I am here with Nick.

"You win, James," I say, and look at my watch. It's 7:10. Fifty minutes to go. In a daring move, I slip off one of my boots, unbutton my jeans, and sink back into the five-zillion-thread-count pillows.

It doesn't take long before I have to turn over and straddle my fist, humping it as if it were Nick. I shimmy out of just my right pant leg, letting it and my underwear dangle around my left knee.

Imagining Nick's face, sweaty and ecstatic, picturing his body, every one of his well-defined muscles taut with excitement, creates a rising wave of heat inside me. Just as I'm catching the wave to shore, I hear a car door slam outside. Before I have a chance to get my pants back on, "Hello? Maddy?" comes ripping up the stairs, and it's Nick's sexy yet climax-destroying voice. Oh, the irony.

I keep yanking at my underwear, but my panties are tangled in the leg of my jeans. I grab my boot in one hand, keep yanking with the other, and hop toward the closest door I see, praying it's a bathroom. It's not. I'm hopping on one foot in a walk-in closet that easily takes up more square footage than my entire apartment, but I don't have time to snoop. Nick's voice sounds closer now.

"Maddy?" he calls, and I hear the steps creaking. I crack open the door and open my mouth to shout something, a logical response of some sort. But nothing comes out. How in the world am I going to explain my current circumstance? Finally, I manage to untwist my underpants and hike them and my jeans leg up in one fell swoop. I dig my heel down into my boot and run out of the closet, zipping up just as Nick walks into the bedroom.

"Maddy," he says, sporting a fresh question mark in his beautiful crinkly eyes.

"Oh, hi!" I chirp, and my voice, to me anyway, shakes like the Cyclone at Coney Island. Maybe he won't notice. "I was looking for you guys and I came in here and . . ." My voice trails off as I look around the room for the last part of my sentence. I scan the bed quickly for signs of my digression, and there on the top sheet is a circle of wetness the diameter of a silver dollar. I glance at Nick then to see if he's seen it, but he's still looking at me. He's so beautiful that I almost forget about the rest of my sentence, but then I find what I'm looking for. "The sculpture!" I shout, rushing over to present it like Vanna White. "It's just . . . so brilliant, it *beckoned* me over. I'm a big fan of nudes. Nude sculpture. And, um . . ." Does he look amused?

"And?"

"And . . ." I stall, searching wildly around the room. "I, um, love rooms done in white! And it was so quiet and peaceful, so I thought I'd . . ."

"Yes?"

"Meditate for a while. Until you arrived."

"Really?"

"Oh God yeah! Meditation. Just . . . keeps me sane! You know?" Nick nods slowly. I can't tell if he believes me or not, so I start yammering away about the chakras, spinning wheels of energy, all the colors of the rainbow, the power of "om," anything I can remember from my brief foray into yoga, before I finally trail off. I decide to be quietly mortified. He must know I was schtupping myself on his bed. It's probably written all over my face.

When he seems certain that I'm done, he says, "At any rate, I'm sorry to have kept you waiting." Then he puts his hands on his hips and offers to show me around.

The last room he takes me to is the basement rec room. Lola's got her Rollerblades on and is speeding around in circles. I'm guessing one lap equals an eighth of a mile, judging by the size of the room. Who needs the outdoors when you have mansion to go with your penthouse?

"Maddy! Look! No cast!" she says, whizzing by.

"Congrats, kiddo!" I say, and try not to worry that she'll break another bone. I turn to Nick and say, "She's quite the daredevil." I can't tell whether I sound casual or like a nervous wreck. I chew on a cuticle, pondering this.

"Yeah, well, she got it from her old man," he says, stretching. A ribbon of flat belly peeks from beneath his short black down jacket and I salivate like Cujo. I'm in need of release in a major way.

As if he's reading my mind, Nick says, "Why don't I show you to your room?" My heart does a double axel, even though he's staring straight ahead when he says this, eyes following Lola around and around. There is no hint of a pass, no trace of a play for my affections, but then, this is a man who could hock a loogey on the floor and most women would get down on their knees to lick it up. I am not well.

It takes about five minutes to reach my bedroom. By comparison, it could be in a different dimension, let alone a different house.

"It's not the choicest of boudoirs, but we're having the north wing, which has the better guest rooms, renovated. Hey, at least you won't be breathing sawdust!" The room looks like it hasn't been touched since the Johnson administration: floral wallpaper, Oriental rug, satin bedspread, antique spindly dressing table, and matching night tables. It reminds me of my grandmother's old house.

"I love it," I say, and I do. I was fearing more brushed steel and concrete orbs.

By the end of the first week, we settle into a routine. Lola wakes up and has a bowl of cereal, what she calls her "first breakfast."

Then around nine o'clock, Nick makes a "second breakfast" for the three of us. And, honey, it ain't no Bönz diet. Rather, it's an omelette, or scones, clotted cream, and fresh raspberries, or crepes with real maple syrup and, especially for me, Morningstar Farms vegetarian bacon strips, my favorite. So what if I gain twenty pounds in two weeks? They have a gym.

Nick, it turns out, is quite the accomplished chef, as if his smoldering looks and charm aren't enough to send any woman into a frothy lather of desire. After a quick lesson on the cappuccino machine, I'm put in charge of beverages, and I make a mean steamed milk for Lola. If I didn't know any better, I'd say I was a part of this family.

After breakfast, Nick goes into his office or works out with his trainer and I work with Lola on her writing in Shelby's office, which looks more like a shrine devoted to the Orient. If that proves to be too distracting, we'll go down to the basement screening room. Lola and I take turns with the remote control.

Most kids can't stand working in the handwriting book, tracing the same letter over and over. Lola, though, seems to enjoy it. With her newly mobile fingers, it takes all her concentration.

A grocery delivery arrives during lunch, and then Lola either blades laps in the rec room or we venture outside in the cold, down to the beach to throw a Frisbee or build a sand castle. Then there's tea while Lola and I read together and Nick goes back to his office. Dinner could be takeout, or Nick will grill steaks for himself and Lo and supply me with fish. He offered to order me my very own Bönz meal plan for the duration, but to be honest, I prefer Nick's cooking any day of the week. Nick, thankfully, also prefers to cook. He says, "Brad's got his architecture and I have my kitchen," and then he chops and sautés, and I melt.

Sometime during the day, I'll run on the treadmill in the gym, which is its own wing, an addition to the already-cavernous mansion, which Nick tells me was originally a potato farmer's house. The gym is state-of-the-art, filled with the latest cardio and weight-training machines, plus one medieval-looking contraption that I know can only be for Pilates. An expanse of windows faces the beach and mirrors line the opposite wall. The gym is equipped with its own kitchenette with full bar, a shower room, a steam room and sauna, and just outside, down a few winding flagstone steps, is a bubbly Jacuzzi. Nick keeps telling me to use it, but I haven't gotten up the nerve. I guess I'd feel like I was taking advantage of his hospitality. I promise myself that I'll take the plunge, so to speak, before two weeks have passed.

When we finally settle into our separate bedrooms for the night, after a kiddie comedy or a Disney animated feature starring Nick as the genie of the sea, I stare at the ceiling and force myself to believe that what I'm experiencing is real, even if Nick isn't my real boyfriend, even if he's not remotely close. Then I hump my fist, and I fall asleep.

The other thing I do when I get the chance is work on *Golden Ghost*. But as the days slip by, every minute I spend typing on my laptop seems like time I'm wasting—time that I could be spending with Nick and Lola. It made sense to write when my life consisted of a tiny apartment shared with a lovey-dovey couple. But now in the Hamptons, I feel like part of a lovey-dovey couple, and I don't want to miss a single second.

I'm tapping away on the keyboard one night before bed, when there's a knock at the door.

"Come in," I say. Nick pokes his head in the door and my heart leaps a little.

"Hey, I'm not disturbing you, am I?"

"No, not at all." I close the cover of the computer and look at him expectantly. He's wearing an olive green wool crewneck sweater, which is fraying at the neck, a pair of wide-wale corduroys, and heather gray wool socks. Yummy.

"What are you working on?"

"Oh, it's just this story. No big deal. Just, um, experimenting." I decide not to give out the details of my project. If he was anything less than enthusiastic, I might never look at it again.

"Well, I have kind of a confession to make, Maddy."

Holy moly. My dream is coming true. He's going to tell me he's fallen madly in love with me, that the divorce papers are being served as we speak. I nod my head to urge him on, my heart pounding, causing the most deafening noise in my chest.

"I kind of promised my agent I'd throw a Christmas dinner tomorrow night. It's a black-tie affair, and I kind of forgot to mention it to you. I guess with Lo's cast coming off and all the excitement, I pushed it to the back of my mind."

I nod, crestfallen.

"It's okay. I can probably catch an early bus back to the city. It's no problem, really."

"No, Maddy."

"No?"

"You're invited."

"I am?"

"You most certainly are."

"But, I don't have anything to—"

"Well, that's part of what I'm trying to say, if you'll let me finish." The corners of his eyes crinkle with amusement.

"Oh." I feel like a dope. But a happy Cinderella-type dope. I nod again, encouraging him.

"Well, since I forgot to warn you, can I make it up to you by buying you a dress for the party?"

"Mr. Seabolt—"

"Nick."

"Nick. Um, I couldn't. That's way too generous. I . . . You should throw your party and I'll just hang out in here. Really. It's no bother. I can just . . . work on my"—I grab the edges of my laptop—"story." The last thing I want to be doing while Nick parties in a tuxedo below me is to work on any story. I pray he doesn't take me seriously.

"Maddy. Are you sure? You really don't mind?"

I swallow, then say, "No. Not at all. You have fun. Really." I nod and force a smile. "I'm okay." I mean, what am I supposed to do? Allow Nick Seabolt to buy me a dress? There must be some rule against that in the teacher handbook. It seems so frivolous. So inappropriate. So . . . luscious. Decadent. Sinfully fun. When he leaves, I realize I've never felt so alone in my life.

I'm okay, really. That's what I tell myself as I drift off to sleep, where I dream that I am in this house with no clothes whatsoever and have to spend each day in a ratty bathrobe that once belonged to a maid.

I'm okay, really. The thought continues upon waking. I feel like crap, and it shows. I drag myself listlessly through the day's activities, and watching the house fill with caterers and florists does not help one bit. When the crates of top-shelf booze arrive, I nearly cry from the injustice of it all. Maybe Master will let me fill a plate and grab a bottle before banishing me to the dungeon.

When I can't take one more minute of watching the shrewish caterer bark directions at doe-eyed struggling actress waitresses, I escape to my bedroom. I figure I'll try to write for a while to take my mind off my misery. I open the door, intent on flinging myself across the bed for a good dramatic cry, but something is already on the bed. It is, in fact, a shiny black garment bag, draped diagonally across the down comforter. In gold lettering across the top of the bag, underneath a heavily lacquered hanger, is one name: Versace. My breath stops short. I look around to see if Nick is anywhere in the vicinity, but I am alone. A smile breaks over my face, the storm clouds part, the sun shines, and I slowly unzip the bag.

I know this dress. I have seen it in *Celeb File Weekly*. It is the same dress Shelby Seabolt wore to the International Fundraiser Ball for Injured Equestrians last year. The same dress that prompted me to ask, "What the hell was she thinking?" Michelle thought maybe Shelby was angling to play Jane in a remake of a Tarzan movie. It's a leopard-print dress, sleeveless, with a cleavage cutout and not one but *two* thigh-high ruffled slits. It's lined with black-and-green paisley swirls on a canary yellow background. The dress looks like it needs a substantial pair of boobs to make it work, and mile-long superskinny legs. Suddenly, my life feels like a disaster waiting to happen. As I lean over to sniff the pits, I bump into a box on the floor. Shoes.

Just as I suspected: They're impossibly high, impossibly strappy, and feathered. Now when I appear to Nick's guests, not only will I look hideous; I will fall flat on my face doing it. How can I possibly make this dress work?

"Hey, I see you found the goods," Nick says from the door, startling me from my despair. I pray he can't read my thoughts like Mel Gibson could in *What Women Want.*

"Oh, yeah," I say, trying to sound enthused. "Thank you so much. You really didn't need to do—"

"Ah, I wanted to. You deserve it. I'll bet it'll look great on you."

I squint at him to see if he's lost his mind. But he's so handsome standing there that I immediately feel terrible for hating the dress. I mean, it's Versace, for crying out loud. Michelle would kill half the fifth-grade class for a chance like this.

"Nick. It's gorgeous."

"Donatella's a good friend of mine. She's a real genius." Of course she is, I think, nodding mutely.

After I tuck Lola in bed at nine o'clock, I race to my bedroom and put on the dress. As I inch over to the full-length mirror, I can already feel that the fabric is stretched taut in all the wrong places—across my thighs, mostly. And the shoes are not only deadly but also a size too small. Did Nick really think that I was a size zero and had size-six feet?

In front of the mirror, I cannot bear to open my eyes. But open my eyes I must. I start with my left eye, just to ease the transition. The shoe looks okay. It's my foot that's turning beet red and looking . . . well, quilted. My calves and knees, in all their pasty white glory, are out in the open, taking in the horror of it all. Oh, and there are my saddlebags, cellulite and all, for the world to see. I've never felt uglier. Until I see my chest, a hopeless child drowning in an Olympic-size pool. I lower my head in defeat.

I can hear the grand piano tinkling Christmas oldies downstairs, as well as the din of wealthy voices and every now and then a woman's screeching laughter. I cannot go down there. I refuse to go down there. I—

"You look beautiful, Maddy." I whip around, to see Nick poised in the doorway, looking impossibly luscious in a meticulously tailored tuxedo, his hair disheveled in perfect contrast. Even in this joke of a dress, I feel my insides going gooey. But wait. Did he say I look . . . beautiful?

"Really?"

"Why does every woman on the planet ask that exact question when they receive a compliment on their looks?"

"I don't know, I just— I look okay? Really?" Nick laughs, a hearty, deep laugh and I smile, despite how foolish I feel.

"Maddy, I am telling you—no lie—you are breathtaking."

Now I'm really melting. He can't be serious, though! I know I must look like a trollop.

"I guess I'm not used to wearing such, um, high-fashion, um . . ."

"Couture," he says, a smile teasing his eyes.

"Couture."

Maybe he has a point. After all, Nick sees women in these kinds of getups all the time. Maybe he knows better than I do if I look good. As I ponder the possibility that I actually am breathtaking in this dress, Nick pirouettes into the room.

"How do I look?" he asks.

"You look . . . great," I say, trying not to salivate, or faint. He smiles broadly, obviously satisfied, and refocuses his smoldering gaze on me.

"Turn around, Maddy."

I turn in a slow circle and try not to bunch my shoulders into a tight little knot when my back side is facing his front. I can feel his eyes take in my posterior view, and I would die of humiliation if it didn't turn me on so much.

Then I think of Lola, sleeping innocently in her bed. I wonder what *she* would think if she knew I was destroying her parents' marriage right this minute.

Still facing the wall, I ask, "Do you think we should be getting downstairs? Your guests will wonder where you are."

"Let them wonder." I complete the circle and face him. He's touching his lips softly with the tips of his fingers, making me incredibly nervous. "I almost forgot," he says suddenly, and reaches into his inside pocket. He produces a flat velvet box and gestures for me to come closer. When he lifts his hands around my throat and clasps the necklace, I swear my heart is pounding so loud that he can feel it in his fingers.

"Merry Christmas," he says.

"What?" I ask, eyes bulging.

"Take a look."

I turn and face the mirror. Fastened around my neck is the most delicate golden necklace, a choker that seems to be spun from hundreds of strands of gold filament, studded with tiny beads of jade and carnelian.

"Nick. Wow."

"Lola picked it out. She said it went perfectly with your curriculum."

"That is so thoughtful," I say, turning this way and that, relishing the view.

"Gold rush," he says slowly, letting the words ooze from his lips.

"It's so beautiful. Thank you so much."

Nick walks over to me and places his hands on my shoulders.

"You're so beautiful, Maddy." I stare into the mirror and believe it's true.

He kisses my hand and bids me adieu. Before I know it, I'm left to wonder, Was he just calling me beautiful a minute ago, or did I dream the whole thing?

# Chapter
## Twelve

—

*A*cross the living room, refurnished with cozy tables for two, is a completely transparent grand piano. Alan Alda is playing and crooning Christmas carols. If I'd watched *M\*A\*S\*H\** instead of *Chico and the Man,* this would be a momentous occasion.

Dotted around the vast room are enough flickering votives to light Brooklyn Heights. And for each dancing flame, there must be a dozen gorgeous women, all balancing effortlessly on heels that are impossibly high, dripping with jewelry that looks excruciatingly expensive. I suddenly feel like a cow in my ill-fitting borrowed duds. As I pull at my dress, I see Jaquellinah, successor to the throne of Giselle, captivating an all-male audience with her mile-long tan legs. So what if she doesn't speak a word of English? With a shudder, I turn away. In another part of the room, two of the stars from the latest Australian independent film, *Razz My Truffle,* share a joint, their bow ties undone, their eyes already mere slits. If it weren't for my pasty thighs, I'd think I'd died and gone to heaven.

A group of about five colorfully dressed people huddle near the marble fireplace. Every minute or so, they burst into laughter. Someone's doing imitations, or telling jokes—I can't tell which. One of the women, squeezed into a canary yellow sequined gown, keeps dabbing her eyes with a tissue while she pleads for whoever it is to "stop it!" I crane my neck to see what is so funny.

Eventually, the crowd parts and the jokester emerges. When I see his face, I duck behind a ficus tree, suddenly too nervous even to grab a blini bundle. It's Billy Hawk, player extraordinaire, humiliator of my life. He's wearing a too-tight maroon tuxedo, and his expertly mussed hair sticks to his forehead in pointy chunks.

Through the light-festooned leaves, I watch him saunter from guest to guest, working the room like Austin Powers. Within minutes, he has the *Truffle* stars choking on their blunt, they're laughing so hard. Pretty soon, even Jaquellinah is in stitches. Does Billy Hawk speak Turkish?

I start to feel like a crazy person, skulking behind the tree, spying on a sketch-comedy star. I could use a drink. And anyway, he's an asshole. I stand up straight and make my way back to the bar along the perimeter of the room, just to be safe. I order a double Jack and soda, then guzzle it.

"Big Jack fan, huh?" asks the bartender, a beefy bald man who could give Mr. Clean a run for his money. Peeking out of the collar of his regulation tuxedo shirt is a tattoo of an eel. He sees me looking and rubs it. "From *The Tin Drum*," he says. "Ever read it?"

"Uh, no. I probably should have. I saw the movie, though. My dad actually has an etching of that eel."

"Really? That's pretty cool," he says. I shrug and explain that my father is a bit eccentric.

The bartender, who calls himself Preach, pours me another drink. By the time I've finished my fourth, he knows way too much about me, but at least I didn't crash the party like Alan Alda did. Apparently, he shows up uninvited every year, poor guy.

"Do you really think he likes me?" I ask, leaning my elbows on the bar.

"There's only one way to find out, Maddy."

"You're so right. So wise. Is that why they call you 'Preach'?"

As I'm gushing to Preach about Nick some more, the laughter Billy's been conjuring worms its way to the bar and, all at once, surrounds me.

"I'm going to be so skank when I quit this business!" Billy says, and his entourage erupts. I turn and catch his eye. He gives me a huge smile and I feel like I've just swallowed an ice cube. Does he know it's me?

"Hey, Jane! Me Tarzan!" he says, and the crowd snorts with glee while my eyes widen. There is no hint of recognition on his elfin face.

While Preach makes Billy a Stoli Orange and soda, I open my mouth to stammer a reply but come up short. "What, you only speak the language of the jungle?" My whole body twitches in disbelief. Then Billy starts screeching like a monkey. Does he do this to all the girls he sleeps with? I think very seriously about pouring my drink over his head. But I don't want to ruin Nick's party. Or his floor.

I find my voice. "It's Versace," I say, as if this piece of news will settle the matter once and for all.

While his droogs hunch over, mute with hilarity, Billy touches his cheek and says with mock horror, "Not Versace!" He eyes me up and down then, sizing me up. Then he leans in and says in my ear, loudly enough for his audience to share in the fun, "I know a great cosmetic surgeon who can fix those." He gestures to my size-B cups and a splash of Stoli lands on my breast. That's when I remember the wig—the beautiful, tacky, identity-obscuring white-haired wig. Billy Hawk has no idea who I am.

I take a look around and see that Nick is safely across the room, ensconced in conversation. Then I take a deep breath and leap. I throw my drink in Billy's face and unleash my satisfied smile as whiskey and soda cascades from his face and lapels.

I guess I was wrong in thinking that being a woman would shield me from retaliation, because Billy doesn't miss a beat. Before I can blink, my face is drenched in very cold vodka. Preach immediately rushes over with a handful of towels, handing me a couple. Then he crouches and starts mopping the floor with the rest.

And that's when the crowd parts and Nick appears, creating an extraordinarily awkward triangle. I'm going to be fired. Kicked out. Excommunicated. I feel just like Michael J. Fox in *The Secret of My Success.* Oh . . . yeah.

Billy straightens up and says soberly to Nick, "Sorry, man," and the crowd dissolves into the rest of the room. Then to me, he says, wildly shifting gears, "I'm sorry. Have we met?" What, is Nick the Godfather of Tinseltown?

Nick says, "Maddy, is everything okay?"

Billy says, "Maddy, nice to meet you." And holds out his limp little hand.

"Maddy needs to change," I say, glaring at Billy. I hold my arms out from my sides and away stiffly. I'm sure I am as far from beautiful as I can possibly be. At least the vodka dripping down my cheeks will camouflage my tears.

Halfway up the stairs, Nick catches up to me and puts his arm around my shoulder.

"I'm so sorry," I say when we get to my room, where I promptly dissolve into hysterics. I'm sitting on the bed, and Nick is kneeling in front of me on the floor. I may as well be five years old.

"Maddy, it's okay. I hate to see you cry. I feel like this is all my fault. I—"

"No. It is not your fault. It's . . . such an expensive dress."

His eyes go soft then and he touches my shoulder. "That's what dry cleaners are for."

I try to smile at him through my tears.

"What happened down there anyway?"

"Um—I was just—" I stammer.

Nick puts his fingers to my lips. "Sshh. I understand. You don't have to say another word. Between you and me, Billy Hawk has quite the reputation. And unfortunately for the fairer sex, he works hard to preserve it."

I blink and then nod. And then thank God he wore a condom. If Nick knew I was one of the women who keep Billy Hawk's reputation intact, he'd probably throw me out. I'm such a slut.

"Maddy, what you did down there was act like the lady you are." He leans back, my hands in his, and takes a good look at the lady he thinks he sees before him. "God, you are a breath of fresh air, Maddy." He stands up. "Now, do you want to change?"

"If it's okay with you, I'd just rather go to bed."

"Sure, it's okay, but Shelby has a lot of clothes. I'm sure there's something you'd look great in. And Maddy, I'd feel terrible leaving you up here. Please come with me. I'm begging you."

The corners of my mouth curve toward the ceiling despite the tears still streaming down my face. "All right. But what about . . ." I can't bear to say his name, so I just point my chin toward the door a few times.

"Maddy. I promise you—"

"I can't go down there. I'll just go—"

"Maddy—"

"No. I can do this," I say, changing my mind again. "I'm not going to let him ruin my night."

"There you go."

"Oh my God, who am I kidding? I can never show my face to those people again. They think I'm—"

And that's when Nick kisses me. The most romantic, luscious, tender, best kiss ever.

I close my eyes, swooning with ecstasy, Billy Hawk a distant memory.

"I'm sorry," he says, removing his lips, waking me from my reverie. "I shouldn't have done that, Maddy. I just . . ." He just what? I tilt my head toward him questioningly. "This is so wrong," he says. "But I like you." He likes me. He likes me! Nick Seabolt likes *me*!

"I like you, too!" I exclaim, overjoyed. Suddenly, Vera Wang wedding dresses dance before my eyes.

I gaze into his eyes, a smile of the utmost elation plastered to my face. Now I know what Julia Roberts meant when she told Oprah she was "drunk with joy." I am, right now, her soul sister.

"Maddy, let's find something for you to wear," Nick says, holding my hand and standing up. He leads me down the hall, and I don't think my feet touch the ground once.

Shelby's closet, which is two times the size of my Brooklyn bedroom, is a shopper's heroin. It's like being inside *Celeb File Weekly.* Every outrageously priced item is arranged by color and size. The half a dozen oval-shaped racks in the center of the room rotate by remote control. One whole wall is dedicated to handbags from every era, of every shape, size, and style. Another wall is devoted to denim. Shoes soar up to the ceiling on a third.

Nick sits outside on an overstuffed chair while I make a mess in the closet. Most of Shelby's clothes are teeny, not intended for a human girl with hips. I decide on a metallic Prada top and a long, flowy, tan Chloe skirt, which is long enough that I don't have to worry about shoes, since there are no size eights to be seen anywhere.

"What do you think?" I ask, entering the bedroom.

Nick touches his lips and squints.

"No good?"

"No. I think it works. I do. I'm partial to Versace, but this definitely works as well." He stands and comes toward me. When he's about a foot away, I instinctively hold my breath. "You look great." He nods, tucking my hair behind my ears, smiling into my eyes.

"Thanks," I whisper. Does this man have any idea the effect he is having on me?

And then it happens again! With his index finger, he tilts my chin toward him and lightly, sweetly, kisses me on the lips.

We head back downstairs, my mind whirring. Even though I couldn't care less about Billy Hawk at this point, I'm relieved when I don't see him anywhere. I hope he's gone for good.

A waiter appears before us and Nick takes two flutes of champagne. He hands me one; we clink and then sip. Nick says with authority, "Billy's gone."

"Are you sure?"

"Yeah. All his friends are gone." I look around the room and realize he's right. He adds, "Well, at least it'll be a memorable party," and I giggle, because he has no idea how memorable it will be for me, and not because of Billy. I touch my lips briefly, remembering.

That's when the front door bursts open, the heavy wooden door nearly falling off its hinges from the force.

Standing in the doorway is Shelby Seabolt, who's wearing a floor-length shearling coat, her hair slicked tight to her scalp, her lips a ruby slash on her preternaturally white face. My gooey bubble of romance implodes. Oh God, please let Shelby not have just gotten off the phone with Dionne Warwick. Please don't let her kill me in front of these fabulous people.

"Nick!" she shouts, looking wildly around the living room. "Where the fuck is my husband?"

Nick shoves his champagne glass into my hand without looking at me, and then he's gone, the crowd parting to let him through. He rushes toward Shelby with a look of determination on his face that reminds me of *Nights of Plenty*, the spy thriller he did with Denzel.

He reaches out to take her arm and starts whispering something in her ear.

"Don't you touch me!" she shouts, pulling away, a strand of hair falling across her face. "I want everyone here to know what a monster you are." Oh my God, here it comes.

"Shelby, I really don't think—" Nick looks flustered. He runs a hand through his silvery streaks.

"He's ruining my career!" she shouts to the crowd, leaning forward, the cords on her neck stretched taut and red. I breathe a sigh of relief. The crowd stares, riveted. Shelby starts bawling then, huge sloppy tears running down her face, cutting pink tracks through her alabaster foundation. "He's trying to ruin me!" She falls to the floor, racked with sobs.

"You are out of your fucking mind," he hisses, grabbing her upper arm and hauling her up to a standing position.

"Fuck you!" she spits.

As he drags her away, she shouts, "You're getting old, Nick! You can't be a heartthrob forever!"

As soon as Nick and Shelby are out of sight, the crowd's volume swells in a frenzy of instant gossip.

"What *was* that?"

"She's shit-faced!"

"Do you think it's true?"

"I heard something about Shel at lunch the other day. . . ."

As I look around the room, it begins to slowly spin. Swirls of sequins. Plumes of blue smoke. The murmur of gossiping voices. Flashes of inflated cleavage, bleached teeth, twinkling white lights. Ice cubes shift in chunky lowball glasses while columns of champagne bubbles snake their way to the top of crystal flutes. I put my hand to my forehead. I'm suddenly overwhelmed, and exhausted.

Out of sheer nervousness, I start collecting empty champagne flutes and carrying them back to the bar. Preach and I share dumbfounded expressions. After about five trips back and forth, Nick reenters the room.

"Hey, what are you doing?" he asks, gesturing to my hands, which are filled with a bouquet of lipstick-rimmed champagne flutes. I shrug mutely. "Put those down and come with me." I look back over my shoulder at Preach as I let Nick guide me out of the living room.

We wind up in the library, sitting apart on a distressed brown leather sofa. Nick leans back and covers his face with his hands. He lets out a long audible sigh that morphs into a frustrated groan. I stare at him, wishing it were appropriate to throw my arms around his neck and cover him with kisses.

After he loosens his tie, he turns to me with a pained expression, which makes me want to straddle him immediately, despite the drama that is his wife.

"Well, I guess it's obvious that Shelby is not well," he says, defeated.

I nod carefully, not knowing exactly what my role is in all this.

"She's been battling drug addiction since she was seventeen," he says. "You probably know that part. She had it licked for a while, but lately, since we've moved back to New York, she's just flipped out. I don't know. Ever since she became a new marketable type. She's not the sex goddess anymore, you know? She's 'the mom.' And she's not good at taking a backseat to the latest goddess. And with all the prescription pill parties, she's having a renaissance, I guess. We're supposed to announce the Academy Award for Best Cinematography this year. If her problems upstage that, we're going to be a fucking joke."

While Nick goes on and on, I listen quietly, leaning my head on my arm on the back of the sofa. He confesses that their marriage has been a facade for years, for the sake of the media and their careers. He doesn't mention Lola. Nick and Shel get a lot of mileage out of being a solid couple in a world where the weddings usually last longer than the marriages. I know it's wrong, but my heart does a little dance of joy when I hear this.

"What about what she said? About you ruining her career?"

"She's ruining her own career. I'm the one trying to save it. The more she gets fired, the smaller her chances get for the next role. Do you know how many directors are dying to team us up? Do you know how good that could be for both of us? If she doesn't get her shit together, no one's going to want to work with us as a unit and she'll be doing infomercials for face cream, which will throw my career right into the shitter. If she doesn't check herself into rehab, she's going to destroy both of us." He burns a hole through me then with his eyes. Then, just as quickly, he looks away. "It's probably best if you go back tomorrow."

"Okay," I whisper, trying to hide my disappointment.

"Hey, you okay?" He reaches his hand out and touches my cheek. The leather creaks as he scoots closer to me. "You are such an angel," he says, reaching his other hand to my face so that it's completely cradled. "You know that?" He leans in and kisses me, and now I do wrap my arms around him.

\*     \*     \*

Hours later, instead of going straight to my room, I let my feet guide me to Lola's wing of the house. I need perspective, stat. I've just had the hottest make-out session of my life and need to remind myself that this man is not divorced. Yet. Oh God, please let there be a yet.

Slowly, I open Lola's door. A pale pink star-shaped night-light illuminates the room just enough for me to see Lola, who is contentedly asleep on her back, her hair a tangled halo around her peaceful, adorable face.

I sigh, my eyes surprising me by welling up, and enter the exquisitely quiet room. Picking up a plush rabbit, I sit on the edge of her bed and watch her sleep. Tears start streaming from my eyes, fat, slippery ones that seem to be unstoppable. I wipe them with the bunny's ears. When I hiccup, Lola stirs, opens her eyes, and asks, "Mommy?"

"No, sweetie, it's Maddy," I say.

"Why are you in Mommy's clothes?" she asks, straining to open her eyes.

"It's a long story, sweetheart. Go back to sleep."

She closes her eyes.

"Is it okay if I just sit here, though?" I ask. She lays her warm small hand on my knee in reply.

"Thanks," I whisper, and sob as quietly as I can into the bunny.

# Chapter
# Thirteen

———

$H$oly shit," Michelle says, looking unusually impressed.

"I know."

We're at 718 Slash, a vintage clothing store that just opened on Smith Street, around the corner from my apartment.

"Did he make you sign some sort of confidentiality agreement?"

"Oh, I signed one of those on the first day of school. He gave me a Christmas present, though."

"Penis on a platter?"

"Gold choker."

Michelle squints, purses her lips, and nods as if she's savoring an expensive Chianti. It's traditional for parents to give teachers gifts at winter break and at the end of the year at City Select. I've gotten good stuff before—silver-plated housefly earrings from Barneys, a Swiss army watch, a silk scarf from MoMA. So it's not out of the question to receive something nice, something you wouldn't dream of re-gifting.

"If I were you, Maddy," she says finally, fingering a vinyl miniskirt, "I wouldn't be so quick to accept any more gifts. You should keep the choker. It's standard parent-teacher bullshit. But if he starts sending you flowers, I'd just act like it's no big deal. You may be his mistress, technically speaking, but you're not a prostitute unless you act like one. And if you don't manage to keep some sort of professional relationship, you may wind up suffering. Like a lot." She emphasizes the "a lot" by widening her eyes at me. "And no more jewelry. And no furs. God, do they even do that anymore?" She seems to be having this conversation with herself, so I just nod, taking mental notes. "Just tell him it isn't appropriate. Now, if he wants to wine and dine you, then by all means. A girl has to eat." She laughs and then, almost in the same instant, sighs, forlorn. I know she wishes she were in my shoes. Then she perks up and continues. "And Maddy, this is the most important thing. Forget, with a capital *F,* that he is a celebrity. *Starstruck* is no longer in your vocabulary. Don't ask him what it's like to be famous, or rich, or powerful. Don't ask him who he knows, who his friends are, how much his T-shirts cost. Just act like he's a regular schmuck off the streets, and he'll go insane with desire for you. They're all masochists. As soon as you treat him like a star, he'll shit all over you. It's an exact science. It's been proven."

I nod, digesting her expert advice. Michelle holds up a fur vest in front of her. "Whaddaya think?" She sniffs the collar, which is brown leather, cracking and stiff.

I shake my head.

"Yeah, well, it stinks anyway," she says, and squeezes it back onto the rack. "I swear it doesn't make sense to buy used anymore. Anything good has already been bought and sold at least twelve times these days. Terrible karma."

"You wanna grab some lunch?" I suggest. The odor of burning incense at the cash register is starting to give me a headache.

In less than five minutes, we're settling into a table at Zaytoons, a Middle Eastern restaurant. We order a veggie platter to share. After eating Nick's gourmet fare, I have completely and utterly given up on Bönz.

Michelle laughs her ass off about the stupidity that is Billy Hawk and vows to out him as a small-penised individual for the rest of her days. But we quickly return to the subject of Seabolt.

"So did you fuck him?" she asks, her tone businesslike.

"No. I think I could have, but I didn't want to ruin the illusion."

"That you're virtuous?" She laughs.

"Well, it's almost true," I whine.

"He's almost right," Michelle says, a twinkle in her eye. "You're a goody, that's what you are."

"A goody?"

"What my mother calls a good person."

I nod, grinning. "Thanks, Michelle."

"And that has nothing to do with being a slut."

"Michelle!" I say with mock anger.

"Hey, girls need orgasms, too," she says, slathering some babaganoush onto a pita point.

That's when I lose all composure. "God, Michelle, he is so hot, I think I could have an orgasm just making out with him. He wouldn't even have to unzip."

"I've done that," she offers nonchalantly.

"Really?"

"Yeah. When I was sixteen. He was my manager. Back when I had a manager. But then he dropped me for Jennifer Connelly." Michelle sighs, shoving a huge forkful of tabouli into her mouth.

"Oh Michelle," I say.

"So what about Shelby?" she says, changing the subject. "Did he put her in a straitjacket? Lock her up?"

"No, but I didn't see her at all the next morning. She was probably sleeping it off." I take a sip of my mint tea. "She was so out of it."

"This could be really good for you," Michelle says, her eyes widening.

"You mean—"

"You could make a mint on an exposé."

"Are you serious?"

"No. You signed an agreement anyway. But the money sounds nice. Besides, why should one percent of the world's population get to have all the fun? It must be the biggest high to bring an icon to his knees. . . . Not that you or I would ever—"

"I would never." And here I thought Michelle was going to tell me I could be the next Mrs. Seabolt.

"Anyway, you should have fun while it lasts," she continues. "All the ingredients are there. He seems totally into you. You're young, pretty; his kid loves you; his wife is a fucking loony tune. . . ." Michelle pauses long enough to flag the waitress for our check. "So when are you going to see him again?" She raises her eyebrows seductively.

"I have no idea!" I wail. "When he put me in the car, Lola was standing right there. It wasn't really a good time." I don't tell Michelle that I spend every waking moment willing Nick to call me. I probably don't have to. I look at her then, pleading. "God, Michelle, am I awful?"

"Not at all, Maddy. You are human."

"Promise?"

"Cross my tits and hope to die."

"Thanks," I say, pulling out my wallet. "Hey, do you wanna see a movie tonight?"

"Sorry. Can't. Date."

"Ooh, with who?" This is where I'd usually feel a familiar stab of fear that Michelle would leave me behind for a man. But now that I have someone, too, I can finally feel completely happy for her. "Did you meet a new director?"

"Nope," she says coyly, withholding the valuable information.

"Dylan Hover didn't call you, did he?" I lean over, bug-eyed.

"No, but you're close."

I think for a moment and then it hits me. "The security guard from the benefit?"

Michelle nods then, her smile illuminating the whole restaurant.

"Wow, Michelle, that's great!"

"Yeah, Lawrence is taking me to dinner at his brother's restaurant in Fort Greene."

"Cool."

"Yeah, I figure I'll give the common man a chance. You know, take a break from the temperamental theater types."

"Sounds like a plan." I nod approvingly. I wonder if Michelle is going soft on me for a second when she adds, "Plus, you know what they say. Once you go black . . ."

Amanda Porter remembered her pa's last words to her: "Don't cry, Mandy. I'll be home by suppertime. . . ." Amanda looked up at the sky in the days that followed, at a vast field of blue dotted with puffs of white clouds. She prayed every day that her pa would get out of jail and they could be together again. She was lonely, but her cough had subsided and the rain had stopped. She clutched her riding crop and shouted, "Hyaa!" and the horse picked up speed. . . .

"Maddy?"

"Yeah?" I look up from my laptop as Kate cracks my bedroom door open.

"Are you busy? I can come back later."

"No, it's okay. Come in." I save the file and put the computer to the side.

"It's just that I've hardly seen you since you've been back. And I thought we could catch up."

"Sure," I say, and force a smile. It's not that I don't want to talk to Kate. It's just that if I get into a conversation about my winter break, I'm afraid that she might write me off for good.

"So did you have a good time?" she asks innocently.

"Yeah, it was really nice."

"Did Lola's skills improve?"

"They did," I say, and then we lapse into awkward silence. If I tell Kate what happened, she's going to put a negative spin on it. Then I'll get all freaked out and develop a negative attitude. Then the next time I see Nick, I'll be all weird, and then he'll wonder what he ever saw in me, and then I'll never forgive Kate for ruining it. But then I sneak a peek at her and she's just sitting there looking so sad in Casey's bathrobe, twisting a lock of her strawberry blond hair into a tight coil. Then I think, What if Nick and

I get serious and I've kept the whole thing a giant secret? Then Kate will never forgive me. She'll think I'm an awful friend.

"Kate," I finally blurt out. "Look. You are one of my best friends. And I'm really sorry I've been scarce. It's just that, well—"

"It's okay," she says, cutting me off.

"Really? You don't even know what I'm going to say." I can't believe it. I'm off the hook.

"It doesn't matter, Mad. You don't have to justify anything to me. I've been a real bitch."

"No you haven't. You're just being a friend. You're concerned about me. And I appreciate it. I really do."

"No! Thank *you!* You've been nothing but accepting of me." Kate spreads her arms, and before I know it, we're hugging and crying.

"Maddy, I have something to ask you," she says through her tears.

"Yes?" I say, still hugging her.

"Will you be my maid of honor?"

"*What?*" I sit back, and she sticks out her left hand, and there on her finger is an engagement ring. "Wow." I gasp and inspect the ring, a small round diamond set high on a band of yellow gold. "Kate! You're getting married!" I say, and we hug each other again.

"So will you be my maid of honor?" she repeats as we rock from side to side.

"Yes!"

Kate tells me the whole engagement story, how he proposed to her at the Central Park Zoo. She says that they'll be married in June, somewhere in Brooklyn, maybe near the bridge. She's already got her dress picked out, or the design anyway. She's got a list of caterers and florists to visit, bands to interview, vows to write, seating to arrange, so many decisions, so many plans, I get dizzy just trying to keep up. I nod and smile, but as I do, I can't help but feel a blanket of loneliness surround me. By the time the school year is over, I'll be out on the street. Casey will move in with Kate, and where will I go? And what if Michelle and Lawrence get serious? Who will I talk to? And what if Nick never leaves Shelby?

"I'm so happy for you," I say to Kate, and when she finally leaves, her face flushed with excitement, I put my head between my knees and breathe deeply.

"Happy New Year, guys," I say. We're having our first morning meeting of the new year, and I have to say, I've missed these faces more than I thought I would. In fact, it feels good to be back at City Select Academy.

To get reacquainted after the two-week break, the kids take turns telling the class about their time off.

"I went to my country house in Nantucket," says Lucas.

"I went to my country house in Martha's Vineyard," says Fiona.

"I went to my country house at Lake George," says Stella.

"I went to my country house in the country," says Daniel.

"I went to my country house in East Hampton," says Lola. "Maddy came with!"

Through the deafening sound of blood rushing to my face, I carefully explain how I tutored Lola over the break. We talk about how muscles need to gain strength after not being used, and Zachary delights us all with tales about how some people need physical therapy after operations like liposuction and face-lifts. His father is a cosmetic surgeon. "And people who have the fat sucked out of their butts have to wear special shorts called a girdle!" The class erupts in a fit of giggles, but I am enrapt and want to know everything. I wonder if there's a way to get Zachary to bring in some before-and-after photos for afternoon sharing.

"Hey, guys, it's Nina's turn. Let's listen, please," James says, obviously uninterested in the perils of cosmetic surgery. He's sitting on the corner of a table, freshly grunged after two weeks away.

"I went to my grandmom's house in New Jersey," Nina mumbles into her hands. The class looks perplexed.

"New Jersey?" Raffey asks, scrunching her nose. "Where's *that*?"

Nina shrugs. "In the country, I guess," she says, and starts licking her palm.

"I went to Louisiana to visit my auntie for four days and then to the Caribbean for seven days!" Raffey announces, crossing her arms defiantly. She starts ticking off her adventures on her fingers. "I snorkeled, water-skied, sailed, swam, and made a giant sand castle. It was as big as this whole room!" Her eyes widen as she spreads her arms. I make a gesture to cut her off, but she's on a roll. "Then I dug a hole! It was so deep, I could hear Chinese! Do you get it? China is on the other side of the world!" The class gasps, putty in her hands.

"Thank you, Raffey. *Next!*"

"I went skiing in Colorado," says Zachary, a competitive gleam in his eye. "I'm a terrible skier." He gets up to demonstrate, standing in the center of our group. He waves his arms frantically, shouting, "Whoa!" and then lands on the floor with a thud. The class resumes its uproarious laughter and I send a very smug Zachary to sit in the hallway.

"I went skiing in Italy," says Max, clearly unfazed. "I didn't fall down, though."

"No need to demonstrate," I warn.

"I went skiing in Switzerland," says Kylie. "That's where my country house is."

Of course it is.

"Where did James go?" Raffey asks.

"James?" I say. "You want to tell the class about your winter break?"

"Sure. I went to Paris."

The class erupts again into a chorus of "I've been there!"

"Okay kids, you had your chance. Now it's James's turn."

"Well, I took my guitar and went around to all these different, um, music venues and played and sang. People came along and they listened, and if they liked it, they put some coins in a giant glass for me. Anybody know what they call European money?"

"Euros!" shouts Eden.

"They used to be francs in France!" shouts Lola.

"Good!" James and I say at the same time, and then laugh.

"Are you rich now?" asks Stella.

"I made a hundred and fifty American dollars in tips," he says, smiling.

The children's eyes light the room. A collective "*Wow*" whispers its way among them as the kids look at each other in amazement. James looks at me and we smile from the cuteness of it all.

At dismissal, James elbows me and says, "So? Can I expect a glowing dedication page?"

"I have to finish the book first," I say, unable to suppress my grin.

"Wow, you really owe me big time." He moves away from me then, about an inch, so that we're no longer touching. I hope I haven't insulted him.

"So when can I expect a song?"

"I don't know. I don't speak French. If somebody told me I winked, I wouldn't know."

"How convenient."

We shake Lucas's hand and then Kylie's, and then go back inside to take down artwork and put up the chairs.

"So, like, what's going on with you and the Seabolts? You guys doing a three-way? They looking for a little spice?"

"James!" I say, and swat him with a rolled-up bundle of watercolors. "It's nothing like that."

"What *is* it like, Maddy?" he teases.

"It's like this: Lola needed help with her writing. I was the hired help. Nothing more."

James says, "Hm," like he doesn't believe me, but he doesn't push the issue, either. We roll up the rest of the paintings in silence, so we can send them home with the kids the following day, when James starts his curriculum on New York City.

After a few minutes, the door bursts open and Rachel bounds in, looking shiny and new in her latest designer hand-me-up. She flings her arms around James, who drops a batch of Nina's artwork to the floor.

"James!" she cries. "It's so good to see you! How was Paris?" James politely extracts himself and collects Nina's papers. I'd go over to help, but I'm too busy staring at well-heeled *über* bitch. "Are you ready to go yet, James? It's almost four," she mewls.

"Happy New Year, Rachel," I say between clenched teeth, more to get her to acknowledge me than anything else.

"You, too," she says, not even glancing in my direction. "God, your classroom is so small," she adds. "I never noticed it before. Mine is so big, sometimes I don't know how we ever keep the walls filled."

James comes over to me and whispers, "Sorry about this, but I kind of promised her I'd—"

"No, it's okay," I say, cutting him off. "Go and have fun. This shouldn't take too much longer."

"Okay, so I'll see you tomorrow," he says, Rachel dragging him toward the door.

"Yup. Bye," I say, and start putting the chairs up.

When I get home, I'm thoroughly depressed. Rachel has a way of bringing out the worst in me. The fact that Nick hasn't called doesn't help matters. After a festive meal of frozen lima beans and a veggie burger, I settle into bed with my laptop. At least Amanda is in New York City now, which coincides nicely with James's curriculum.

After toiling over the same paragraph for about an hour, the phone rings, saving me from my misery. In the space of an instant, my hopes soar, but then, to save myself from heartache, I decide that it's probably only Michelle calling to give me last-minute info about her date. And that is why I answer the phone, saying, "Lay it on me, sister. My life sucks balls."

"Maddy?"

"Nick?" My heart thunders into action.

"Are you okay?"

"I guess not," I say, trying to make a joke. He doesn't laugh. "I thought you were my friend from school," I add weakly.

"What are you doing tonight?"

I guess we won't be discussing my good friend Michelle.

"Just hanging out?" Why am I asking him? Oh my God, I'm reverting to high school. God is cruel. Man, I'm nervous.

"Can you meet me at Wooster Hotel in an hour?"

"Nick, I don't think I'm ready to—"

"No, I don't mean to spend the night. I mean for a drink. They've got a great VIP lounge. It's got a Zen waterfall. Really beautiful. And it's casual. I need to get out of the apartment. I'm getting a little claustrophobic after studying a script all day. What do you say?"

Looking around my shoe box of a room, I'd say he doesn't know the meaning of the word *claustrophobic.*

"Okay," I say, knowing that this simple affirmative reply carries with it the power to transform destinies.

When I arrive an hour later, a very pretty woman is standing at the entrance. I smile politely and walk past her to open the door.

"Hi, Miss Braverman?" she says, stopping me in my tracks. I nod.

"I'm Lainey, Nick's assistant. It's great to finally meet you. He's told me how wonderful you are with Lola." While we shake hands, I marvel at how similar we are in age and stature. Youngish, darkish, thinnish. I want to ask her how she knows who I am. How much does she make a year? Did *she* have to sign a confidentiality agreement? But Lainey is moving fast, herding me through the echoing lobby, through the dark bar, and to a massive gleaming wood door. "Okay, Miss Braverman. You can go right in. It was really nice meeting you."

"You, too, Lainey. Thank you." And then she's gone, walking at an efficient clip, her wide-legged trousers swooshing.

Inside the room feels like outdoors in Japan. If I'd been in Japan. There is indeed a Zen waterfall. Even the air feels different. Charged. I can smell cherry blossoms.

"Maddy." I pass the waterfalls and find Nick seated on a cushion on the floor, leaning against what looks to be a boulder. The table in front of him is about five inches high. Candles in red votive holders flicker everywhere and an Asian waiter in a black satin kimono and matching beanie comes over immediately with a tray, deftly sinks to his knees, and deposits two martini glasses on the table.

"Lotus Blossoms," Nick says, lifting a glass. I sit down next to him and pick up my glass, which is encrusted with jade-colored sugar, the liquid glowing a milky pink in the light of the flickering candles.

"I met your assistant," I say, sipping. The drink tastes as sweet as it looks, like a red-bean smoothie mixed with sake and rum. My lips start to go numb almost immediately, and I find myself looking cross-eyed into the bottom of the glass far too soon. Slow down, Mad, I tell myself.

"Yeah, she was in Poland, working on a documentary. Her passion. Shel hated her, but now that Shelby's . . . well, now that she's so . . ."

"Lainey's back in action."

"Yes. Exactly." I wonder if Lainey and Nick ever had anything together, but he takes my glass from me and kisses my mouth, and then I'm not thinking much of anything, except for how much I want to get naked with him.

"I missed you," he says, sounding so vulnerable and raw that my best Target underpants start to drip.

The waiter replaces our drinks. Nick tells me all about his rise to fame, the early days, which he misses, the simplicity of Hollywood in the late eighties versus now, the rush that fame and fortune brought him back then, and how special he used to feel.

"Sometimes I think it'd be better to pack it in and move to Alaska before I embarrass myself by sticking around for too long, you know?"

"Really?"

"Or Tibet. I could do the whole Buddhist thing."

"Doesn't Richard Gere have that market cornered?"

"Yeah, I guess," he says, and laughs. "You are so refreshing, you know?" And he sticks his tongue in my mouth. Before I know it, we're horizontal, grinding against each other. Music starts to play, or maybe it's been playing the whole time and I'm only noticing it now. It's a curious combination of crickets and a drumbeat. I can feel Nick's erection through his jeans and I know my panties must be soaked. The room is twinkling, glowing red; the waterfall is gushing.

"I can get us a room," he says, breathing heavily in my ear.

"Uh—I—" I stutter.

"You're not ready?" he asks, lifting his head. I can't tell if I'm disappointing him.

"It's not that I don't want to. It's just that—"

"I'm married."

I nod. "And—"

"Lola."

I nod again.

"Maddy, you are such a . . ."

"Tease?" I offer.

"No! No, not at all. I was going to say that you are such a *good* person."

I'm beginning to wonder, even though he's the second person to call me a good person, if I have any right to the title. "If I were a good person, I wouldn't be here right now."

Nick reassures me that I am indeed a good person, and that I am by no stretch of the imagination a home wrecker. "Our marriage was a piece-of-shit facade long before you entered the picture," he tells me, in between nibbling my earlobes. "Besides, Lola loves you." I shiver with satisfaction and lean in for another kiss, when he adds in a singsong voice, "I have something for you."

We sit up, my heart pounding in my ears. This is so soon. Things are moving too fast. Still, if it's a ring he's about to present me with, how could I possibly say no to this megawatt sex symbol? Who could possibly say no? I've never swooned so much in my life.

Nick presents me with a small gift-wrapped box, bigger than a Tiffany ring box, and not robin's egg blue, either. The paper is silver and the box is roughly the size of a . . . a . . .

"A cell phone?" I ask, extracting it from the box.

"Sprint PCS," he says, as if this is all the explanation I need.

"Thank you," I say, and kiss him on the cheek. "It's . . . beautiful. But what's it for?"

"Maddy. You're cute. You really are. Seriously, I don't know how you live without one."

"I have indoor plumbing, though. Just got it last week."

He squints at me, confused. Then he takes the phone from my hand, flips it open, and shows me how he's entered all his phone numbers into it. "It's so I can reach you anywhere, anytime. Romantic, huh? And check this out." He pushes a button and the theme from *Dot Communist* plays. "This is what you'll hear when it rings." He raises his eyebrows at me and pushes another button. This time, the theme from *Nights of Plenty* plays. "This is what you'll hear when I've left you a message. Pretty cool, huh?"

I nod, grinning at my fabulous luck. "It's like you'll be in my pocket," I say.

"I don't know about your pocket, but *my* pocket's already full," he says, putting the phone down and guiding my hand to his crotch, where I feel that his pocket is very full indeed.

# Chapter Fourteen

*H*ey, glassy eyes. Did you hear what I just said?"

"Huh?"

James and I are resupplying the pencil and marker bins.

"What the hell are you thinking about? You've been in the fourth dimension for the past ten minutes. No. Since winter break."

"I'm fine. I'm right here," I say defensively. "I just have a lot on my mind." The truth is, I am not fine. Or I am more than fine. I am a changed person. I am no longer a run-of-the-mill Brooklyn gal. I am seeing a Hollywood celebrity. Of course no one knows I'm seeing him, but I am, even if I'm still waiting for him to call. But I know he will. He wouldn't have bought me such an expensive phone if he weren't going to use it.

"What are you, master of the obvious?"

"I don't know," I say absently, and sharpen another pencil.

I haven't spent time with Michelle in awhile. But we always say we'll catch up soon. And Kate's so busy with work and wedding plans, we barely get a chance to hang out. Until today, that is— half an hour from now, we'll be shopping for my maid-of-honor dress.

"So what do you think about what I asked you earlier?" James says on his way to the garbage can, hands full of dried-out markers.

"I'm sorry, James, what was it again?"

"Where do you think we should go for a New York City field trip?"

"Statue of Liberty?"

"I thought you were going to suggest a place that wasn't such a cliché."

"What about the Tenement Museum?"

"That's good. I'll research that. And what about that other thing I mentioned?" James says from far off.

"Huh?"

"My gig Saturday night. At Two Boots."

"I will be there, James. I promise." I smile and squeeze his shoulder for emphasis, and so that he'll leave me alone already. But James is right: I'm not here, not really. Tomorrow morning, first thing, I will work on being in the moment.

"I'm thinking green. Celadon. What do you think?" asks Kate, flipping through the rack of handmade dresses at Curtsy, a teeny boutique on Warren Street, off of Smith Street.

"I don't know. I've never worn it," I say. "My major color is denim."

"I think you'll look great in it. With your dark hair and pale skin? God, I love this!" Kate says, and pulls a dress from the rack. She holds it up in front of me and tilts her head, thinking. "Straps or no?"

"Well, considering I don't have much to hold it up—"

"That one has a hidden drawstring," a voice says, interrupting us. Kate and I turn as a mousy wisp of woman with rimless glasses walks over to us. She takes the dress from Kate's hand and turns the fabric so we can both see. Kate beams.

"Maddy, this is exactly what I had in mind. Aren't you excited?"

"Totally," I say, and return her smile.

Kate and I sit down with the woman, who turns out to be the designer and the owner of this boutique. While they discuss fabric, prices, and shoe possibilities, I drift off, chewing a cuticle, imagining what my bridesmaids would wear. I imagine Michelle and Kate standing beside me in matching Ungaro or Calvin Klein. Something flowy. Or simple. It's so hard to decide. Maybe Nick would send Lainey to help me. I'm just about to draw blood as I ponder this conundrum, when my phone rings.

I look at Kate, very much the canary-filled feline. I fumble through my bag for the phone, which is playing the *Dot Communist* theme shockingly loud. Maybe I should ask Nick to change the ring tone to something less . . . scarlet. I finally find the phone and then have to figure out how to flip it open. By the time I finally do that, Kate and the owner have stopped talking and are staring at me.

"I'll just take this outside," I say, and run for the door.

"Hey, you," he says sexily, as if almost a week hasn't gone by without a word. "I've missed you."

"Me, too," I say. "It's been awhile." God, why do I have to be so needy? I could kick myself.

"Yeah, I know. It's been so hectic. You know how it is." Then he switches gears, his voice growing husky and full of tantalizing promise. "I can't wait to see you again."

"Me, too," I say again, my resentment melting away like cheese fondue.

"You like your new phone?"

"Yeah."

"Good. So how's Friday night?"

"Great!" Damn. I probably should have played harder to get. I can practically hear Michelle cluck with disapproval. This time, I do kick myself.

"Great," he repeats. "I'll call you with the details. Gotta run. Big kiss, Mad."

I make a kissing sound into the phone, finishing just in time to see Arthur Wilcox, the head molester, heading straight toward me.

"Is that the lovely Maddy Braverman, star of the first grade, Ah see?" he says, sauntering over.

"Hi, Arthur." We enter the store together. I introduce the head molester to Kate while the owner heads back to the counter. Arthur lights up when she tells him she's marrying a writer.

"A wordsmith! A man of letters! What could be finer?" We give Arthur exaggerated shrugs of agreement. Arthur's voice is so loud, the barrettes and bracelets are vibrating on the glass counter. "It's just too bad that marriage is such an archaic institution! A vestigial tail of patriarchal exploitation, if you will. But you might want to ask my exes about that." He winks. Then he leans close to Kate, who sneaks me a wide-eyed look. "You're young yet. Perfect time to experiment!" And with that uplifting sentiment, he bids us adieu and heads to the counter.

The head molester purchases a lavender scarf, a gauzy rectangle encrusted with glass bugle beads, which makes Kate's and my eyebrows rise with suspicion.

"Who do you think it's for?" Kate asks me when he's gone.

"His assistant? She's definitely in his preferred age range."

"Which is?"

"Eighteen to twenty-five," I answer flatly.

"No wonder he doesn't believe in marriage," Kate says. "Well, at least he's up front about it." She shrugs at me and I stiffen despite myself. Was that an insult? Even if it wasn't, I deserve it.

Suddenly, I feel even lower than Arthur, even if I don't have a nickname to prove it. While Arthur's running around in broad daylight with teenyboppers, I'm sneaking around behind everyone's back, having an affair with a married man. Who'd have thought it would come to this?

The light on my answering machine is blinking when we get home. My heart starts to race with anticipation. Could Nick have called twice? Could I possibly get the added bonus of hearing his beautiful voice again? While Kate's in the bathroom, I squat close to the machine, press the play button, and turn the volume down.

"Maddy, this is Shelby Seabolt. I need to talk to you. Call me at nine one seven—"

I smash the stop button on the machine. I can't bear to hear any more, as if just her voice on my answering machine could have some lethal effect on me. Poison me somehow through my ears. Then I bolt upright and look around the apartment, as if maybe Shelby is here with me. Stalking me. Or having me followed. Is there a private eye taking my picture right now? God, I hope I look okay.

Kate is still in the bathroom. Taking a deep breath, I rewind the tape and play it again, all the way through this time. Shelby hangs up after she finishes reciting her number. Mercifully, she doesn't condemn me to a slow and painful death. I've been spared—at least for now. I write down Shelby's number with a shaking hand. Then the doorbell rings and I scream.

"Maddy? Are you okay?" Kate calls, bursting out of the bathroom.

"The doorbell scared me," I explain, entering the living room. It's half true. "Is it getting louder?" I ask her.

"I don't think so," she says, and looks at me curiously. "Are you sure you're okay?"

"Yeah." I gulp hoarsely. I hear footsteps ascending the staircase and am convinced it's Shelby, or maybe a large henchman coming to snipe me right in front of the bride-to-be. Kate will never forgive me for ruining her wedding if I get killed. Oh God.

I swallow again, hug myself, and squinch my eyes shut as the door opens. I can't move, even to hide under my bed.

"Don't act so happy to see me," says Casey as he enters the apartment. I open my eyes and exhale loudly. "Long time no see, Mad-Mad," he says, and greets me with a kiss on the cheek.

I start to laugh uncontrollably then, sort of a knee-jerk reaction to not being shot to death by a henchman, I guess. Both Kate and Casey say at the same time, "Are you okay?" which makes me laugh even harder.

Through tears of hysterical laughter, I tell them I am definitely okay.

"Work got you down?" Casey asks, flopping on the sofa, his curls bouncing.

"Yes!" I shout, doubling over. "No, it's just that . . ."

Kate and Casey look at me expectantly. I have to make something up, and quick.

"Mazel tov on your engagement," I say to Casey, using the distraction method. People always seem to forget about whatever strange things you're doing if you start talking about them instead. I force myself to straighten up, wipe my eyes with the back of my hand, and flop on the couch with Kate and Casey.

"Thanks," Casey says, and adds, "So, how's your love life?" And I lose control all over again.

When I finally sequester myself in my bedroom, I pick up the phone, then hesitate. As much as it kills me to call her, I know it's the right thing. She might be a drug addict and her marriage might be over, but she's still the one with the ring, and I am her daughter's teacher.

I dial the number.

I'm thinking she won't pick up. She's Shelby Seabolt, after all. She should have better things to do than answer a phone. She should—

"Seabolt," she barks. Oh God.

"Mrs. Seabolt? Hi, this is Maddy."

Silence.

"Lola's teacher?" I remind her. I sit on the bed and brace myself.

"Oh Maddy! Sure. Listen, my behavior at Christmas. I want to apologize for that. I want to take you out. You know, 'girls' day of beauty' kind of thing. Can you be available Saturday at eleven?"

"Um, I have to look in my planner?" What is going on? Is this some sort of sadistic joke? Like when kids are forced to smoke a whole pack of cigarettes after their parents catch them in the act? I mean, *does she know*?

"Well, my publicist thinks it's a good idea. You know, clear the air, make a fresh start. And my healer concurs. So can I send a car for you at ten?"

"So ten and not eleven?" Her *healer*? "Mrs. Seabolt, I really don't know. I—"

"What? Shit. No. Let's do . . . um . . . How about nine-thirty? We can do an hour massage, then mani-pedi. Maybe we'll have lunch. No. Make it brunch. A smoothie. I've got a meeting at two.

I'll send the car for you at eight-thirty. Be outside, okay? I'm in a hurry that day."

"I'm not sure I'm free that day," I manage to say, stunned.

"Well, then get free," she says emphatically.

"Um, I—"

"Great! Can't wait! Gotta run!" she chirps, and then she clicks off. With the dial tone buzzing in my ear, I say, "Okay, Mrs. Seabolt. See you then."

I lie back on my bed and bring my knees up to my chest, hugging them. Actually, it doesn't sound so bad. I've never had an hour-long massage before. And I've only had one manicure in my life. But there is the niggling fact that I'm scared to death to be alone with Shelby Seabolt. Not to mention the fact that she's squeezing me in for an appointment I didn't even make at eight-thirty on a Saturday morning. But, most important, she doesn't seem to know a thing about me and Nick.

Shit. Nick. We're supposed to get together Friday night.

Deciding that this qualifies as an emergency, I pick a number from the list in the cell phone and dial. It's a beeper number, so I wait an interminable five minutes until he calls me back.

"What's up, sweetie?" he says, and I have to take a moment to go all gooey before continuing.

"Shelby called me. She wants to get together Saturday morning."

"She does, huh."

I explain her proposal and Nick laughs. "Her healer told her she should do this? She's worse than I thought. Shit. That's the other line. Can you hold on?"

"Sure." While Nick answers his other call, I inspect my fingernails, which I hope will grow quickly by Saturday, chewed nubs that they are.

"That was her," he says, clicking back over to me. "She's spending Friday night in SoHo, at her healer's. She says it'll help ease her into the intuitive zone or something, I don't know." He sighs.

"So should we reschedule?"

"Absolutely not. You are my respite, little girl. In fact, why don't you come to the penthouse Friday night and I'll have Frank drive you home early on Saturday, so you're ready at your doorstep for Shel."

"Okay," I agree, and try not to keel over from excitement.

"Sweetie," he says, opening the door for me. He gathers me into his arms and kisses me. Before I know it, he's taking my bag from my hand and leading me into the bedroom.

"Where's Lola?" I ask, looking around the huge penthouse.

"She's shopping with Lainey."

"Sounds like fun."

"Yeah, if you like that sort of thing, spending the day at Barneys on Big Daddy's credit card." He reels me in for a kiss then and I just about die from anticipation.

"Maddy," he says when we reach the bedroom. He places his hands on my shoulders and shakes his head at me. My back is toward the bed, and before I know it, he's gently coaxed me to lie down. We're kissing on the bed and it's wonderful, but isn't there some other bed in this vast dwelling to do this on? Would it be rude to ask?

He's tugging at my T-shirt, and suddenly I tense up, realizing that Nick's not making any plans to move this operation to a less overt place. He doesn't seem to notice until I gently push him away.

"Hey, you all right?"

"I don't know, I'm just—"

"Apprehensive?"

"Yeah," I say, sighing with relief. He gets it.

"Still?"

Uh-oh. Have I annoyed him?

"Kind of," I admit, growing a little uneasy.

"Well, I can assure you that you won't be disappointed." He kisses me wetly and then adds, "See?"

"Can we do it on the floor?" I blurt out.

"Oooh, the floor," he says, coming up for air. "I didn't know you were kinky, Maddy."

"Mmm," I say, not disagreeing.

I push all thoughts of Lola and Shelby out of my head as we roll onto the floor and continue making out. My shirt disappears, then my jeans, and then Nick's clothes vanish and he rolls on a condom. It's so sweet of him. I didn't even have to ask.

The moment has arrived.

At the Wooster Hotel, I was practically coming from anticipation. Now, though, it's different. Maybe because of the years I devoted to dreaming of this very moment. But in my dreams, it was never clandestine. It was pure. It was beautiful. I wasn't a home wrecker. On the other hand, we're talking Nick fucking Seabolt! God, I wish everyone from my high school could see me now. Wait. No, I don't. I don't want them to see me on this Turkish kilim; I want them to see me on the red carpet. When Nick and I are on our way into the People's Choice Awards. The Golden Globes. The Oscars.

Nick pumps away on top of me, sweat gathering on his upper lip. But then I'm on the red carpet, decked out in Zac Posen, Harry Winston, and Jimmy Choo. The kilim is giving me one hell of a rug burn and my right knee keeps knocking against the bed frame. But wait! Dick Clark is stopping us for an impromptu interview. I'm twirling for the camera. I'm stealing the show! In the name of starstruck fans everywhere, it's my duty to be here as their ambassador!

I begin to grunt. I'm twirling, twirling! The flashbulbs are popping. Exploding. I shudder and quake. Ashley Judd asks me who did my hair. I push Nick in deeper, so deep that his bright, famous, beautiful cock is nudging against my brain. The fans are screaming for our attention. They love us more than Brad and Jennifer. More than Ben and Jen! I howl from pleasure. Gwyneth asks me for fashion advice. Nick collapses on top of me. I am a star. I've arrived.

From far away, I hear, "Now *that* is what I like" over and over, like a steam engine drawing near. I look at Nick and tears well in my eyes. It's too beautiful to be true, that I've made love with this hero of the silver screen.

Nick gets up, walks to the bathroom, and flushes the condom down the toilet. His ass is surprisingly hairy. I'd have thought he would have had it waxed. I curl into a ball and stuff some fingers in my delirious mouth, keeping my smile a secret.

Nick doesn't return to our little nest of forbidden love right away. He has paused at the gargantuan mirror in the bathroom.

"Honey?" he asks me. "Do I look . . . different after achieving orgasm?" He turns his face from side to side, investigating himself.

I take a guess, pulling the fingers from my mouth. "You look, um, more peaceful?" He called me "honey." I'm over the moon.

Nick smiles, satisfied. "I think I glow," he says. Then he turns from the mirror and adds, "You bring me peace. Do you know that?"

"I do?" I bubble. I didn't know such happiness was humanly possible. And wow, look at his penis! Just hanging there, limp and spent and small. He is so *human*.

"You do." He comes toward me and his manhood begins to reawaken. Before I know it, it's stiff and ready, and the fans are screaming for more.

I open my eyes and sit bolt upright when I hear the rumble of garbage trucks far below on the street. The clock says 7:45. I have exactly forty-five minutes to get home, get upstairs, and get back downstairs in time to meet Shelby. And everybody knows that it takes twenty minutes to get anywhere traveling only within Manhattan, at least an hour to get to the outer boroughs. I am screwed in more ways than one.

"Nick." I poke him. "I gotta go." He barely stirs, and when he does, he smiles as if he hasn't a care in the world.

"Nick. It's seven-forty-five. I gotta get back to Brooklyn." God, he's so beautiful. I wish I could stay. But alas . . .

He gropes the night table, finds his cell phone, and punches a couple of numbers. "Frank. Nick. I need you, buddy," he mumbles, and then clicks the phone shut. Then he turns away from me and continues to snore.

I leap out of bed, frantic, and start twisting on my clothes. Why does his wife have to ruin my perfect clandestine liaison?

Five minutes later, when I'm finally ready to leave, I debate as to whether or not it's a good idea to wake him.

"I'm leaving, Nick," I say finally, my voice practically inaudible from the doorway. He doesn't stir. I venture closer. The clock glares at me: 7:58. I lean over his stubbly face and kiss him on the cheek. "Bye, Nick."

He stirs and then turns over. "Bye, sweetie. Have a good day. And honey?"

"Yes?" I say, hopeful for some tidbit of encouragement, a good-luck wish, a "May the force be with you" sort of thing.

"Try to get there before she arrives."

"I will," I say, deflated.

# Chapter
# Fifteen

New York City must be the only place in the world where the delivery trucks vie for curbside space at eight o'clock on a Saturday morning. Frank navigates Broadway like a true veteran of the streets, but that doesn't stop my heart from doing triple axels in my chest every time we have to slow down. I start chanting "nam-myoho-renge-kyo" under my breath, promising to devote my life to the law of the Lotus Sutra if only I can arrive at my apartment before 8:30.

We're practically on the Brooklyn Bridge, but then we get stuck behind a taxi. A mother and her infant are trying to get in. She has at least three diaper bags, plus the baby, plus her own bag, plus some kind of giant Tupperware container. I groan and sink down into the leather seat.

"You okay, Miss Braverman?" Frank asks from the front seat.

"Yeah, Frank, thanks. I'm just late for an appointment."

"Don't you worry, Miss Braverman. We'll have you home in no time." Frank flashes his high beams at the taxi, and it lurches ahead once the woman is finally inside with all her belongings. We're just in time to catch the light, and then we're on the bridge, coasting across the East River. I continue chanting anyway, just in case.

When Frank turns onto my street, I can see Shelby's own limousine idling in front of my building. I blurt out for Frank to stop the car. Thankfully, it's a one-way street, which means that Shelby is facing away from us.

"Frank, I know this might sound strange, but would you mind dropping me off here and then waiting a few minutes before leaving? Like until that limo ahead is gone?"

"Sure thing, Miss Braverman. Not a problem at all."

"Thank you so much, Frank." I wonder how much he knows, and secretly, maybe perversely, I hope that he *does* know, and likes me despite it. Before I get out of the car, I rummage through my bag for the cell phone so I can turn it off.

As if he's reading my mind, Frank clears his throat and says, "Yup, I've worked for Mr. Seabolt seventeen years now." He turns around in his seat then and faces me, as if we're right in the middle of a conversation. Looking at him now, I realize he's much older than I previously thought, sixty at least. Deep creases traverse his forehead, and his sideburns are almost pure white. His light blue eyes, though they're shadowed by the bill of his driver's cap, twinkle with a light that seems to come from inside. "You're a class act, Miss Braverman, a real nice lady. I can tell you got a lot going for you." He punctuates his speech with a wink, and suddenly I feel tears welling up, but I swallow them back down, as if they've arrived by mistake and weren't meant for me. In his thick Queens accent, he continues. "I'm not getting any younger. I'll turn sixty-one in June. I have three wonderful grandkids. But I seen one too many sad ladies in this car, and I've always kept my mouth shut. None of my business—you know how it is, smart lady like you. But I ain't gonna be around forever. The Lord has other plans for Frank Caruso, that's for sure. So before I'm lying there on my deathbed—sorry to be morbid, Miss Braverman, but that's the way it is—I'd like to say to one nice lady in the backseat of this car, it's not worth your pain. No disrespect to Mr. Seabolt, and all the respect I got in my heart and soul to you."

I stare at him, nodding, and a tear manages to escape. I wipe it away, embarrassed. His grandkids are incredibly lucky. I'd cast Robert De Niro to play his part. Or Anthony Hopkins, if he could do a Queens accent.

But I, Maddy Braverman, am the world's biggest chump. I stare down at the seat beside me for a moment and try to imagine all the other women Frank has escorted all over town, here and in L.A. I wonder what they would have thought if they'd known their final destination wasn't ever going to be a mansion in Bel Air or a penthouse in Manhattan, but smack-dab in the middle of their own beds, crying and more alone than ever.

But aren't I different? I'm Lola's teacher, for God's sake. We have a special bond, the three of us. We're like family, a great, shining, happy family. I was there when she broke her arm. I helped nurse her back to health. Nick confides in me. Calls me his "respite." Calls me "honey." No one's ever done that before.

Frank swivels back around and faces the windshield with a heavy sigh, unburdening a lifetime's worth of sad memories. "Miss Braverman, I'm so sorry. I made you cry. That wasn't my intention. Not at all."

"No, Frank. I'm glad you said what you did. I really am. Thank you." I don't know what to think anymore. I just know that when Nick looks at me, I dissolve into a heap of goo. How does a girl fight that special feeling, even if it's wrong?

He turns back to me once more and smiles, touching the brim of his hat briefly. "Now, you go have a good time, Miss Braverman, and remember what I told you. You are a class act. With a capital *C*!"

"I will." I wish him a good weekend and then gather my courage and step out of the car. I put my bag over my shoulder, press my hands to my lips, and repeat under my breath, "I am a class act." But I don't believe it. Not yet anyway.

When I arrive at Shelby's car, I bend down and peer into the smoked glass until I see her unmistakable shape barking inaudibly into her cell phone and trying to light a cigarette at the same time. When she turns and sees me, she jumps, startled. Then the door opens, and I have to leap backward to avoid being smacked with it.

Shelby holds up her index finger at me and continues to talk on her phone, interrogating the poor soul on the other end.

"Look, Gregory, I know it's his first film. That's why I'm so concerned. Don't you see that? I mean, can you pull your head out of your asshole long enough to see that I need to be *nurtured* here?" I stand outside, trying not to stare at Shelby, shifting from foot to foot, wondering when she'll scoot over so I can get in the car.

"Yeah, well, if he acts like that last snot-nosed kid, I have no problem making this his last film." Shelby rolls her eyes at me, as if I'd know all about her plight and be able to sympathize. "Lawsuit my ass, Greg. I should have sued that last kid for emotional damages. I looked so old in that film, he could have ruined my good name!"

I can tell that Shelby's talking about *Blind Deaf Stupid,* the only independent film she ever made.

"Fine, then. Just get Larry to DP and I'm on board, okay?" And with that, she clicks her cell phone shut and fumes.

I remain standing, waiting. It's starting to rain. "I hope you weren't waiting too long?"

Shelby looks up at me as if she's seeing me for the first time.

"Maddy, what are you doing out there? Get in the car." Shelby remains seated near the door, so I climb over her as gingerly as possible. I'm surprised to see that we are not alone. Sitting opposite me, her stiff back to Shelby's driver, is an older woman—in her late fifties perhaps—with a mulelike face and a chin-length black bob. There's something like a Modigliani painting about her, as if she were made of taffy and had been stretched into an unwieldy rope. The turquoise beads around her neck are the size of giant gum balls and look excruciatingly heavy, as if at any moment their weight alone could slice her head clean off her pashmina-clad shoulders.

The car pulls into the narrow street and turns the corner, the windshield wipers flattening the new raindrops.

"Oh Maddy, this is Dr. Kiki Joypain," Shelby says, presenting her other guest with a formal flourish of her well-groomed hand. "My healer. My friend. In many ways, my personal savior." Shelby's voice quivers a bit then with unmistakable reverence.

I smile warmly and hold my hand out to shake Dr. Joypain's, but she reaches beyond my outstretched hand and grasps my upper arm instead. She has the force of the Terminator.

"It's a real pleasure to meet you, Maddy. Forgive my not shaking your hand. I know you work with children, a hugely noble profession. But I also know that children carry with them many different strains of bacteria, and I must protect myself. You understand."

"Of course," I say quietly, feeling like a leper.

"Maddy," Shelby continues, placing a hand on my knee. "Dr. Joypain has a gift for healing. She's intuitive. Do you know what that means?"

"She has good intuition?" I say, playing the docile and dim-witted student she seems to see me as.

"Yes, that, and so much more." Shelby pauses, searching for the right words. Then she continues. "Kiki has helped me through so many dark places. She's like a light in the forest, or a beacon of some sort. . . ." Shelby trails off, searching for the words that will do her idol justice.

"What Shelby is saying, Maddy," Dr. Joypain interjects, "is that God has given me a gift. And my duty is to share that gift. I can see things that everyone on this wondrous planet has the *ability* to see but that they mostly choose *not* to see. Do you understand?"

"I think so," I say, growing annoyed, despite the star wattage in my midst. Dr. Joypain stares at me in a way that makes me think she's got X-ray vision. She clenches her jaw and lifts her chin, eyes shrinking, nostrils flaring. "That's so wonderful," I add, realizing that I'm probably supposed to be awestruck about now.

"It *is* wonderful," Dr. Joypain agrees. "But it also can be excruciating."

"Like your name," I say, growing giddy for some reason, as if I'm guessing the right answers on a pop quiz.

"Yes, that's exactly right, Maddy," she says, smiling, showing her long and slightly gray teeth. I can see that her lipstick has pooled in the chapped cracks of her lips, giving them a striped appearance, like a tiger's coat. After stroking her bangs a few times, she continues. "I visited a Native American village in New Mexico a decade ago, and as I sat in a sweat lodge with a medicine doctor, he had a vision. He told me to change my name; said it would bring me to the next level, so to speak. When I questioned him further, he told me that the name would begin with a *J*. When I returned home, I opened myself up to all the possible *J* names. One particular day, when I was meditating"—Dr. Joypain touches her twiglike index fingers to her thumbs, demonstrating—"images flooded my brain. With my openness, this happens all the time, of course. But on this day, the image repeated itself. I saw not just one but thousands, millions of women, from every corner of this magical, beautiful globe. All of them were sweating, writhing in pain. Do you know what they were doing, Maddy?"

"I have no idea," I confess, becoming riveted by this story despite my cynicism.

"They were giving birth." Dr. Joypain opens her legs then, which, thankfully, are covered in an ankle-length maroon velvet skirt. She reaches her hands out as if to extract a newborn, as if perhaps I don't understand her complicated language. "I realized then that the pain they were going through was crucial." She snaps her legs shut and pokes a bony finger toward the roof, her bangs shimmying furiously. "And this is the important thing, Maddy. The pain is *imperative*. For without it, one cannot experience the *joy*, and if you've ever seen a woman who has just given birth, then you know what I'm talking about. Isn't that right, Shelby?"

Shelby nods, glassy-eyed, her mouth slack with wonder.

"And so I went right down to City Hall and changed my name that very day. And within a year, Maddy, I had a best-seller, and I met some of the most extraordinary people. Like Shelby here." Dr. Joypain squeezes Shelby's shoulder. I think the two might actually kiss each other, but then Dr. Joypain sits back and strokes her giant turquoise beads.

"So who were you before?" I ask, dying to know what Dr. Joypain's real name is. Probably something ethnic, something that wouldn't let her forget her roots and the sensible family who probably wanted to have her committed. Paulina Polznitsky perhaps. I wonder what her family calls her now. Coo-coo for Cocoa Puffs?

"That is beside the point, Maddy. I've shed the name my parents gave me, for it no longer fit. Don't you see? You have the ability, Maddy, in this one precious and brief lifetime, to *become who you really truly are*. That's the name of my third book, by the way. Have you heard of it?"

"I have," I say, lying eagerly. But I should have. I don't know how her books escaped my self-help radar. I've spent many an hour in that aisle, and many a dollar, too. *Drowning in the Drama of I Can't*, by Amy Marinelli, Ph.D., is a particular favorite. I return to it time and time again.

Dr. Joypain smiles, showing her stripy lips. It reminds me of a quote, something about a tiger never changing its stripes. I promise myself to look up Dr. Joypain on-line.

"Kiki's joining us today because you and I could both use the strength, Maddy. Don't you think?" says Shelby. I nod, not understanding. "In other words, sometimes it's okay to lean on others for support, you know? Kiki's taught me that."

I nod again, wondering if Dr. Joypain is truly here to help me, or if she's just here for Shelby, and if she charges by the hour. And if so, is Shelby the world's second-largest sucker? Has Dr. Joypain convinced Shelby that she has no strength without her constant companionship? Should I be asking myself these very same questions?

"Why don't you tell us about the struggles you face, Maddy," Dr. Joypain says, leaning forward so that her giant beads swing to and fro in front of her boardlike chest. What is this, I think, an emotional sting operation?

"Well," I stammer, looking for something innocuous to feed them, "I don't really make a lot of money?" I present my "struggle" like a question, the way I always seem to these days, and silently curse myself for sounding so weak.

"Maddy, you must *choose* money," the doctor says authoritatively.

Is she a real doctor? Where is her degree from? I want to ask her these questions but sense it wouldn't be nice. Then I think of Nick telling me that his was the life he chose, all those months ago, the first time I was in his apartment.

"Okay," I say. "So I choose money." I shrug and sit back, waiting for crisp green dollar bills to float down to my lap from heaven. Dr. Joypain and Shelby laugh openly. The doctor is about to correct me, but Shelby jumps in.

"You have to really mean it, Maddy. And you have to affirm it. Every day," Shelby says.

I sigh. If they could see my journals they'd know I've tried. I've written it over and over again. Hell, I've read Shakti Gawain, M. Scott Peck, Dr. Phil. . . . Quite frankly, this "doctor" isn't saying anything I haven't heard before on *Oprah*.

"That special someone you're looking for, Maddy. You've already found him," Dr. Joypain says slyly, and my eyes widen in horror. I sneak a glance at Shelby to see if she's in on it, or if she can sense any underlying meaning to the doctor's "intuition," but she's busy lighting another cigarette, covering us both in a blanket of blue smoke. "I sense it very clearly," Dr. Joypain continues. "He's an artist, and he likes you very much. But there's an obstacle, isn't there?" Dr. Joypain lifts her narrow head and closes her eyes, shutting out any distraction. She's getting closer to the truth. "Another woman . . . or . . ."

"Where did you say you went to medical school?" I blurt out, anything to get Dr. Joypain to stop this madness. I realize with a shudder that nobody knows where I am right now. Shelby and Dr. Joypain could shoot me right now, or stab me, or inject me with poison. Yes, poison. Dr. Joypain probably has a case full of the stuff. They could take me under the Brooklyn Bridge and dump my body in the river. It would be so easy. Nobody would suspect them. It would be the perfect crime.

"University of Chicago," Kiki answers levelly, opening her eyes. I gulp. Nobody from the University of Chicago could possibly botch the perfect crime. Could they?

"Top of her class," Shelby chimes in like a parrot. Is she mocking me?

"You know, Maddy, when you change the subject like that, it makes me think you're not ready for true love," Dr. Joypain says smugly.

"You're so right," I say, my heart pounding. "That's exactly it." Maybe I can throw her off the track. Make her think I'm unworthy of her sixth sense. Or shut my brain off so she wouldn't be able to read me so well.

"Yeah, well, true love," Shelby says, scraping her doe eyes at the roof.

"There there," Dr. Joypain says, stroking Shelby's back.

"You know I have this rule now: If the old sod doesn't have a rubber handy, he can forget it, with all the places his dick has been."

*What?*

"That's right, Shelby. You look out for *you*," Dr. Joypain says, now grasping Shelby's hand.

Oh God. Is he like the neighborhood STD dealer? No. No. I can't believe it's true. He's the one who rolled on the protection. And *Shelby's* the one with the drug habit. She's the one who's so out to lunch that Nick's trying to undo her mistakes as fast as she makes them. If he slept with someone else, it was only because Shelby hasn't been there for him. I decide not to believe a word of her lies. But then there's Frank. Didn't he say what amounts to the very same thing? Jesus. The atrocities of my contact with this family stack themselves up like flapjacks at the IHOP.

I crack the window and stare out at the city, trying to rid my brain of all thought. It's really pouring now, and I'd rather be out there with no umbrella, getting soaked, than in here with these two.

The car maneuvers west, through SoHo, and I let out a long sigh. As we pass the Wooster Hotel, I glance at Shelby and Dr. Joypain, but I don't see any flickers of recognition in their eyes. This hotel holds no significance, a good sign. Shelby's smoking away while Dr. Joypain massages her jaw, eyes closed, deeply engrossed in the needs of her own flesh.

When we arrive at Mercer Studios Sky Spa, the newest and most expensive day spa in Manhattan, according to *Celeb File*, I'm relieved to learn that each of us will get her own personal spa treatment. I gaze around the front desk area, which is lacquered in pale blue from floor to ceiling, giving the slightly dizzying feeling of floating in the sky. Points of shimmering light shine from the ceiling like little stars, and I notice that there are no right angles here. The floors curve into the walls and the walls into the ceiling. Even the serpentine front desk seems as if it grew from the blindingly polished floor.

The three of us are barely there a minute before Shelby and Kiki are escorted away by a statuesque woman in a white lab coat. Shelby takes one last pull from her cigarette and Dr. Joypain's fingers remain fused to her jaw as they recede down the long, curved hallway. Then a squat woman, Russian maybe, wearing a mint green wraparound lab coat, white stockings, and white Birkenstock clogs, greets me and I am briskly herded toward the back of the spa.

The woman smiles warmly, showing me a mouthful of very white, very opaque teeth. I smile back and notice immediately that I am suddenly so sleepy and so sad that I could fall into her masculine arms and weep the afternoon away while she murmurs Russian fairy tales in my ear and strokes my hair. The wonderful, simple, silent woman gestures me into a small private dressing room where a pale blue waffle-weave bathrobe and matching paper slippers await. I feel like the joke's on me, as I put the slippers onto my feet. I expected to feel sexy and European somehow, but I only wind up feeling clumsy and overweight.

In the space of one hour, I am greased, kneaded, pummeled, and flogged. I am salted and rubbed like a fish that Nick might roast in the oven for me. I groan in ecstasy, my eyes closed, trying to appreciate my privileged glimpse into the world of celebrity, and to not die of jealousy on the spot, realizing that people like Shelby enjoy such treatment on a daily basis.

Unfortunately, though, the massage ends, and I enter into the hallway again, dazed and dreamy, until I see Shelby and Dr. Joypain striding toward me.

"Come on, Maddy, chop chop! We have nails to be done, and then I am out of here," Shelby says, practically knocking me over on her way past.

Kiki drapes a long arm around my shoulder as we follow. "How was Sabina, Maddy? I picked her especially for you. She's one of Sky's finest pair of hands, you know. Magical."

"She was great," I say, surprised that my good fortune had anything to do with Dr. Joypain.

"Mmmm," she murmurs, squeezing my shoulder as if it's a washcloth to be wrung. I can feel my muscles transform from jelly back to the tangle of knots they usually are. So much for lasting effects.

Shelby decides that I should do something daring—"to get your life flowing in a more affirmative direction" is how she puts it. Before I can protest, I find myself seated at a small white table, my hands splayed before me, held hostage by a highly skilled, acrylic-wielding nail technician.

I watch in horror as my nails grow to twice their length. As if that's not bad enough, Shelby chooses the color for me, something called Haywire. I learn that Haywire is Sky Spa's own patented nail lacquer. It is the blackest shade of red I have ever seen, with an iridescent neon blue shine to it, and is the last color I would choose for myself, even if I wore nail polish. When Shelby explains that Sky Spa makes "eye grime," "lip tarnish" and "body lube in a tube" in the same shade, I realize with a jolt of terror that Haywire is the same color Christina Aguilera wore in her last music video—on her ass cheeks.

I watch, mesmerized, as the manicurist hunches over my hands, fiercely committed to her mission of making my hands look as if they came from another planet, filing, shaping, and polishing my new talons with the deftness of a crime-lab technician and the silence of a monk.

When it's over, I stare at my hands, turning them this way and that. I feel disembodied, as if Sky Spa is really Dr. Frankenstein's laboratory and I have just been given a hand transplant.

As I shrug on my jacket, careful not to smear the nail polish, Shelby thrusts her Fendi handbag into my arms and asks me to extract her cell phone, explaining that her nails are still wet. I get the feeling it wouldn't be a good idea to tell her that my nails have also just been painted. I force a smile and accept the bag, not allowing my fingers to touch it. It's heavy and stuffed so full that the latch pops open. Of course I can't help but peek. It's right under my nose, after all.

Sitting beside Shelby's sleek little phone are a bevy of prescription bottles, at least three bottles of Haywire nail lacquer, and a rubber-banded bundle of pale blue paper slippers. The owner of the Fendi bag, I decide, peering into its gaping maw, is a binge-eating, pill-popping klepto. And they thought Winona was bad.

Shelby, oblivious to my discovery, wangles her phone out, and I notice for the first time that her pupils are unusually large. That's about the moment when Dr. Kiki Joypain, teeth ablaze, swoops in, taking the purse.

"I see Shelby's taking the vitamins I prescribed for her," she says to me, smiling conspiratorially and reminding me uneasily of Jim Carrey in *How the Grinch Stole Christmas*. Shelby punches buttons on her cell with a silver pen while Dr. Joypain extracts the purse from my arms, snaps it shut, and hugs it to her chest.

# Chapter
# Sixteen

Maybe it was the massage, or maybe it was escaping an untimely death, but I can barely keep my eyes open by the time I get home. Kate's at Casey's parents for the weekend, so the place is mercifully quiet, lonely even.

I nap for the rest of the day but can't seem to get away from the Seabolts and Dr. Joypain, even in my sleep. I dream that I am covered from head to toe in Haywire nail lacquer, that the makeup girl was supposed to be painting me with body lube in a tube and got mixed up. I'm trying to tell her she's made a mistake, when I realize with horror that the makeup girl is Lola. I try to apologize for sleeping with her dad before she kills me, but the polish is drying, paralyzing my face, and I can't move my mouth. When I'm about to suffocate to death, I start flailing around wildly. I wake up panting and sweating. It's dark out and I feel disoriented and hugely guilty.

I pad into the kitchen, willing myself to stop thinking about the dream. The streetlights outside cast an otherworldly glow in the apartment through the fogged windows.

There's nothing to eat. Even the pasta leftovers are gone. There's no milk, and no cereal to pour it on anyway. My stomach growls in protest and I look at the stuccoed ceiling, half praying, half feeling sorry for myself.

I start rummaging through the menu drawer. Chinese—too sugary. Indian—too buttery. Mexican—too cheesy. Middle Eastern—too oily. Cajun—hmm. I open the menu for Two Boots and it hits me like a vat of boiling gumbo. James's band is playing tonight and I promised him I'd go.

I run to the phone, frantic, and stumble like a buffoon over the coffee table. Cursing and rubbing my shin, I punch Michelle's number and chant to Buddha for her to answer.

She answers on the third ring. Thanks, Richard Gere.

"Michelle, you don't by any chance want to go out tonight?"

"Is that the lovely and talented Miss Maddy Braverman from Union Street U.S.A.? How've you been, sweetie?" Michelle sounds unusually chipper.

I ask Michelle to go with me to James's gig, and start getting dressed as well, no easy feat with my new nails, with or without the multitasking element. I can't button my jeans, or my top. If this is the dress-up montage of my life, I'm in deep trouble. The only shoes I can handle, literally, are a pair of Michelle's platform sneakers, Velcro-tabbed, mauve suede. Oy vey. Meanwhile, the gig starts in fifteen minutes and Two Boots is fifteen minutes away.

"Lawrence is here," she says in her patented bedroom voice. "Wanna say hi?"

"Um, no thanks. Tell him I say hi, though. Listen, Michelle. The gig starts in like ten minutes and I promised James I'd go. Lawrence would probably love it. Why don't you both come?"

Michelle yawns luxuriously, nary a care in the world. "I don't know, Maddy. We're pretty comfy right here." I pull on a pair of sweatpants to the sounds of kissing and cooing.

"Michelle? Michelle?"

I hear fumbling. Then a man's voice: "Mmm . . . get over here, hot stuffin'."

I would curl my hands into a fist if I could. "Michelle, I have to go. But if you change your mind, it's on the corner of Seventh and Second in Park Slope."

"Okay, sweetie, give James a standing ovation for me."

"I will." I hang up, grumpy and starving.

If I don't show up at this gig, I will have some major explaining to do to James. He'll know not only have I lost our little wager but that I'm unreliable, as well, and I take pride in being the reliable one in our relationship.

Plus, I could use a drink. I could use a six-pack.

The car service dumps me off in Park Slope and I enter the restaurant. I spot James immediately, setting up on the tiny stage in the back, by the kitchen. I decide not to bother him. There's an empty seat at the bar by the front door, which is strung with chili pepper lights. I sit down and the bartender comes right over. I order a white sangria and ask for a menu.

Two Boots is like a slice cut from *Pee-wee's Playhouse,* if Pee-wee celebrated Mardi Gras every day of the week. The walls are painted turquoise and the bar is cast in resin, with all sorts of glittery treasures trapped inside, like scarabs in amber. Old metal street signs are nailed to the walls and the booths are made of glittery red vinyl. The tabletops are patterned with fifties-style pink-and-yellow boomerangs and have shiny chrome edges.

My drink comes and I immediately wolf down the orange and apple slices garnishing it. The white sangria is a house specialty. It comes served in an old mason jar with a striped bendy straw, and when I take the first sip, I get a mouthful of crunchy sugar crystals that have settled on the bottom. I suck down half of it while I stare at the menu, getting distracted every once in awhile by my new fingernails, which gleam with the reflection of the multi-colored Christmas lights strung everywhere.

When the bartender returns, I order fried calamari with sweet 'n' spicy dipping sauce, a salad, and another sangria, and my stomach grumbles its approval.

The drink goes down smoothly, and I feel like I'm finally starting to let go of the weirdness from this morning. I close my eyes and smile, proud of my ability to "let go" and "live in the moment," and when I open them, I see Rachel and her famous sister, Felicia Tepper, walking into the restaurant with the rest of James's band. Rachel doesn't see me because her gaze is fixed straight ahead of her—on James. My first impulse is to be annoyed at the sight of her, but then I make the conscious choice not to let Rachel Tepper bother me—anymore, ever. And why not? Especially when she's got her famous sister with her and I would just love to meet Felicia, maybe get her autograph on a bar napkin, and ask her what it was like to kiss Sam Rockwell.

Felicia Tepper, star of such edgy indies as *Thinking Room* and *Nuller and Voider,* is taller than Rachel. Her skin is smoother, her limbs longer, her teeth whiter, her smile brighter. All in all, she's got that star power, and she's sucking the wattage from everyone in the restaurant, the same way Nick and Shelby did on the first day of school, way back in September. Bitch. I still want to meet her, but my food and second sangria are arriving and my stomach isn't about to let me leave this bar stool.

Before I turn to my calamari, I take a moment to watch the patrons' faces as they register a genuine superstar in their midst. As Felicia snakes her way among the tiny tables and booths, each customer glows with that eureka moment of a celebrity sighting. Then, like clockwork, they turn to their partners and nod, grinning. Then the whispers begin. I can't hear what they're saying, but it probably goes something like this: "Did you see who just walked by? Do you think it's really her? What do you think she's doing here? Did you see her last film? She's so beautiful." Or "She's not as pretty as I thought she would be." Or "She's so much prettier in person." Each of them will be dying to tell a sister, a brother, a mother, a best friend, a therapist, an Al-Anon support group, an E-group, an ex-girlfriend, or an ex-boyfriend about this.

Now if it were Nick entering Two Boots unannounced, the poor saps would be drooling in their beans and rice. And if he were to approach yours truly, slip a strong arm around my waiting waist, and plant a passionate smack on my mouth, I'd know what it was like to be despised for my celebrity proximity. I'd be able to butter my dinner roll with their jealousy. How cool would that be?

Rachel and Felicia slide into a booth near the stage and shrug off their tight denim jackets, revealing equally tight tank tops. Now I wish I'd worn something nicer than this schlumpy sweater and my baggy sweats. If it weren't for Shelby and her stupid dream to make my life all positive and flowing, I could have worn something decent. I scowl at my fingernails.

James walks over to the Tepper sisters, giving each one a kiss on the cheek. He must feel pretty good about himself to have Felicia in the audience, but, I have to admit, he seems utterly unfazed by her blinding star power.

Once I figure out how to eat with these nails, I start to maul my food and slurp my drink like a medieval soldier. I'd throw the bones on the floor if there were any. Instead, I spear four calamari rings on each talon, angle my head, and drop them in my ravenous jaws. I eat the rind of my lemon section just to prove I can, or to torture myself—I'm not really sure which. James can have his superstar fans, for all I care.

"I didn't think I'd see you tonight."

I turn, swallowing the last of my waxy yellow peel in agony, and there is James, tipping his cowboy hat at me.

"I told you I'd be here," I say, wondering if he saw me eating a lemon peel. If he did, does he realize I live on the edge, or does he think I'm a nutcase?

James is wearing an old threadbare white T-shirt. Sipping my sugary cocktail, I realize that I've never really looked at his body before, and that it's pretty nice. Thin but toned. He's wearing a red-white-and-blue-striped terry-cloth wristband, a pair of torn Levi's, and his battered cowboy boots, which must be his only pair of shoes.

"Well, it's great to see you. You wanna move up there? Better view," he says, grabbing an orange wedge from my plate and popping it in his mouth whole. "Rachel has a booth." He doesn't wince as he chews the peel, and I cock my head, impressed. He winks, then wipes his eyes and says, "That wasn't a wink."

"Uh-huh," I say, spearing another calamari ring.

"Nice," he says, impressed with my dining style. "So you coming?"

"I'm waiting for someone," I say. The truth is that I'd go up there in a second if I had the right outfit on. I could barely comb my hair, for God's sake, let alone smear on a dab of lip gloss. I feel like a troll.

"Oh yeah? Cool. Well, if you change your mind," he says, and then adds, teasing me, "You could meet a celebrity."

"Thank you," I say derisively, "but I'm fine."

James nods, trying to figure me out maybe. "You want another one of those?" He points at my almost-empty mason jar.

"Okay, thanks." I can tell I'm already tipsy, because I'm starting to think James is kind of sexy, in a scruffy, inappropriate way.

"Whoa," he suddenly says, somehow noticing my daring manicure for the first time, even though he watched me spear my food less than a minute ago. Now he really looks confused. "What, um, inspired you to do that?"

"Insanity." I sigh. James looks concerned. "No, really. I'd tell you, but then I'd have to, you know . . ." I make a halfhearted slicing gesture at my throat.

"Uh-huh," he says, shrinking his eyelids down to scrutinizing slits. "Something you need to confess to me, Maddy?"

"Not at all," I say, waving my fingers slowly in front of his face. "Hypnotic, huh?"

James fakes the heebie-jeebies, gets me another sangria, and invites me once more to sit near the stage. I refuse politely again and he goes back to the stage. But as I'm sipping, I realize that I'm all alone in this festive place and that Felicia "Indie Queen" Tepper is sitting a mere ten paces away. So what if I look like an agoraphobic middle-ager? At least my nails are bootilicious.

I grip my third sangria, let my Velcro-tabbed sneakers slide to the floor, and gain my balance. After a deep and hopefully sobering breath, I take my first tentative step toward the Tepper table, telling myself that it is okay. Rachel and I are going to get along just fine. This is the weekend, after all, and after a harrowing near-death experience, I can handle a brat like Rachel Tepper effortlessly.

"Are you drunk?" is the first thing she says as I approach.

"Are you *not* drunk?" I reply effortlessly. "Can I buy you a drink?" This is going to be a piece of cake.

"What is going on with your nails?" She scrunches her nose at them, as if they smell bad.

"They were a gift," I say cryptically, which causes Rachel's face to transform from a look of disgust to one of bewilderment. Suits me fine. "Mind if I sit down?" I add, sliding into the booth and cozying up to Rachel, who does not seem pleased. But what do I care? "Hi, I'm Maddy Braverman," I say to Felicia, and extend my luminous talons across the table. "It's so nice to meet you. I love your *work.*" I hope she appreciates how hip to the lingo I am.

Felicia and Rachel share a glaring glance and then Felicia smiles jadedly and tentatively holds out her cold, limp hand. "Nice to meet you, Maddy," she says, and then turns to face the band, who are adjusting their microphone levels. Maybe not the best time to ask for an autograph.

When the waitress comes over, I order a fourth sangria. I'm going to need it. "Can I get one for her, too?" I ask the waitress, thumbing a claw at Rachel.

"Sure thing, doll. Red or white?"

Rachel answers red as I answer white. "Whatever the lady wants," I declare.

The waitress nods, chomping her gum. "I *love* your nails," she says then, tucking a pencil behind her ear. "By the way, I'm Doris. If you gals need anything else, just gimme a holler."

"Thanks!" I say, beaming. Finally, someone who treats me with respect. Cyndi Lauper will definitely play her in the movie of my life. She could use the comeback.

I click my talons on the festive tabletop. Felicia and Rachel look at me with disgust, Rhea Perlman and Linda Hunt. Doris arrives with our drinks. I offer a toast. "To new beginnings!" I say, but no one lifts a glass except me. I toast to my water glass, me, myself, and I.

"There she is! My little Maddy!" I turn, and there, saving me from myself, is my dear, dear friend and confidante, the glowing and irrepressible Michelle Zucker, sheathed from cleavage to thighs in shiny black spandex.

"Oh Michelle, thank God." I signal for her to lean in close. "Did you get a table?"

She gestures over her shoulder, where a busboy is clearing dishes from a booth across the room. Michelle stands up straight then and bellows in a ceremonious way for me to join her.

Drunkenly, I declare, "Well, ladies, it's been a scene from the depths of hell. We must do it again never, ever. Ta ta!" I wave my magic fingers at them and follow Michelle over to the booth, bumping into a couple of tables on the way.

Lawrence walks over with two margaritas and Michelle introduces us again. Lawrence is tall and smooth and taut. He's wearing extra-dark blue jeans, a bright white T-shirt, and a brown leather jacket. And he smells good, too. A flicker of envy lights in my chest, but when I look at Michelle, she is so glowingly giddy that I just shake my head and smile.

"Have you eaten, Maddy?" Lawrence asks graciously, sliding into the seat opposite Michelle and me, and I realize then that the trick isn't to tolerate people who treat you like shit; it's to hang out with people who treat you like gold.

"I wish I hadn't, Lawrence. I'd love to break bread with you."

Michelle raises her glass and this time we do toast—to love and excellence and all that is good in the world. "Basically, to everything except Osama bin Laden and that booth over there," Michelle says, shrugging at the evil Tepper sisters. "L'chaim!" she adds, and we drink.

"Maddy, I love your new manicure, but they're a little long, don'tcha think?" Michelle says.

I tell Michelle about my "day of beauty" with Shelby and Dr. Joypain, and while I do, Michelle, businesslike, extracts a pair of golden nail scissors from her sequin-covered tote bag. After receiving Lawrence's approval, she commences trimming my nails down to a sensible length, which I must admit makes them look damn good. Maybe Haywire is my color after all. She trims silently while I talk and talk.

When I've reached the part about the pills in Shelby's Fendi purse, Michelle says matter-of-factly, "You know, Maddy, you and James would look great together." No pearls of wisdom for dealing with an insane celebrity. No tips on how to conduct a discreet affair. No scheme on how to cash in from the tabloids. It's as if she didn't hear a word I just said. She just drops the nail scissors back in her bag and crumples my clippings into a napkin while I look at her in disbelief.

"That irresponsible . . . child?" I sputter, unable to contain myself. "What about Nick?" I whisper that part, eyeing Lawrence, but it comes out sounding more like a grunt.

"Oh Maddy, Lawrence and I don't keep any secrets from each other. Right, sweetie?" They rub noses. I look over at James, who's crooning away. He's handsome all right, but he's my assistant teacher. And he's so young . . . so carefree . . . so grungy.

"I'm not saying you have to marry him, Maddy. I'm just saying he's a better prospect than what you've got going. Plus, he's a goody."

"But how can James Watkins, 'goodyness' notwithstanding, be better than Nick Seabolt?" I ask, clenching my disagreeable jaw.

"Maddy." Michelle sighs. "All I'm saying is that you have a greater chance of contracting Ebola from a mascara wand than you do making it work with Nick Seabolt."

After a moment of silence, during which I fume and Michelle and Lawrence inspect each other's tonsils, our conversation resumes. Even though Michelle's being completely unsupportive and irrational, we make the requisite jokes about strapping the Tepper sisters to nuclear warheads. Meanwhile, Lawrence studies the menu and Spur launches into another number, that same song about the actress who made the narrator's life a living hell. Michelle leans across the table and plants another long kiss on Lawrence's lips. "Just like me, honey bunny!" she squeals happily.

Everyone in the place seems to be enjoying James's band, but I can't believe that a few people don't think there's anything wrong with getting Felicia's autograph during the set. Have they no shame?

"What a bitch ho," I mutter to Michelle.

"If she doesn't get her RDA of adoration, she'll shrivel into a fish flake," Michelle says, as offended as I am.

"Have you ever seen someone so insecure?" I ask.

"Never," Michelle says.

"Not like us."

"She's pathetic."

"Sad, really."

Felicia signs every bottle-imprinted bar napkin handed her way. I wouldn't be surprised if people started lining up. I know the names of half the people in this place, she's talking to them so loudly. James is so cool about it, though. He keeps on playing and even glances at me once in awhile. Go James, I think, and hope he picks up on my positive vibes. Not that I think he's hot or anything.

"I just wanna thank y'all for coming out tonight," James says at the end of his third song. "We're called Spur, and I hope you'll sign our little mailing list, if you haven't already.

"For our next little ditty, I'd like to invite a very special guest up here to join us. This is her first time onstage, so be gentle! And she's a performer I hope we see a lot more of in the future. Ladies and gentlemen, please welcome Rachel Tepper."

The audience applauds politely, while I nearly spew sangria all over myself. Michelle and I look at each other, stupefied. Felicia starts clapping wildly and shooing autograph seekers away. Rachel scoots out of her booth.

There's a guitar on the stage. Rachel picks it up and then loops the strap around her neck, acting like she knows what she's doing. She steps up to the microphone. James nods at her and begins playing a slow song. Rachel looks kind of nervous, which is weird for me to see, since nervousness is one of those vulnerable emotions and would signify that she is actually human.

James sings a few bars—about a loner who's in love with an overnight waitress at the twenty-four-hour café—and Rachel starts harmonizing and strumming like a real musician. Michelle and I are dumbfounded and show it by staring at the stage with our mouths wide open.

When the song is over, the audience resumes its polite applause and Felicia leaps out of her seat and runs up onto the stage to hug Rachel. The audience applauds much louder now, and Felicia turns toward us, her admiring followers, beaming. She grabs a microphone and shouts into it, not realizing its purpose, I suppose. "That's my big sister!" And the audience claps furiously, matching her volume level. Even Lawrence gets in on the act, until Michelle silences him with a kick under the table.

Felicia remains on the stage, beaming and hugging Rachel. James looks a little flustered as he leans into the microphone and says, "Rachel Tepper, ladies and gentlemen," as if his vague announcement will return things to their former middling state.

Felicia lifts her ashtanga-toned arms to the band like a conductor and they repeat the bars of the chorus. Rachel smiles with contrived humility and resumes her playing while Felicia sways, beaming, center stage. Even some of the kitchen staff begin to trickle through the swinging red door to see what all the commotion is about.

"You can go back to your seat now!" Michelle shouts over the din, standing up on her seat and banging her hand on the wall to get Felicia's attention. The band stops playing, Felicia freezes midsway, and everyone turns to stare at Michelle. She registers this and sticks her tits out for emphasis. "We see you all the fucking time—in the movies, on TV, in magazines. . . . Isn't that enough for you? You have to steal everyone else's thunder? Are you that pitiful that you have to upstage a fucking bar band?" She looks briefly at James. "No offense." Then she refocuses on Felicia and Rachel. "But you played your little song. Now it's time to give the stage back to the band." Felicia and Rachel are the ones whose mouths hang open now. Michelle rolls her eyes then, obviously aggravated by their simplemindedness. She says slowly, so they don't miss a syllable, "It's called *grace*. Look it up. Learn it. Use it."

A collective gulp ensues. Near the bar, a waiter drops a check, and we can hear it whoosh to the ground. A cockroach scuttles somewhere in the storage room and we can hear its legs click on the wall.

In an effort to be humorous, maybe, or simply trying to break the ice, James says, "Michelle Zucker, ladies and gentlemen," and gestures toward her with a guitar pick. A few people clap, clearly confused.

"That's all. Thank you, everyone," Michelle says, and sits down, beaming as if she just won an Academy Award.

Rachel and Felicia creep off the teeny stage and put their jackets on in silence. James glances at his band mates and, without saying another word, they begin their next number. The audience stares into the bottoms of their empty mason jars as Rachel and Felicia skulk out of the restaurant, glaring at Michelle on their way.

"Wow, Michelle, you're like a superhero for the pedestrian masses. The superstar to end all superstars."

"If it could get me an agent, in a few years some other jealous nobody could give me the same speech. That's my life's dream." She gazes at the ceiling, melodramatic tears brimming in her eyes.

Lawrence puts his hand on Michelle's. "Baby, you got a lot a juice in that beautiful body of yours. Somebody's gonna notice it soon enough. Just don't let all that attention go to your head. You don't want to wind up like that skinny-ass bitch Felicia Tepper. That's no way to act appreciative for all God's gifts."

"Baby, I promise to use my powers only for good," she purrs, and then they're tonguing each other above their empty plates.

# Chapter
# Seventeen

Amanda called for her grandmother, but there was no answer, only the same old howling of the wind. She crept into her grandmother's bedroom, where she had been forbidden to enter. There on her four-poster bed, on top of the covers, were two golden nuggets, each the size of a fist. Amanda gasped and tiptoed over to the bed. This was the answer she'd been waiting for. Her father had finally come. . . .

"Okay, that's it for today."

A collective groan erupts from the peanut gallery.

"Read just a little bit more, Maddy, pleeeeaaase!" Raffey wails, and the chorus sings, "Yeah, pleeeaaase!"

"Sorry, guys," I say, beaming with pride. It's amazing how energized I feel after every installment of the latest *Golden Ghost* chapter. Or, maybe it's because spring break is almost here. Still, I can hardly believe it, but I'm actually almost done with my first draft.

"Anyway, it's time for our New York curriculum. I think James has something pretty special planned." I look at James, who is busy clearing the tables and stacking the chairs so that the kids can get to work on the floor, painting giant murals of the five New York City boroughs. It's time for brown paper and acrylic paint.

"I think smocks are in order," I say, and start sending the kids, four by four, to their cubbies for said smockage.

The kids are all busy putting their fathers' old Brooks Brothers work shirts on backward. They form a makeshift line in front of James and me so we can button them up and roll the huge sleeves.

"So I hope you're not mad about Michelle," I say to James, buttoning up Lucas's smock.

"Mad? No, it was cool. The guys loved it."

"But what about Rachel and Felicia? They were so pissed."

"Eh. They'll get over it." He pats Kylie on her head and sends her on her way.

Wow, he's so unfazed. I wonder if there's a bottled version of his coolness. I'd buy a case. "So you're okay?" I ask.

"Yeah," he says, and smiles at me. "No worries."

Zachary and Eden pretend they're ancient Romans in their oversize garb.

"No. Wait! This is so much better," Zachary says, winding the lavender-and-white-striped shirt around his head like a turban. He touches his hands together in prayer position as he tries to balance the heap on his head.

"I will grant you three wishes," he says to Eden, who jumps in the air with delight.

"Um . . ." She pauses, touching her mouth and looking at the ceiling. Raffey walks over then, hiking up her huge sleeves.

"I want a chocolate cake, a million dollars, and to be famous!" she says.

Eden begins to cry. "Those were my wishes! Maddy! Raffey stole my wishes!"

I sigh. "Eden, I think the swami has wishes to go around for everyone."

"But it was my turn!" she wails.

"You took too long, kid," James interjects. "How's about you get your wishes now, instead of crying? You're wasting the swami's time." He taps his naked wrist. "Time is money, you know." Of course James wouldn't own a watch.

Eden blinks at James and repeats Raffey's wish, but she adds a "jillion zillion" dollars to her request.

"Your wish is my command," Zachary says solemnly, and the next ten minutes are devoted to refocusing the kids' attention on James's project.

When we finally settle each kid in front of a section of brown paper, I slip out the door with my cell phone and check for messages. There are none. Damn. I'd finally resolved to keep the phone turned off so the *Dot Communist* theme wouldn't blare my transgressions, but Nick hasn't even called. Was it something I said? Maybe he can't get through to me with it off. I know that there's some way to make it vibrate instead of ring, but I haven't figured out how to do that. Or maybe he has no intention of calling. "Screw it," I mutter, turn the phone back on, and return to the classroom.

"Maddy! Look! I'm painting the Statue of Liberty!" Stella says, her eyes huge with zeal, as I stuff the phone into my bag. Stella's fellow artistes view this announcement as their cue to publicize what they are doing.

"Maddy! Come over here!" demands Raffey.

"I'm painting Yankee Stadium!" Max says, his hands already covered in thick globs of cobalt blue.

"We're doing the subway!" Eden and Zachary cheer.

"I'm painting a spider monkey in the Bronx Zoo!" says Tyler.

"Can you show me how to make a horse?" Nina asks, at a loss as to what to paint.

Then the phone in my bag actually rings. Or rather, it blasts.

Lola sits up on her knees. "That's the song from my daddy's movie!" she shouts, and James whips his head in my direction so fast that he manages to get a streak of red paint on his cheek.

I grimace and head for the door, phone in hand. I can feel James's eyes practically boring holes into my back.

My heart is hammering.

"Mad, I've been thinking about you," Nick says when I answer.

"You have?" I'm swill. Suddenly the fact that it's been eight days, four hours, and twenty-three minutes since he's called matters nil.

"You bet I have, babe." Babe. *Babe.* He called me "Babe." And not like the pig in the city.

"Come over tonight, Mad. I need to see you. Had a rough day."

"You did? Are you okay?"

"*Essential Insanity* didn't do too well this week. It just came out on DVD, and well . . ."

"Nick, I'm so sorry."

"Yeah, it was my first producing credit, so . . ."

"Oh Nick."

"Yeah, I know. So I could really use that mad Mad mojo tonight," he says, and then growls. He actually growls. For me.

I'm floating by the time I hang up. Nick's had a hard day and he called *me* for comfort! I'm going to his apartment to comfort him tonight. I've got Mad mojo!

When I return to the classroom, I try, I swear I do, to adopt a neutral expression, one that doesn't betray the fact that I am in love with a Hollywood superhunk. But the kids are painting away like little Picassos, the most glorious murals I have ever seen. I knew they were cute and cuddly, but not this cute and cuddly. The light in the room seems brighter now. James crouches on the floor with Nina, helping her with her glorious horse in Central Park. What a saint.

I plop down beside Lola, who's painting gravestones in Brooklyn's Green-Wood Cemetery.

"James says Green-Wood Cemetery is one of the tallest places in Brooklyn," she informs me, eyebrows raised to the sky.

"Wow," I say. "You're doing a fantastic job!"

For the next twenty minutes, I float around the room, cleaning spills, rerolling sleeves, refreshing water cups, and handing out extra paper towels. For the first time all year, I don't feel like a maid to these precocious youngsters, but like a guide of some sort, an educational guru in my own right, helping the precious angels to reach their fabulous destinies.

When art period is over, I walk over to the lights and flick them, beaming like Vanna White on *Wheel of Fortune.* "When you've washed your hands and have put your smocks away, please get a book and a spot on the floor for quiet reading," I announce.

James is sitting on the edge of a table, helping the kids off with their smocks, and I go over to join him. "You look like one of those Moonie people," he whispers, not nicely. But who cares about that? I'm in love!

Leaning in close, I whisper back, "You look like Sitting Bull. Not that there's anything wrong with that."

"What?"

"You have paint on your cheek."

He wipes at his cheek with the palm of his hand.

"The murals look great, James," I say, getting up and flicking the lights again. "Kids, you all did a fabulous job! But let's bring the volume down. Emma, great job of quiet reading!" Hopefully, the compliment will lure the rest of the mini Monets to the floor with a book.

James shrugs. "Yeah, but you still look like a Moonie."

I sigh. The old Maddy would be insulted at such hostility, but the new Maddy couldn't wipe the smile off her face if she tried. "James, not that it's any of your business, but I'm happy to dedicate *Golden Ghost* to you." I start to giggle then. I can't help it.

"Maddy, I . . ."

"Don't know how to thank me?"

"No—"

"You know your moods turn on a dime, I swear."

"Yeah, well, so do yours," he says accusingly. "Listen, I don't want the dedication anymore. Forget about the bet, okay?" The kids are thankfully engaged in their books. Maybe the art project exhausted them.

"Ooh, testy. That's not like you James," I say teasing him.

James gets up and heads over to the sink with a handful of gloppy paintbrushes.

"What, no pithy reply?" I say in a stage whisper as I follow behind, taking care not to step on the kids.

"Are you and James married?" Nina asks, squinting up at me from her *Where's Waldo?* book. James and I stop and stare at her.

Max gets up on his knees, laughing and pointing at Nina. "PP thinks James and Maddy are married!" he says, and the rest of the kids start laughing at Nina, too.

"Maddy and I are *not* married," James says curtly, turning the faucet on full force and staring into the sink.

"That's for sure," I say. "Now read your books, and not another word."

James and I don't speak to each other for the rest of the afternoon, except when forced, and then it's only in clipped monotone chunks. He really knows how to steal my thunder. Or burst my bubble, or put a thorn in my side. He makes me so mad, I can't even keep my damn clichés straight.

Then, at the end of the day, as we're ready to go our separate ways, he has the nerve to ask me to go to another gig.

"Oh, what, so you can just ignore me all afternoon, and then I'm supposed to show up tonight at some smoky dive to support your cause?"

"Forget it," he says quietly.

"Oh, no, I can't wait, really," I say, but he just walks away without saying another word, the brown suede fringe swaying with his gait. As if I don't have better things to do.

But then I'm standing in Nick's doorway. He takes my jacket and bag and hangs them by the door, and then I'm wrapped up in his arms. He tells me how much I mean to him, how seeing my face lights up his dreary days, how nobody understands him except me, because I am *different*. He's looking into my eyes and brushing the hair away from my face, and I forget all about that asshole James.

Nick's just about to kiss me, when Lola materializes. "Maddy!" she shouts, and runs over to me, practically knocking me down with the force of her enthusiasm. Nick and I each take a step backward and my heart free-falls to the floor. I glance at him and see that his jaw is clenched with fury.

Lainey dashes over, not far behind, in hot pursuit. "Sorry about that, Nick," she says quietly. He shoots her a look, which she fails to catch. Then to Lola, she says smoothly, "I'll bet I know who wants to make sushi!"

"I do, I do!" Lola says, jumping up and down. "Can Maddy come with? Maddy, do you like sushi?"

"I do, sweetie," I tell her, "but I'm not really staying." I smile down at her and feel my cheeks redden with shame.

"What are you doing here?" Lola asks then, as if she's just realized that it's out of the ordinary for me to be standing in her father's vestibule, let alone in his arms.

"I, um, I just came to tell your dad . . . how great you've been doing since your cast came off. He was concerned and so . . ." Lola looks over at Lainey, sticks a lock of hair in her mouth, and chews.

"So you can't make sushi with me and Lainey?"

"Sorry, kiddo," I say. "I'm just going to . . . finish telling your dad how . . . great you're doing and then say good-bye."

"Okay," she says, and stands there, staring at us, befuddled.

"Lola, I need your help in the kitchen," Lainey says, coming to take Lola's hand and glancing at me apologetically. They walk off to the kitchen, Lola looking back over her shoulder at us, still chomping on her hair.

My body, as if possessed by an unseen force, starts to tremble. I want to put my head in my hands and scream, "What have I done?" until my voice is wrecked.

"Listen, Nick—"

"Don't worry about that, Maddy," he says, but his jaw is still tight. "I'll talk to Lolo, smooth it out."

"Nick, it's not that."

He looks at me expectantly. Then the words are coming out of my mouth faster than I can reign them in, as if they've been waiting by the door this whole time and finally figured out how to unlock it from the inside.

"Nick, I can't do this. I thought I could, but now I think—I mean I *know*—that this whole thing is . . ." I gesture toward the kitchen.

"Yes?"

"Wrong. Really wrong. I mean, I've been trying to put this . . . thing we're doing into some kind of positive light. I've been trying to make it work . . . make it seem okay somehow. And I've been working so hard at it, but it's wrong, really wrong. There's just no way of making it right!"

"Maddy, shh. . . . Let's step out in the hall."

Once we're in the hallway and I see that the door is shut behind him, I'm on a roll.

"Nick, I am not a good person. And I want to be one. I really want to be a good person," I say, and try not to sob.

"Maddy, you *are* a good person. Haven't I told you that?" Nick looks incredulous, as if he can't believe I'm saying these things.

"You think I'm a good person because I'm not a drug addict like your wife," I whisper. "I'm not a serial nympho like Billy Hawk. I'm not in the movie business. I'm your daughter's teacher. I'm . . . wholesome, some kind of . . . novelty. Oh my God, that's exactly what I am!" I realize what I've just said is absolutely true.

"That is not—"

"Yes, it is. But Nick, but I am not novel. Novel would be refusing you. *That* would be novel. And I'm *not* wholesome. I'm having an affair with a married man! Oh my God, that's the first time I've said it out loud. It sounds so terrible. How can I possibly be a good person?" I'm talking more to myself at this point, and I'm almost hyperventilating now.

"We're not having an affair."

I look at him, furious. "What is it, then?"

"We slept together one night. That's not an affair, Mad."

"Who cares if it was one night or one year?" Nick starts to say something, but I cut him off. "And I love Lola, and this is how I treat her? By sleeping with her dad and then having to lie to her face? That is not okay, Nick." I'm squeaking now, my voice high-pitched and feverish. Now I do start to hyperventilate.

"Maddy, you are so naïve," Nick coos.

"What?" I say, my tears freezing in their tracks.

"You want so much for the world to make sense, Maddy. It never will. And you'll only wind up frustrated every time. Stop trying to make everything right."

I blink at him.

"C'mere, precious," he says, holding out his arms.

Slowly, I find myself moving back toward him. Why are my feet betraying me at a time like this?

"That's my girl. Now you don't feel so bad anymore, huh?"

I shrug underneath the weight of his embrace. How can he not see how wrong this is? After seeing the look on Lola's face? And how can I not extract myself from him right now and get the hell out of here?

"You just follow your heart, Maddy. It will never lead you astray." He kisses me then, a long and deep and tender kiss, just like he did with Lara Flynn Boyle in *Junction 666,* right before he stabbed her in the eye with an icicle he ripped from the highway guardrail.

# Chapter
# Eighteen

——

*The* hardest part to believe isn't that Nick can't see my point. It's that I don't run out right there and then. A little red devil perches on my shoulder, but mine doesn't look like Homer Simpson, or Itchy or Scratchy, or Tom or Jerry, or even Ally McBeal. Mine looks more like Sandra Bullock, playing me in the horror movie of my own sorry life. And she's bludgeoning the little white-robed Sandy Bullock angel with her pitchfork.

Nick grabs my things, lets Lainey know he's going out for a while, and before I know it, we're whizzing off to SoHo, to the Wooster Hotel. He grips my hand the whole time, while I stare out the window, incredulous that I'm doing this. I hear him on his cell, getting us a room. He's stroking the inside of my wrist, and I just sit there like a useless lump.

The room is every bit as gorgeous as I knew it would be. The spread on hot hotels in *Celeb File* couldn't come close to doing it justice. It's a modernist's wet dream, with its Eames furniture, *Sputnick* lamps, and red shag rug.

Nick points at the rug and wiggles his eyebrows. "You want to do it on the floor again?" he asks.

"You have no idea," I say, shaking my head.

"What?" he comes closer and kisses my neck.

"I didn't want to do it in your bed, where you and Shelby sleep. That's why the floor."

"My little Mad," he says. "Sweet innocent Maddy-mad." He kisses me on the lips, and it still feels good. What is the *deal*? "Mmm," he murmurs. "You taste so good. Listen. I'm gonna start the Jacuzzi, order up a bottle of wine, and we'll put this whole thing behind us. Get you up to speed so you can give me that magic mojo, okay?"

I nod robotically, my panties heating up despite myself. Nick leaves me standing there in the middle of the room. I bite my lip. The two Sandras on my shoulders are pulling each other's hair out. I can hear him on the phone in the bathroom, a din above the whoosh of running water.

"Mad? I'm ordering champagne instead," Nick calls from the bathroom suite.

"Great," I answer, my voice quavering.

"Maybe after we can go downstairs and have a massage?"

"Sounds great!" Tears are streaming down my face. Sandy One and Sandy Two halt their bloody battle to wipe them away from my cheeks.

"I'm hard just thinking about you, honey!" he calls. I take a step to my left, lean over, and peer into the bathroom. Nick's got his clothes strewn around the room and he's sitting on the edge of the Jacuzzi, stroking his Hollywoody.

Devil Sandy throws off her horns then and stomps them to bits. In a puff of smoke, she disappears. Angel Sandy blows me a kiss and flits back up to heaven. And I run for the door.

Wooster Street is dark and quiet. The stores are closed and the shoppers have returned to the suburbs. I take a deep breath, briefly wondering what Nick will think when he sees I've left.

I head farther west, toward Sixth Avenue.

The nights are getting warmer. There's a hint of spring in the air. I lift my head and take in my surroundings, willing myself to concentrate on what's in front of me, not what lies behind in smoldering ruins.

The phone rings in my pocket as I'm passing a homeless man sitting on the sidewalk. Even though the temperature is in the fifties, he's huddled in layers of dirty wool blankets, his long gray hair matted into one colossal dreadlock. His skin tone, hair, and rags blend into a depressing colorless bump on the dark sidewalk. I lean down and hand him the phone, which he answers.

"Whaddaya want?" he snarls into it as I back away. "Am I supposed to know you, man? You somebody special, calling on your fancy cell phone?" I mouth the words *thank you* to the homeless guy and continue on my way. I can still hear the conversation as I walk up the avenue. "No, you called *me,* man. No, *you're* crazy! You're a crazy motherfucking *nobody*! Now quit hogging the line, asshole. I got calls to make. . . ."

I have no idea where I'm going, so I keep walking north. I walk as fast as I can, as if speed will wipe away the image of Nick sitting on the tub masturbating. As if it will erase all those months I've been under his spell.

It's not until I reach Fourteenth Street that I know where I'm headed.

Finally Fred's is practically empty upstairs. I go over to the bar and get a bottle of Bud from the bartender, then make my way downstairs. James is onstage, playing to an audience of one: me. I raise my bottle in a half-assed sort of salute, or surrender, and take a seat along the wall. He lifts his eyebrows at me and then returns his gaze to his acoustic guitar.

I order Bud after Bud from a cocktail waitress, half-listening to James play. Mostly, I'm watching the wall opposite me and wondering how I could have been so blind, and why I never gave therapy a fair shot. Could I have avoided this pain and shame if I'd analyzed everything into neat little pieces? Could Frank Caruso have possibly been right about me? Could I possibly be a class act, even after what I've done? If so, it's time to start acting like it. Another beer should help.

"You drink a lot, you know."

"Hi, James." He's stepped off the plywood stage and now sits down beside me—who knows for how long.

"So, do we have to make another bet? No more drunken escapades for you?"

"I'm sorry. I just thought the bar could use some business. You haven't exactly packed this place." I gesture around me with my half-empty bottle. "Meanwhile, maybe you want to thank me for coming, before you dive in with the AA pitch."

"You're right. I'm sorry. Thank you, Maddy. I just worry about you."

"No need, and you're welcome," I say, swerving my lips into what I hope is a sober-looking smile.

"I didn't think I'd see you here tonight, after this afternoon."

"Well, a lot has happened since then."

"Huh," he says. "Well, I'm glad you came."

"You know, you were wrong, James. When you said that thing about celebrities, that they're no different from the nonfamous."

"I was, huh?"

"Yeah. They're even worse."

"Do tell," James says, sliding an elbow onto the table and resting his head in his hand.

"I thought they were really special. They, like, glowed. They all glow to me, James. Do you know that?"

"I had an inkling." I look at him, and he's got this half smile on his face, like he's having a lot of fun with this.

"Do I amuse you?"

"Well, yeah. But I really wanna hear what you have to say on the subject." He reaches for my bottle with his free hand. "Mind if I have a sip?"

"No, not at all. Hey, let me buy you one." I lurch over to the yawning cocktail waitress and order James and myself refreshers, then almost wipe out on the way back to my seat.

"Maddy, you are wasted," James says, hopping up to help me. My ankle gets caught around the leg of the chair as I try to climb into my seat. James grabs me, but he stumbles and we slide to the floor. I lean against the wall, giving up.

"Maddy, you should probably go home," James says.

"No. I can't. I'm not ready yet. Just talk to me, please?" Is that a hint of hysteria creeping into my voice? God, help me.

James settles on the floor opposite me and folds his hands in his lap, waiting for me to continue.

The tears start up and I'm helpless to stop them. It doesn't matter anyway. By the time the school year is over, James will forget all about this embarrassing moment, when he's playing his guitar in some other dive bar.

"I did a really bad thing, James." I look at him to see if his face registers sympathy or disgust, but his eyebrows are raised in kind anticipation. "I slept with him."

James says nothing. We're quiet for I don't know how long. A minute? A year? Finally, he responds. "I know."

"You know?"

"Well, I kind of figured, Maddy."

"Does everyone know?"

"No. Just me."

"How?"

"Because I see you all the time. And you couldn't hide anything if you tried. You're an open book."

"I am?" I sniffle. The floor feels comfortingly chilly, almost sobering beneath me.

"Yes, ma'am." He smiles and hands me a napkin.

"I'm so pathetic," I wail, starting to cry all over again. James starts to laugh. "What? You get some kind of sadistic pleasure watching me writhe in pain?"

"No, I don't. But you're funny as hell, Maddy."

"I am?"

"You are. You're all drunk, sprawled out on the floor of some dive, crying your eyes out over a guy you slept with."

"But he's married!"

"Yeah," he concedes.

"And he has a daughter!"

"Yeah."

"And I'm a horrible monster!"

"Yeah."

"What?"

"I'm kidding!"

"It's not funny."

"Maddy, you fucked up, but you're not a monster. I watch you with the kids all the time. They love you. Your problem is that you don't see how special you are. And you have this ridiculous idea that celebrities have this magical DNA and that you're, I don't know, deficient. You gotta take 'em down, give yourself a break."

I've stopped crying and am staring at James. "I'm special?"

"Yeah," he says, sounding almost frustrated.

"And the kids love me?"

"Yes, and can you please tell me why every woman on the planet must clarify every compliment they're ever given?"

"And I'm not a monster?"

"Maddy! Man. You're frustrating as hell, too."

"I know. It's my low self-esteem." I sigh and look at the floor.

James doesn't say anything. But he takes one of my hands and holds it, surprising me. My heart does a drunken shuffle.

"What are you doing?" I say, staring down at our clasped hands.

"I'm holding your hand."

"Why are you doing that?"

"Because I felt like it," he says. My heart shuffles again, stumbles in the dark.

"I really thought they glowed," I say again, shaking my head.

James shakes his head, too, and then we're quiet for a bit.

"So what's going on with you and Rachel?" I ask, breaking the silence, about as smooth as a pile of broken glass. James drops my hand and leans back, adding distance between us.

"See that?" I say, brightening. "You're a celebrity addict, too. But I'm the one who's strong enough to admit it!" I feel smug, self-righteous.

"Anything else I should know about my personal life?" James asks, clearly fed up.

"Only that you're not so different from me. I might be sitting here crying like a fool, but you're crying right along with me. Inside." I tap my heart with a fist.

"I wish you could see inside, Maddy," he says softly, his smile gone.

"What? I didn't quite get that."

"Nothing."

James helps me up from the floor then and soon I'm propped in my seat, and he's packing up his guitar.

I put on my jacket with great difficulty, grab my bag, and start for the stairs. Out on the sidewalk, I try to walk in a straight line, but my legs betray me, the way they always seem to these days. Then James is beside me again. I can smell his patchouli.

"What are you doing now?" I ask, annoyed.

"Helping you get a cab."

"I'm fine," I say, and nearly trip over a garbage can. James hooks his arm in mine and begins to lead me toward Fourteenth Street. I surrender to his stability and allow myself to be led. When we reach the corner at Eighth Avenue, we stop, but he doesn't unhook his arm from mine.

James raises his arm and I watch as the light from the street plays on his jacket fringe. A cab swerves over to the curb and then James and I are standing before the open door, facing each other.

"I'm sorry," I blurt. "I'm such a mental case. I just need psycho-analysis or something."

"I think you need a good night's sleep."

"Yes!" I agree. "Everything will be better in the morning. Every-thing is always better in the morning."

"That's right," he says. "You're going to be fine."

"James, thank you so much," I gush. "You were really there for me tonight. And I really needed someone. Thank you."

"Hey, that's what friends are for," he says.

We stand there awkwardly for a moment, and then he does this thing with his eyebrows—a wiggling sort of move. And I could swear he licks his lips. I realize with a jolt that James is trying to seduce me, and it's a jolt that feels right, nice. Suddenly, I find myself filled with a gust of amorousness, and I lean a little closer to his lips. He leans a little closer to my lips and I make the first move. I kiss him. I kiss him like I've never kissed anyone before, with equal parts passion, urgency, and hunger.

"Okay, sleep tight, Maddy," he says politely, gently pushing me away.

"Oh God, I'm so sorry. I thought—" I say, opening my eyes.

"It's okay," he says, bundling me into the backseat of the taxi. I'm such a fool. "Sleep tight, Maddy," he repeats as he's closing the door. I give him a weak smile, and whaddaya know, he winks.

The cabdriver is nice enough to shake me conscious when we get to my apartment, and by the time I wake up the next afternoon, all I remember, with a shudder and a shiver, is mauling James, being embarrassingly rejected, then herded into a taxi. Could the shame be any deeper?

# Chapter
# Nineteen

───

My hangover seems to last forever. Eventually, it morphs into a kind of flulike virus. Call it "emotional hibernation." Or better yet, "my lost spring break."

When school starts again, I'm not feeling any better. For weeks, I teach class in a Godfatherly whisper, stooped over like Scrooge and wearing dark shades, popping aspirin every ten minutes, as if they're Sprees. My sunglasses become fused to my head, shielding me not only from the glare of the fluorescent tubes but also from having to look James in the eye. I'm still so mortified that I try to repress the whole evening, and every time I get a flash of it, I start chanting affirmations. The most popular these days is "Each day in every way, I'm getting classier and classier."

Nick hasn't tried to call me at home or at school. I've thought about calling him to try to explain why I ran away, but every time I pick up the phone, I realize it may be better for him not to know I've discovered that he's the devil. I worry that hearing such a thing might hurt his feelings. And I don't want to cause anyone any more pain. Lord knows, I'm bearing enough myself these days.

The kids have been great. They have that animal sense not to venture too close, lest they disappear in the black hole of my contaminated aura, and I haven't had to flick the lights more than once. My illness has made them unusually cooperative.

As far as I can see, Lola's behavior doesn't betray any hurt feelings. Out of all the kids, she and Nina have been the most concerned, making me homemade "Get Well Soon" cards with glitter pens and construction paper every day. One day, Lola comes over and hops up on my lap, but I have to shoo her away, because if I let her stay there, I know I'll cry and freak her out.

James, like the cool cat he is, acts as if nothing has happened between us, and I don't know if I should appreciate that or not. He putters to and fro, helping the kids, checking on me, bringing me tea, but I know he's just biding his time until the year is finally over and he can get as far away from me as humanly possible. That's what I would want to do if I were him.

On my way to the lunchroom one day, the older kids stare at me, looking confused. At the salad bar, Rachel saunters over, crunching deafeningly on an apple, and tells me I look like a mental patient. "It's very unprofessional," she sneers. I tell her I'm stark raving mad, and try to procure a little drool for effect, which makes her wince. "What does it matter anyway?" I say, and sigh.

Then the head molester trots up to me and asks to try on my glasses. I refuse. "They're prescription glasses," I tell him, lying. I look back to Rachel, who's still chomping and glaring. It's the most she's ever looked at me in my life, and it's unsettling. Just then, Michelle enters and hurries over. She hisses at Rachel, bats her eyes at Arthur, and slips me a small brown bottle with an eyedropper attached. Rachel scurries away and I manage to crack a smile. She might be a total bitch, but I do believe that Michelle Zucker intimidates her, even if I'm the one who should be locked up. Well, that's one positive revelation.

"It's homeopathic," Michelle says, placing a hand on my shoulder. I throw my head back and unscrew the cap, but she stops me before I get a chance to drizzle the entire contents down my throat. "Three drops, Maddy, okay? It's ho-me-oh-path-ick."

"You are so very very loud, but I love you," I say. She showcases her dental wattage then and I cower like a vampire caught at sunrise.

"I gotta go," I mumble, pat her shoulder, and shuffle back to the classroom with a handful of saltines and the medicine.

At home, I'm no better, but at least I've stopped turning to the razzle-dazzle of celebrity spunk and spirit to help me bear the grinding in my head, the sourness in my stomach. Used to be I'd pore over *Celeb File Weekly,* but if I'm going to do that, I may as well guzzle a bottle of Jack Daniel's and dig myself an early grave. I'm not well enough even to open my laptop. I do manage one evening to crack open a slim volume of poetry, but its effect has me bolting to the bathroom before I finish the first stanza.

While I'm curled over the mouth of the toilet, Kate comes in to check on me.

"Mad? You gonna be okay?"

"Yeah," I say, my voice echoing in the porcelain chamber. "Thanks."

"Vitamin C is really helpful," she says before disappearing into her nuptial laboratory.

In the mirror, I discover I've turned green. Back in bed, shivering under the covers, I pray for sleep.

Okay, I can do this. First one foot and then the other. I think I've worn the same sweatpants for the past month. I've decided that if I have to look at the same four walls one more minute, I'm going to have to check myself in to Bellevue.

So Barnes & Noble it is. One little *Celeb File Weekly* won't kill me, especially coupled with a venti mocha frappuccino. Maybe I'll even browse through Dr. Joypain's book and find out who I *really, truly* am.

The sun on my face feels cleansing, and I suck in huge gulps of air, as if it will dry-clean my insides. I haven't been out and about for so long that I've overdressed, and I quickly unwrap the scarf from my neck, glancing around to make sure no one's seen my obvious fashion gaffe.

Barnes & Noble is the same as it ever was, and I shiver with comfort as I pass by the tables of new arrivals in the front of the store. Being Saturday, the magazine section is packed, so I grab a *Celeb File,* replete with Britney Spears's sultry gaze, and then head upstairs to the café.

I study the magazine cover while I wait for my slushy coffee. I am pleased to see that Britney is becoming more of a woman than ever before. She's not a girl anymore. Power to the cleavage is what I say, even if I don't have any of my own. Britney's will simply have to do.

When I sit down, I feel like I'm meeting an old friend for coffee. Opening the magazine, I feel a giddy excitement, which concerns me. I don't want to be excited over famous people anymore. And though I feel I've demystified a certain element of celebrity after my experiences with Nick and Shelby, I find that I still crave the sight and sound of entertainment royalty as much as the kids crave a special snack.

God, everyone looks so pretty at their premieres—Kate Hudson, Jennifer Aniston, Chloë Sevigny. They are all so little, with such gigantic eyes and heads, like aliens with really shiny hair. Or like cupcakes with way too much frosting, which *is* like a special snack. I take a giant slurp of my frappuccino and turn the page. And there's Shelby Seabolt, a whole spread devoted to her. She's beaming at me and donning a fresh pair of contrived-looking rimless spectacles, something very un-Shelby. I nearly spit out my frap when I read the bold yellow headline at the top of the article: FROM SILVER SCREEN TO *GOLDEN GHOST!* SHELBY SEABOLT BECOMES CHILDREN'S AUTHOR!

Then I start reading the article.

*From the silver screen to the writer's desk, the star of* Pine for Me *and other movies is trading in her screen time to write a children's novel about a little girl who travels alone cross-country during the California gold rush. Who would have thought that Shelby Seabolt, star of blockbuster hits like* Out of My Mind *and* Menacing Straits, *was also a gifted storyteller?*

In the interview, Shelby says, "I wrote about something I could identify with—a little girl who is left alone when her parents die, who has this epic, sweeping adventure, who possesses such inner strength. . . . I really relate to Amanda Porter."

The interviewer asks Shelby what she means, as Shelby's parents are alive and well, living in Atlanta.

"Oh, that's what I like to call a metaphor. You know, I felt like I was all alone during my childhood. Mostly because I was an artist. You know, I was in my head a lot. Thinking in these weird, circuitous paths. I think it's all led me to this moment. I'm so excited!"

The article ends with the interviewer sharing Shelby's excitement and coaxing the reader to buy the book: "Share this sure-to-be best-seller with your kids. Don't miss *Golden Ghost,* coming next Christmas to a bookstore near you!"

I reread the article about seventy-five times, my heart pounding faster each time. How could this have happened? *Golden Ghost* isn't even finished yet. I haven't looked at it in a month.

Wait a minute. When was the last time I used my diskette? I grab my jacket and the magazine, leaving what's left of my frappuccino on the tall round table, and bolt out of there. Only when I'm back on Court Street do I realize I've stolen the magazine. Fuck it. I'll pay double next time.

I throw everything down on the floor when I get home, rush into my room, and start ransacking my messenger bag. No diskette. I slump down on the floor, now ransacking my brain to figure out where I last had it. Then I remember Nick passing me my coat and bag when we left his penthouse, after Lola saw us together. It must have fallen out of my bag. He'd crumpled my stuff into a ball when he handed it to me. Shelby must have found it on the floor when she got home and . . . stolen it. Does she even know it's mine? I wonder.

Heart racing, I pick up the phone and dial Nick. He'll be able to help me set this whole thing straight.

When he finally answers on the tenth ring, I shiver.

"Nick, it's Maddy. I—"

"Maddy. To what do I owe the pleasure?" he asks, his tone malevolent.

"Nick, look. I know this is going to sound really bizarre, but Shelby's somehow stolen my novel. My diskette. It must have fallen out in your apartment. I read the article today in *Celeb File*, and I could really use your help."

He laughs then.

"What's so funny?"

"Maddy, I have no idea what you're talking about. Shelby's been writing that book for almost a year."

"What?" My mind freezes.

"This is exactly the kind of thing that will get her back in action. You know, rekindle her good working relationships in the industry. It's a great thing, for both of us, Maddy. Maybe you should be happy about it."

I slump onto the bed, dizzy.

"Nick. Don't tell me."

"I know, it's a surprise to me, too. I had no idea that she was writing a book, either, but there it was, on a disc, just lying on the living room floor. Shelby could sure use the break, too." He's having a lot of fun with this.

"Oh my God." I don't feel the tears coming out of my eyes, but I can feel their wetness on my cheeks. "There are laws for this kind of thing, Nick," I say.

"Maddy, you're cute. You really are. But do you have any idea who you're dealing with? You can't touch me. You don't have the resources."

"What about us, Nick? She's going to find out!"

"How?"

"If she knows where that disc came from, she'll—"

"She doesn't care where it came from. And even if she knew, she still wouldn't care. What do you think this is, Dorothy, Kansas?" I don't say anything. I can't believe any of this. Then, in a bedroom voice, Nick says, "Of course, if it's upsetting you that much, I'm sure you and I could work out a little private deal of our own."

"What, you want me to fuck you to get my own novel back?"

"No. You fuck me and I'll pay you so much money to keep your mouth shut, you won't have to write, teach, or do anything else ever again."

"And if I don't fuck you?"

"You get nothing. And nothing you do will make any difference."

"You can't buy everything, Nick," I say softly.

"You can come *really* close though, Mad. A naïve girl like you would be surprised at what, and *who,* money can buy."

"I'm sure I would."

"So? Wanna get together tonight?"

"No!"

"You're greener than I thought. I'm almost . . . impressed. But you know, Maddy, there comes a time when that innocent act you put on gets really tiring. You might want to try a different tack. Just to try something new, you know, broaden your horizons."

"Okay, how's this for you?" I say calmly. "Go fuck yourself." I slam the phone down and breathe calmly for about ten seconds before I burst into tears.

Kate and Casey come running.

We spend the rest of the night on the living room sofa, Casey unrolling ribbons of toilet paper for me while Kate strokes my hair.

"Copyright kicks in the moment you set your words down in tangible form," Casey says.

Kate lights up then. "See that? You're protected."

"But it may not be that simple," Casey says. "Did you copyright your manuscript with the Library of Congress?"

"No," I whisper.

"Do you have a copy of it printed out?" he asks.

"No."

Casey puts a fist to his lips, thinking. "Well, how about on your hard drive? You backed it up, right?"

I look up at him, feeling a shame worse than Demi Moore must have when she starred in *The Scarlet Letter.*

Kate explodes. "Maddy, you never backed up your work?"

"I worked on my laptop, and in the computer lab at school. I lost track!" I yowl. "I'm so stupid!"

Neither Casey nor Kate opposes this statement. We sit on the sofa, the silence broken only when I proclaim my idiocy or blow my nose.

"Well, there's got to be something you can do, Maddy," Kate finally says.

"Not with his battalion of lawyers." I sniff, then quietly confess, "I deserved it anyway."

Kate looks at me, incredulous. "Maddy, you did not deserve to have your work stolen from you. Why would you think that?"

"Take a guess."

"Look, Maddy, it's none of my business. But it takes two to tango."

"Kate, I know you don't want to hear this, but I had an affair with him. I slept with him. A married man. With a child! I am totally getting what's coming to me. Never mind the fact that I could get fired for sleeping with the parent of one of my kids!" I start sobbing all over again. "What is wrong with me?" I wail.

"Maddy, how many times did I tell you not to get involved with those people? How could you have done something so stupid?" she says, her anger rekindling.

"I don't know! I'm sorry!" I grab a throw pillow and scream into it. I feel a hand rubbing my back then and I look up. "He promised me his marriage was bogus. Please don't hate me, Kate. I was really stupid. I know that now. I just didn't know. Please don't hate me."

"Maddy, I don't hate you. I just hate the decisions you make sometimes. You are so much better than any of those pricks."

"I hope so," I say quietly.

Casey hands me another toilet paper streamer and I wipe down my face, blow my nose.

Eventually, Kate says, "Look. I hate to say this to you, but you're the kind of person who has to throw her whole body into the fire to see that it really burns."

"It's okay. That's exactly what I am." I shake my head with the realization. "The kids are never going to forgive me."

"Well," Kate says, "if we can't figure out how to get your book back from that total a-hole, then you'll just have to write another book."

I remove my face from the pillow. "Yeah, I can write one about how stupid I am. I can write *Dummies for Dummies*."

Kate starts to laugh at that, and then Casey joins in.

"Shut up you guys," I say. "It's not funny."

"It's pretty funny," Casey says with some effort.

"Fuck off," I say, and leave them there, wiping away their tears of laughter.

# Chapter
# Twenty

The only person I can think of to talk to is Arthur. He's the only one who could possibly do something on my behalf without charging a fee. I've been at City Select Academy for six years. We have a good working relationship, even if he is a sleaze, but then, who am I to talk? Yes. Arthur will be on my side. He's always been loyal to his employees.

I let James know where I'm going, and tell him to have the kids work on some math problems while I'm gone.

Arthur's office is at the end of a narrow hallway on the ninth floor, along with all the other administrative offices. His corner view of downtown Manhattan is practically famous in its own right. Film companies over the years have acquired permission to shoot scenes from there during holidays. With all that's happened, I can't help but think that the entertainment industry has its fangs sunk into just about anything and everything, and that no place is safe anymore from its venomous bite.

I'm out of breath by the time I reach the ninth floor. Just as I'm about to turn the corner to Arthur's hallway, Rachel comes barreling toward me, sunny as a schoolgirl.

Here it comes, I think. She's going to insult me again. I brace myself.

"Hi, Maddy," she says, confounding me with kindness, as if that little scene in the lunchroom never happened.

Then she's passing me, casually tossing a gauzy scarf over her shoulder. "I guess I am crazy," I say under my breath, and wonder why that scarf looks so familiar.

When I reach Arthur's office suite, his assistant, China, nineteen years young, is sitting at her small desk outside the head molester's inner sanctum. She's flirting with an eleventh-grade boy, the grandson of Cavish Menlowe, *Vogue*'s most sought-after fashion photographer.

"Nashy, you're so weird!" she howls.

"Nashy" boasts, "My shrink says I'm *cyclothymic.*"

"Ooh, that sounds dangerous," she says, and gives him a pouty look. I roll my eyes and clear my throat.

China cranes her neck around Nash, who's sporting a carefully contrived slovenly look. She sees me and frowns.

"Just knock on the door, Maddy. He should have some free time." Before I can thank her, though, she returns to her task at hand, namely getting into Nash Menlowe's slouchy cargo pants.

I walk over to Arthur's door, which I find is open a crack. Taking a sneak preview, I spy him gazing out the window and spraying about ten short blasts of Binaca into his mouth. That's when I know where I've seen that sheer lavender scarf with the glittery bugle-bead fringe. Rachel and Arthur are still doing it, I think, and shudder with disgust, even if I'm not any better. I guess I'm not surprised. But meanwhile, isn't she a little old for Arty? That's why she was just so nice to me. She's one of Arthur's chosen flock. That scarf is probably just one in a string of gifts. I will never understand the attraction, or what keeps drawing such young pretty prey into his tentacles.

I knock on Arthur's doorjamb, clearing my throat. He whips around, pocketing his breath spray with his good hand.

"Miss Braverman!" he says jovially. "To what do Ah owe the pleasure? And may Ah say that the view outside my window is nothing compared to the one inside." He smiles grandly at his own cleverness, sits at his massive antique desk, and gestures for me to close the door.

As I do, I wonder if Rachel was naked in here, and if so, *where* was she naked? I sit opposite Arthur and wonder, Am I soaking up her very juices right now? Would wiping the seat be impolite? Can I possibly wrench my mind from the gutter?

"Arthur. How ya doin'?" I ask. I must be nervous. I'm turning into Joe Pesci. Which reminds me: Where has he been lately?

"Couldn't be better, Maddy," Arthur says, and winks conspiratorially. Which reminds me of James. Which reminds me of being wasted with James and humiliating myself. How splendid to think of such things at a time like this.

"Arthur, I have kind of a serious matter to discuss with you," I say.

"You know, Ah keep meaning to add dental to the insurance policy. Ah've got to talk to Shirley about that."

"It's not about health insurance."

"Well, Ah am planning on acknowledging the lower-school teachers more often around here. Hell, if it weren't for you beautiful girls paving the way for our students, where would we be? Certainly not at Harvard." He laughs again at his wit.

"Arthur. Thank you. Really. You're . . . too kind. But I have kind of a . . . private matter to discuss." I fold my hands in my lap like a nun, wondering how I can possibly explain all this. At least I know which parts to leave out. My explanation for the diskette being in Nick's apartment is simple. I was there to share the good news about Lola's progress. Even she can attest to that.

Arthur loosens his necktie and smirks. He runs his veiny flesh-and-blood hand over his yellow helmet of hair in a way I can only describe as seductive. "You want to lock the door, Maddy?" he asks in a gravelly voice.

"Uh, no. But, uhm . . . thank you." I sit up in my seat and wish I had wiped it down.

"Maddy," says Arthur, pulling himself together. "Let's start again. Why don't you tell me what brings you here?" His face becomes serious, devoid of all innuendo and possible flirtatiousness. It seems a difficult task for him, but I explain my problem.

\*     \*     \*

"So, I guess what I'm saying is that if there's anything you can do, it would be very much appreciated."

Arthur squints, stroking the desktop with his fake hand.

"Well, Maddy, it's complicated."

I gather myself. "What do you mean?"

"Well, Ah mean that there's a certain conflict of interest. It's probably best that Ah don't get involved." He leans forward on his elbows and his corduroy blazer stretches unattractively under his arms. Bushy blond hair sprouts at his wrists. "You have to see, Maddy, that the Seabolts are the best PR this school has ever had. And the sweet center of that succulent fruit is that they're paying *us*." He caresses his lips with a plastic finger and continues. "Ah can't rightly risk sullying such a . . . productive relationship. Do you understand that?" He says all of this in a kindly, grandfatherly way, and I have to admit it makes sense. I just wish I'd thought of it before I ventured into Arty's chamber of love.

"Yeah, well. Thanks anyway." I stand up, even though I'm falling to pieces.

"Oh, Maddy. Don't leave just yet." Arthur opens his desk drawer and shuffles around for a bit. He's really good with that left hand of his, I have to admit. "Ah have a newly drafted contract here. Ah thought maybe, while Ah have you here, you might sign it." He pushes the cream-colored stationery in front of me.

While I study it, Arthur says, "It's been awhile since you received financial recognition for your ongoing commitment. Ah think it's high time for you, Maddy."

"You're giving me a ten-thousand-dollar raise?" I ask, looking up from the contract, dubious. "I don't understand." The most this school has ever given for a raise is a thousand dollars.

"You put in a lot of work with those kids. And well, with what's going on with your, ahem, situation—"

"Nick called you, didn't he?"

"Maddy, please. You're creating rapids out of rivulets."

"What did he say?"

"He simply made it clear that you might need some assistance. And Ah was happy to—"

"I can't believe this." I stare out the window above Arthur's head, wondering why Nick didn't just tell Arthur that I attacked him. If he's so hell-bent on stealing my manuscript, why doesn't he go the distance and finish me off for good?

"Did he say anything else?" I ask.

"No. Should he have?"

"No. I was just wondering. Arthur, thank you, but I can't accept the contract. In fact, I resign." Wow, now I'm surprising me. I've been wanting to do this for the past three years, and now that I've finally said the words, even with all that's going on, I feel lighter, freer, hopeful.

"But Maddy, you're one of our best teachers."

"You'll find another one."

"It's quite a good salary. Are you sure you don't want to reconsider this?"

"You know, I've been here for six years. I know that might not seem like a lot to you, but it has been for me."

"Ah don't think there's another school in the city that could match this offer."

"It's not about the money, Arthur," I say calmly. "It's just . . . time for me to go."

"Ah see," he says, clearly distraught, which flatters me a hell of a lot more than that bribe disguised as a raise.

"I'll drop off a letter of resignation tomorrow."

When I finally leave, Arthur looks different, fragile and small, sitting there smoothing his hair.

Before I head back to the classroom, I slip a detailed note into Michelle's mail slot. If anything, she'll be good for some positive vibes, or maybe a job lead. At the very least, she'll congratulate me for finally escaping from City Select Academy.

"You quit?"

"I did," I say, hardly believing it myself.

"But what are you going to do?"

"I have no idea."

James and I are hanging the kids' latest New York City–inspired paintings, depictions of their houses. It's funny how similar they all look, with trees planted in front, even if the dwelling is a twentieth-floor apartment on West End Avenue, as is the case with Zachary.

"But why?" he asks.

"It's a long story. Can I tell you some other time?" The truth is, I don't know how to tell him. Out of everyone, I think James is going to take it the hardest. He was the one who got me started writing *Golden Ghost,* who cheered me on from the beginning. It's almost as much his story as it is mine.

"The kids are gonna miss you," he says, standing on a chair, a batch of paintings in one hand and a roll of masking tape around his other wrist like a bracelet.

"I'll miss them, too. It's just time, you know?" I make sure I've written the kids' names and the date on the back of their work, then grab another roll of tape and search the walls for some empty space.

"You seem almost happy about it. Are you?"

"I am," I admit. "I've been wanting to do this for a long time."

"Why didn't you before?"

I consider this for a moment. "I don't know. Laziness? A place like this ruins you. There's no dress code. Free lunch. Summers off. It's a good deal."

"That's why I'm here," he says, punctuating his good fortune on an imaginary guitar.

"And fear," I add.

"Of?" He turns to me.

"Of there not being anything better out there. Of working in some corporate nightmare. Of a nine-to-five job, panty hose, and the subway during rush hour."

"Yeah, that's gotta blow," he says, faking a shiver.

"I guess I'd like to write. But I'd like to eat, too," I say. Then I panic. "You don't think I just made the worst mistake of my life, do you?"

"No, Maddy. I think you already made *that* mistake."

"Ha-ha. No, really. Should I have taken the offer?"

"I don't know. Why don't we discuss it over a beer? To celebrate your leap of courage."

"How about coffee instead? I don't want to go on any more benders."

James smiles with recognition. "All right, let's get outta here."

"James, I just wanted to tell you that I'm really sorry about my behavior at Finally Fred's."

"Hey, no biggie. Anything to interrupt the monotony," he says charitably, and I smile.

We're shrugging on our jackets when Michelle comes zooming into the classroom, keys and bangles jingling.

"Maddy. I just got your note. I came as fast as I could." She's panting and leaning over, exposing a bright mound of heaving bosom. I glance at James to see if he's leering, but he's looking at me.

"We were just about to grab some coffee," he says. Then he looks at Michelle. "Wanna come?"

"Coffee? *Coffee?* You want to have coffee at a time like this? Maddy, you are farther gone than I thought. What you need is raw fish and hot sake."

I nod. Of course. Michelle's right. The only thing to ingest at a time like this is sushi.

James shrugs in agreement, but he looks confused. "Hey, I thought we were celebrating here."

Michelle stares at James. "What? Superdick and Psycho Bitch stole Maddy's novel, and you want to celebrate?"

"Three large hot sakes, please," Michelle says. "In fact, why don't you just nuke the whole bottle and bring it to the table." The waitress smiles, as if she doesn't understand a word, repeats, "Three hot sake," and bows.

Michelle has led James and me to her favorite Japanese restaurant, Wasabi, on Smith Street, not as hip as the place across the street, Vom Fusion, but the fish is fresher and the service is superior, according to our resident culinary expert.

James and Michelle put the madness at Two Boots behind them on the walk over here. What with James's "anything goes" demeanor and Michelle's supersize personality, they were bound to hit it off eventually.

James stares at the sushi poster on the wall above us, deep in thought. "I can't believe this," he says for the thirtieth time.

"I don't know, Maddy," Michelle says. "I think you should just sell your story to *Celeb File,* or the *Enquirer.* At least you could make some money off those bastards."

"No. She should not sell her story to any tabloid," James says to Michelle. Then he turns to me. "Maddy, don't even think of doing that."

I put my head in my hand and slump over the table. The only thing I have going for me is that the school year is almost over and I can be rid of Shelby and Nick for good. I can honestly say for the first time in my life that if I never see another celebrity as long as I live, it'll be fine with me. Kate was right: I've learned my lesson— big time.

"Maddy, don't give up," Michelle says, reaching across the table and patting my head. I look up and force a smile, which I'm sure comes across as more of a grimace.

"Thanks, Michelle." I sit up. "It's okay, though. Hey, at least I know my writing's worth something. It's good enough to steal anyway." I squeeze a pathetic guffaw out, and both James and Michelle look at me with such a pain in their eyes that I feel guilty. "Okay, stop looking at me like that, you guys. You're making me feel worse."

"It's going to be okay, Maddy," James says forcefully, as if he's trying to convince himself. "Now, what do you want to eat?"

The waitress comes with our sake and takes our order, but I'm not prepared, so James and Michelle order a platter of sushi and sashimi for three. Then Michelle proposes a toast. "To turning tables," she declares, and though I drink to that, I still don't believe it could happen in this lifetime.

"Have you talked to a lawyer yet?" Michelle asks after slurping down two tiny cups of hot rice wine.

"I don't know any lawyers, and besides, I don't want it to turn into some ugly legal battle that I'll just lose anyway." I sip at my sake, suddenly exhausted.

"Okay, look. I wasn't going to suggest this, because she's really more of a corporate lawyer, and she still hasn't forgiven me for the tattoo, but talk to my mom, Maddy." Michelle roots through her fake tiger-skin knapsack and pulls out a transparent blue coin purse. After more rummaging, she extracts a graying, fuzzy-edged business card and hands it to me. It reads, "Ellie A. Zucker, P.C. of Counsel. Zucker Danon & Calderwood, LLP."

"Michelle, you'd really do this for me?"

"Maddy! Duh! You're my best friend! I'd give you the tits off my chest if it'd help." That's when James does take a gander at Michelle's boobs, but I forgive him for it. I mean, how can anyone not look at that gleaming load?

"Michelle, you have no idea how much this means to me," I say, tearing my eyes away from her chest.

"Great. Lemme call her now. She should be getting home any minute."

"Now?" I say, flustered. "I thought I could—"

"The sooner the better," she says, and starts punching buttons on her cell, causing the Hello Kitty charms to boogie in time.

Our miso soups arrive while Michelle is calling her parents' house on the Upper West Side.

"Okay, she'll be right over," Michelle says after a few minutes of earsplitting conversation peppered with Yiddish, then says good-bye. My heart starts to pound in anticipation.

"Now? But I haven't eaten. And I can't go alone. Will you go with me?"

"James," Michelle says, gathering her things. "You can go with her, right?"

"Sure," he says. "We can get the food to go." He pours himself another sake and gulps it down, now that we're stretched for time.

"But what about you?" I say to Michelle.

"I'm meeting Lawrence," she says as coyly as ever. "You guys take the food and go meet my mom." Michelle scrawls out her parents' address on a Sapporo coaster and tosses it to me.

James downs another swig and then gets up, alerting the waitress to our change of plans. Apparently, the food is almost ready, and a few minutes later, it is being shepherded gently into three rectangular foil trays. I gulp down my own sake to calm my nerves.

"Michelle," James says, handing her one of the containers. "Take it to Lawrence."

"Oh, he hates sushi," she says, then swings an orange cape around her shoulders, kisses both of us on the lips, and blazes off. James and I step outside, tipsy and tentative. At the end of the block, Michelle turns around, shouts, "Break a leg!" and then continues on her way.

Ellie Zucker shows us into her home office, on the garden level of her enormous brownstone, while I try to keep my head from swiveling right off my shoulders. She is still in her work clothes, a putty-colored tailored suit jacket and pencil skirt, and four-inch black patent pumps pointy enough to skewer kittens. I could probably buy a BMW with just the gold on her right hand. The rock on her wedding finger could no doubt pay for a helicopter. I wonder why Michelle doesn't just stay here instead of in the rat's nest she calls home, but then I remind myself that we're talking about living with the parents here. No matter how amazing they might be, they're still mom and dad, with the nagging or the neglecting, always reminding you of your darkest hours just by their breathing patterns. A thousand miles from my own parents seems to be working out just fine. Michelle is lucky she can live so close and yet remain happy and unscathed.

"You'll have to excuse the mess," Mrs. Zucker says, gesturing for James and me to sit down. "Stan's doing a little renovating, so I don't know where anything is anymore." The dark office, with its low ceilings and striped wallpaper, is crammed with boxes.

"Call me Ellie," she says.

"Ellie," we say, nodding politely. I clutch the strap of my Manhattan Portage bag and James clutches the food, as if we're about to take off for deep space.

"So what's this about a stolen novel and evil celebrities?"

Ellie listens intently, and when I'm done, she purses her matte mocha lips and looks up at the beamed ceiling.

"Do you have any hard copies of your work? Or any proof that you have been working on this novel?"

"I never saved any of the printouts. I threw them away after I made changes. The only copy I had was on that diskette. I've been reading the story to the class this whole semester. The children and James can back me up on that. They did some illustrations, but I sent them home with the kids. They do a ton of work, so I can't hold on to everything." I realize how ditzy I must sound. I lower my head, embarrassed.

"I see. Well, Maddy, the word of a few six-year-olds and your coteacher's"—Ellie gestures at James—"won't hold up against the type of legal power the Seabolts will have."

I touch my forehead, as if it'll stop the tears that are welling up. James touches my arm reassuringly.

"Tell me again how Nick got hold of your work," Ellie says, and I shift uncomfortably in my seat.

"I went over there after school. Lola, as I told you, broke her arm in October." I can feel James staring at me. "I wanted to tell Nick about the amazing progress she'd been making."

"And you had to go over there to tell him?" Ellie seems bemused, and rightly so.

"Well," I begin, and then realize I have no good explanation.

Ellie nods, and I can practically see the lightbulb flick on over her head. "Did they have you sign a confidentiality agreement?"

"Yes, on the first day of school."

"Well, that's good. This way, any, uh, personal transactions will be kept secret. You had relations with him, then?"

I grimace and nod. "Just once," I whisper. Now Michelle's mom knows I'm a home-wrecking slut. Maybe she can offer me a suicide pill, a little black triangle in a glass container, like the one they gave Jodie Foster in *Contact*. "It's fast and painless," they told her. I'm salivating for it.

"Does anyone else know?" Ellie asks, jolting me out of my despair.

I nod and count on my fingers: Kate, Casey, Michelle, James. "Four friends," I say.

"So there's nothing we can do?" James asks, leaning forward as he interrupts this line of questioning. "Without some concrete proof that Maddy wrote *Golden Ghost*?" He seems annoyed with Mrs. Zucker, and I silently thank him for it.

"Look," Ellie says, clasping her hands on top of her mammoth antique desk. "Miracles still happen, but I haven't seen too many lately. These fucking celebrities. They have all the resources. Without a manuscript or some other tangible evidence, these Hollywood characters can and *will* screw good goddamn people like you. Uh, no pun intended." She laughs at her own joke. I can see where Michelle gets her personality. Ellie inclines her head toward me. "And I'm sure you have as many reasons to keep this to yourself as Nick does?"

I nod.

"I'll see what I can do. But I can't promise anything. Good luck to you both." She rises and extends her bejeweled hand.

After we finally emerge from the subway in Brooklyn, James sits down on the deserted staircase outside Borough Hall and unknots the plastic bag with our food in it. Across from us, the Parks Department has started prepping the oval-shaped garden for tulips of every hue. A few giant garbage bags are scattered about, and even in the dark I can see rich soil peeking out from their open tops, reminding me of the barrels of grain at the corner market in *Amélie*. God, I wish I were in France right now.

I plop down beside James and help him open the containers.

We eat in silence for a little while, and I realize that hopelessness really fuels my appetite.

"Why didn't you tell me about this sooner?" he finally says.

"I don't know. I was afraid you'd hate me."

"Nah. I just wish there was something I could do."

"Yeah, me too."

We reach for the same piece of yellowtail and briefly touch fingers.

"You take it," I say.

"No, you."

I take the pearlescent piece of sushi, dip into some soy sauce, take a bite, and hand the remaining half to James. He wolfs it down.

We look at each other for a few seconds, chomping away.

"You have an egg," he says, touching his lip.

"What?"

"*Tobiko,*" he says, and plucks a poppy seed–size orange fish egg from my lip, then pops it into his own mouth. I shiver, despite the fact that it's a warm evening.

James stares at me for what feels like a long time and then rubs my back. "It's going to be okay," he says, and my thighs turn to plum paste. This is no time to go gooey over a boy, I scold myself. Not now. Not ever again.

"Thanks. But Ellie didn't seem too optimistic."

"Well, I am," he says.

I dip a piece of tuna into wasabi and soy sauce. "You sound so hopeful."

"I'm just saying it's not the end of the world."

"Well, it sure feels like the end of my world," I say after I swallow. "Do you have any idea how hard I worked on that book?"

"I know exactly how hard you worked on that book. I was really excited for you." He stares intently into my eyes again and I start getting really nervous.

"God, that sounds so depressing."

"What?"

"That you *were* excited for me. It's like my life is over."

"Your life isn't over, Maddy," he says, smiling now. He leans close to me then and kisses my forehead. Impulsively, I grab onto his jacket and hide between the lapels. It's leathery and smoky and warm, and I just know I could hide out for years in here.

"Hey, you okay in there?" he says after a minute or so.

"Oh, sorry."

"You want the last piece?" He holds out a piece of salmon.

"No thanks." I pull my knees to my chest and rest my chin on my elbows.

"So, why didn't you back up your work?" he says, still chewing.

"God, James, haven't we been through this? I was stupid, trusting, naïve. I fucked up. Why does everyone keep reminding me about it?" I bury my head again, my anger revived.

"Fine," he says, wiping his mouth on his sleeve.

"You're goddamned right it's fine. I've just had my novel stolen, quit my job of six years, and turned down a ten-thousand-dollar raise. That novel and money could have come in really handy right now."

"That's fine," he repeats, suddenly annoying the hell out of me.

"Don't get into one of your self-righteous kicks. I'm not in the mood, okay?"

"Maddy, I said I understand."

"No you didn't. You said 'fine.'" I mimic him, in case he doesn't get the point. "Meanwhile, if it weren't for you, I wouldn't even be in this situation."

"What does that mean?"

"It means that you were the one who told me I should write it down."

James stands up, annoyed. "Hey, don't pin this disaster on me. I'm not the one who screwed you over."

I wait for him to say "no pun intended" and I can see he's thinking it, but instead he stuffs our empty trays into the plastic bag and chucks the whole lot into a garbage can. When he returns, I get up and walk toward the garden.

"Where are you going?" he asks.

"I need to think," I say, hoping he'll get the hint that I mean alone.

"Good. I love to think," he says, and starts to follow me.

I step over the low iron fence, take off my boots and socks, and feel the new soil on my bare feet. "You know, the kids are more mature than you are."

"Yeah," he agrees proudly, as unapologetic as ever. "What's that, some new spa treatment?" he asks, pointing at my feet.

"You're a real wit," I say, stomping around. "I'm just frustrated, okay?"

"Hey, whatever rocks your Kasbah. Does it help?"

"No." I lean over and grab a handful of soil.

"All right, you obviously need to be alone. I'm gonna go," he says.

"Oh look, I've finally pissed off Mr. Cool." I rub some soil between my hands.

When I realize that he's really leaving, I blurt out, "You know your girlfriend is doing the headmaster."

"My what?" An angry question mark blossoms on James's face when he turns around.

"Rachel. God, do I have to spell it out for you?"

He flings his hands in the air and keeps walking away.

"I saw her today," I shout. "Coming out of his office. With this scarf he bought her." As James turns toward me again, I mimic the way Rachel tossed it over her shoulder.

"Maddy. For your information, Rachel is not my girlfriend, but your compassion overwhelms me."

"Hey, I have a lot of compassion," I say, indignant. James is silent. "So then why is she always hanging all over you? It's completely gross."

"I was giving her *guitar* lessons."

"Guitar lessons?" I laugh. "Is that what you call it?"

"Jesus, Maddy. Not that it's any of your business."

"It's my business if she's constantly a total bitch to me, and hangs on you like you're—"

"Like I'm what?"

"Like some rock star."

"Well, did you ever think that maybe you're jealous?"

"Jealous? Of what?"

"Forget it, Maddy. Good night," he says, and storms off, leaving me standing ankle-deep in a pile of dirt.

# Chapter
## Twenty-one

*I* would be impressed that James has planned a field trip if I didn't want to shove my foot up his ass every time I glance in his direction. Of course he's acting as if nothing happened between us, taking the so-called high road. He knows how furious it makes me.

Anyway, City Select field trips are well beyond the call of duty for assistant teachers, especially given the pittance they're paid. I should be especially impressed, since he barely needed any guidance, but I'm not.

During morning meeting, I gather the kids together and we go over the rules of conduct. It's good to see that everyone is chipper (except me), and, more important, that no one's forgotten their bagged lunch.

"So when we get to the Tenement Museum, you'll do what?" Every hand stretches toward the ceiling. "Max?"

"Zip your lip and hold your partner's hand," he says stoically.

"That's right. And we're all going to remember that we're guests, and behave in a polite manner."

Heads nod in agreement.

"We follow directions and don't interrupt," Raffey adds.

"That's a good rule to follow. Thank you," I say.

"And we raise our hand if we have a question!" says Stella.

"Or if we have to go to the bathroom!" Lucas adds.

Every kid begins shouting at once, adding new rules to the list. Finally, I cut in. "Okay, guys. I'm not in the mood. And if we sit here listing rules all day, we'll miss the bus." This logic seems to work and the kids settle down again.

We gather in a line at the door, two by two. James invites the kids to practice their exemplary field trip behavior and we silently make our way downstairs to the waiting yellow school bus.

"Why are you bringing your guitar?" I ask James as we're herding the kids up the steep bus stairs. It's the first thing I've said to him this morning.

"I thought I could play during lunch. You know, we'll sit in Battery Park and keep the kids occupied." He smiles at me warmly.

"Good thinking," I say through clenched teeth.

As we travel down Eleventh Street, I lurch up the narrow aisle, making sure the kids are doing okay. James is holding court in the back of the bus, teaching the kids to sing "New York, New York," by Ol' Blue Eyes.

"Why don't you play your guitar?" I ask, stabbing a finger at the case on the floor. "We still have a little while before we get there."

"Nah," he says. "I'm gonna make these guys suffer a capella for a while." The kids groan in an exaggerated way and I roll my eyes, turn around, and head back to my seat.

While everyone giggles and sings with James, I notice that the bus is turning north on the FDR, instead of south.

"Isn't the Tenement Museum on Orchard?" I ask the bus driver, and he tells me to talk to the gentleman in the back. Hmph.

Again, I get up, trying not to fall on my face as I make my way toward James. "Hey, are you aware that the Tenement Museum is in the other direction?" I whisper, hoping the kids won't hear me. They might get worried if they see I'm not in full control.

"I thought it'd be nice to take in a little curriculum-related scenery beforehand," he says in a normal voice. A couple kids turn and watch us, but James seems unconcerned, as always. "Our tour doesn't start for another half hour anyway."

"How dare you not ask me about this first?" I demand. Then I make an announcement: "Kids, James has planned a kind of . . .

surprise. Before we get to the museum, we'll be taking a little tour around the city. Does that sound like fun?" I'm going to kill him.

"Yeah!" the kids scream in unison at the tops of their lungs. I rush over to the bus driver to apologize for the ruckus.

The road trip continues, James quizzing the kids on various New York landmarks while I devise ways to get rid of the patchoulied pop star. The bus takes us to midtown, where James points out the Plaza Hotel and Central Park. Then we go south on Broadway, where the blinding wattage of Times Square reflects in the kids' overjoyed eyes. The bus heads north on the Avenue of the Americas then east on Fiftieth Street. When I finally get into the swing of things, we turn into an underground parking garage.

"Um, James?" I call. "Is this part of the tour?"

The kids cover their mouths and giggle.

"Something funny I should know about?" I ask them sternly.

"Kids?" James says, and the kids say in a very rehearsed way, "It's a surprise. Sssshhh."

"Oh, okay," I say, pretending to know what's going on. James is probably going to show us the skating rink at Rockefeller Center, or Saint Patrick's Cathedral. Still, he could have told me. I am the head teacher, after all, and ultimately responsible for these guys. Throwing him off the Brooklyn Bridge is too good for this guy.

When we've all disembarked, I say to James, "I'm going to have to report you for this."

"Go ahead, Maddy," he says with so much confidence, it actually startles me.

"Well then, do you mind letting me in on your little surprise? I have a right to know. These kids are my responsibility."

"Maddy, you're just going to have to trust me on this one."

"I hope you know what you're doing."

I count the kids and partner up with Lola at the back of the line. "You know what this is all about?" I ask her when James starts leading the way.

"Uh-huh," she says. "But I'm not supposed to say."

"Hey, are you okay?" I ask. "You look a little blue."

"I am." She sighs. "But James told me everything would be okay."

"He did, huh," I answer, not having the slightest idea of what she's talking about.

"Yeah. Now stop asking questions." She looks up at me then and shows me the new gap in her front teeth, melting my heart like she always does, no matter how out of control I feel. I zip my lip and throw away the key.

James leads us to the front entrance of one of the many enormous office buildings on Sixth Avenue. He turns around and faces us. "Okay, we're here. We're going to go in, wait silently while I check in at the front desk, and then we're going to head to the elevators. Give me a silent thumbs-up if you understand."

Nineteen little thumbs point toward heaven, and we enter the building.

In the cavernous lobby, James converses briefly with a blue-suited security guard. The kids and I look up toward the ceiling, which seems about five stories high. Then James leads the way again, heading to one of many elevator bays. Since it's after ten o'clock, there aren't too many people waiting to ascend, and we only have to torture one businessman on our way to the thirty-first floor. People would be surprised to see that nineteen kids and three adults can actually fit in an elevator together. It's too bad I can't make money from this circuslike talent.

"Okay, kids. I'll bet you guys can't hold your breath for the entire ride," says James, and the kids nod furiously, defying him. "Okay then, show us. Ready? One, two, three!" All of us suck in a gulp of air and puff out our cheeks. The lone suit along for the ride smiles broadly at us.

When the elevator opens on the thirty-first floor, we all sigh audibly, then exit and head down an all-white corridor with shiny marble floors. The kids immediately begin comparing notes on their performance, their voices echoing loudly.

"I held my breath the entire time!" Raffey announces.

"Yeah, I could've held my breath to the fiftieth floor," Max boasts.

"I could've held my breath to the hundredth floor!" Raffey shoots back.

James and I quiet the kids down. I might want to slip a heaping helping of cyanide into his morning brew, but until that special moment, we're a team.

"Okay, kids, we're here," James says. Wherever here is. "Now, like I told you before, they're not going to let us in if we're making any noise. It's a regular business day, so everyone is very busy. Give me a thumbs-up for understanding."

Thumbs shoot in the air.

"Okay. Let's go."

James and I line the kids up in their former order and walk toward a heavy-looking set of glass double doors at the end of the hall. I am more confused than ever. Maybe James is taking us to a record company? The lettering on the door says CONHEADY, MURRAY & BROWN. Never heard of it.

At the reception desk, James lets a perky blonde with a button nose and squinty blue eyes know who we are. She smiles and nods, then punches a number on her vast phone console.

After a couple moments, during which I'm terrified that the kids are going to lose their composure, another beautiful young woman appears and leads us down a wide carpeted hallway. Where are we? I wonder. The Miss America office?

We are herded into a large conference room. There's an oval white-topped table with seating for about twenty. A wall of glass overlooks other gargantuan midtown office buildings, and packed bookshelves fill an interior wall. At the far end of the table sits a chiseled older woman in a tailored plaid skirt and jacket that seems to match her fiery hair color. She smiles and gestures for us to join her at the table.

"Welcome. James? Maddy?" She stands and steps forward to shake our hands. "I'm Carolyn Conheady." Then she turns to James and says, "They should be here any minute."

Who should be here any minute? What is going on? I look at James, but he seems to be deliberately avoiding eye contact.

Carolyn passes the time by shaking each student's hand and learning their names. The kids are delighted with such special treatment and beam at Carolyn, James, and me before clamoring for seats around the egg-shaped table. Kylie and Eden thankfully seem only mildly disappointed when they have to double up on one seat, and for the most part, the kids keep quiet, busying themselves by drawing on sheets of photocopy paper with gold-stamped pencils that Carolyn has expertly procured from a hidden drawer. She must have kids of her own.

I'm just about to ask James what the hell is going on, when the door opens and Nick and Shelby enter the office. My jaw takes the plunge. Now I am going to kill James. Right after I kill myself.

I instinctively lower my head to avoid meeting Nick's eyes, but not before I quickly assess his attire. He looks like he always does: camera-ready in designer jeans, a black T-shirt, and new Puma slip-ons. Only now, my underwear isn't steaming up the way it used to whenever I laid eyes on him. Instead, my insides feel as if I've just swallowed a mouthful of sand.

Shelby, on the other hand, is dressed ever so academically in a sober navy A-line skirt and a crisp white oxford-cloth shirt. She's sporting the same pair of glasses she wore in the *Celeb File* article. Something tells me we won't be making it to the Tenement Museum today.

When I sneak another glance, Nick is looking at me. For an instant, it seems that he doesn't know what to make of all of this. Then, as if I hallucinated his momentary unease, he morphs into the slippery-smooth operator I'm used to. As he regards me calmly, I realize he hasn't been cast as a villain three times for nothing. My knees are going to give out any second.

I look at the rug again, but I can't exactly close my ears. "Carolyn, you're looking well. Love the new cut. It suits you." Nick says this all so calmly that I shiver. I look over to get a clue from James, but he's too busy setting his guitar case on the table to notice.

"Carolyn, what is this?" Shelby says, rushing toward us. Then she sees Lola. "Lolo, what are you—" She stops and gazes around the table, then her face softens into a smile. "Oh, I get it," she says. "You all came here to see me! Is this a field trip? Are you learning about the publishing industry?" Shelby turns to me. "Maddy, you are so clever, I swear. But why didn't you call me? I could've made reservations at 'Twenty-one'!"

"I-I-I," I stutter, and then gesture to James, who is unlatching his guitar case.

We all stare as he opens it. There's no guitar inside the case. Well, I guess I didn't really think a serenade was appropriate. Instead, James extracts a thick stack of paintings and drawings done by the kids. He places those on the table and then signals for Kylie and Eden. They get out of their shared seat beside James and begin spreading the pile of artwork out over the table, remaining as silent as before.

"What's this?" Shelby asks, scooting her glasses down her nose.

Nick begins to laugh, shaking his head. "This is priceless," he says, clearly enjoying himself. When our eyes meet and that thousand-watt smile is directed at me, I wish I could take cover, hide under the table. Anything to escape his dangerous looks.

Carolyn ignores Nick and watches with deep interest as the scene at the table unfolds. Kylie, Eden, and about half of the other kids continue organizing the drawings and paintings on the huge table. I stare at the collection. Amanda Porter looks back at me in all her various forms—playing at the side of the creek with her father and his miner friends; riding atop a stagecoach in the sun; arriving at her grandmother's mansion on Eleventh Street, circa 1850; holding hands with her mom and dad in heaven.

"Are you illustrating my story?" Shelby asks, suddenly smiling with pride.

"It's not *your* story," James says to her, and then glances at Nick and then at me. "It's Maddy's." My guts do a nosedive. I gulp and brace myself. Here we go.

"What?" Shelby looks at me, incredulous. She's completely clueless. Maybe she really believes she wrote the book.

"It's Maddy's story!" Raffey says, gesturing in front of her, as if she's squeezing a bagel in each hand.

"Sweetheart, this is my story," Shelby insists. "Right, Nick?"

"That's right, sweetie," he says, taking a step toward her and grasping her hand. His smile disappears.

"Well, I'm not so certain anymore," Carolyn says. "You know, this could be pretty serious."

"But Carolyn, you're my publisher! My trusted friend! You're supposed to help me! It's my story! Mine!" If I closed my eyes, I would swear she was one of the kids. "Nick?" Shelby pleads. Nick squeezes her hand tighter.

"Shelby. Calm down," Carolyn says. "These are some pretty serious allegations here, and it's my job to look into them before we go any further. If this book is really yours, you've got nothing to worry about, so why don't you settle down so we can get to the bottom of this. This carrying on is not helping your case."

Shelby's head quivers furiously, like a pan of Jiffy Pop about to burst, and she snorts a few puffs of air, indignant. Carolyn Conheady, I decide, looking over at her, is my new hero. And she's not even famous.

Carolyn looks at James and asks him to go on. James takes the corner of one of the many pieces of art and holds it up. At the bottom of the colored pencil drawing is a caption carefully written in the special D'Nealian technique we teach at City Select. It reads "Chapter 4: Amanda Gets Sick." A little girl is shown in profile, lying on a blue bed, one crescent-shaped eye closed.

"Whose is this?" James asks, and Zachary raises his hand. "Care to describe?" James says in a lawyerly but endearing way.

"It's Amanda Porter, from *Golden Ghost.* I drew it the day Maddy said we could illustrate the book. Drawing the pictures was *my* idea," he adds, patting his chest.

"This is bullshit," Shelby says, planting two white-knuckled fists on her narrow hips, finally getting it.

Nineteen pairs of eyes widen in wonderment at Shelby's word choice. "You said a swear!" Raffey exclaims, and points. The kids are eating it up. Nick drops Shelby's hand. A thick vein begins to throb in the center of his forehead.

"And when was that?" James asks Zachary, ignoring the commotion.

"Mmm." Zach thinks about this, craning his head sideways. "Before Halloween, that's for sure!" he says finally, remembering.

"Very good," James says. "Now, who came up with the title of the story?"

All hands shoot up.

"Raffey?"

"Well, I wish it was me, but it wasn't," she says, exaggerating a frown. "*I* thought we should've called it *The Little Millionaire,* but everyone voted on *Golden Ghost* instead."

"And who came up with the title *Golden Ghost,* Raffey?" James asks.

Raffey points a reluctant finger across the room. "It was Nina." She sighs. Nina smiles at me, spreads her arms like airplane wings, and twirls.

Nick breaks in, sweat blossoming on his flushed forehead. "Maddy, I can't believe you would try something like this after we put our trust in you and let you into our home. I thought we discussed this. I feel so betrayed."

I stare at him. "*You* feel betrayed?" I all but shout. It's a lucky thing for him that there are children present. *We discussed this?* God, he's good.

"I mean, do you really think that this stack of scribbles means that Shelby didn't write this story?" he says, but I can swear his voice has less conviction than before. The kids scowl at him, which is quite justified, in my opinion. I look at Nick in disbelief. I have never seen him look so panicked, not even in *Bluebell,* when his mistress was hemorrhaging.

"Dad!" Lola yells, exasperated. "It's *artwork.*"

"Yeah," a few kids agree. "Artwork."

Way to go kids, I think.

"Oh, okay. Sorry, Lolo," Nick says, but he's clearly distracted by his own venom.

Shelby nods in agreement. "You can bet Barney's fat purple ass that no court of law is going to take a bunch of crayon drawings into account. Right, Carolyn? Right, honey?"

Nick nods, stroking her shoulder in agreement, but I can see the wheels spinning in his head. Carolyn says nothing.

I don't know how James is keeping so calm during all this. I can hardly breathe from all the pressure in this room, but he just casually reaches into his guitar case and pulls out another pile of papers, so rumpled this time that they look as if they've been salvaged from the trash. He gives them to Lucas, who delivers the pile into Carolyn's waiting hands.

"James," I gasp. They're manuscripts, early ones of mine, installments of *Golden Ghost* from the very beginning, a pile of typewritten pages, each with a footer that includes my name, the title, and a date, a massive pile of pages I threw away at the end of each reading period because I didn't want to carry them home. James must have taken them out of the garbage.

Nick and Shelby look on in growing horror as Carolyn looks over the first page and then flips through the pile, nodding. I stare, too scared to move a millimeter.

"What the hell is this?" Nick spits out then, finally losing his cool for good.

Carolyn shushes him by holding a palm up in the air while continuing to go through the stack of papers.

"Carolyn?" Shelby's eyes look so pleadingly desperate, it's a wonder they don't fall out of her head. "Nick?" Her voice is papery.

This is the longest moment of my life. When Carolyn finally looks up, I realize I've been holding my breath. For how long? Minutes? Months?

"Well, James, you're absolutely right. This certainly establishes more than enough proof that Maddy is the author of *Golden Ghost*." To Nick and Shelby, she says, "It's a good thing you two can afford the best lawyers. You're going to need them." Then she looks to me and says, "Maddy, you will have an official apology from Conheady, Murray, and Brown. And I"—she places a hand on her chest—"am so sorry about this. Of course, I am prepared to offer you a contract immediately and to make sure *your* book gets the recognition it deserves." She finishes by shaking my very sweaty hand, and I think I'm going to faint.

Shelby slumps into an empty seat between Nina and Stella. "You told me this was a done deal!" she shouts at Nick, who tries to console her. "Get the hell off of me!" she shouts, flailing her spindly limbs in every direction before cradling her head in her hands and sobbing loudly enough to frighten us all.

The kids are agog, and some of them even start to whimper. Nina and Stella run over to me and cling to my jacket.

Nick stands back and fumes. "Shut up, Shelby. You're making it worse," he says.

Lola bursts into tears and runs over to James, who scoops her up into his arms. She weeps into his shoulder. Shelby glances up at Lola then, an unusually defenseless look on her blotchy face. James whispers something into Lola's ear and sets her down. Lola walks with some trepidation over to her mom and looks at the floor. Then she says, "Mommy, you can write a book, too. Just like Maddy. You'll see."

I stand there, feeling dizzy, while Shelby continues to cry and Lola climbs into her mom's lap and strokes her hair. "It'll be okay," she reassures Shelby, and Shelby hugs Lola, rocking her back and forth.

Nick places his hands on his hips, glares at Shelby, then points a furious finger at me. He looks as if he's about to say something, but no words escape his lips when he opens his mouth. Finally, he just storms out of the room, slamming the door in frustration and rage. I look at James again for some signal, and he's staring at me, his eyes searching for my reaction.

After thanking Carolyn and saying good-bye, we quietly usher the kids back to the hallway, leaving Lola in the conference room with her mom.

There's no need to hold our breath in the elevator again, as we're all pretty stunned into silence, but when we're out on the street, the floodgates open. I start crying and babbling so much, I begin to resemble the fountain we're standing beside.

"Thank you so much, guys," I shout over the din of water and traffic. "I can't believe you planned such an elaborate rescue mission. I can't believe it. I am the luckiest teacher—no, the luckiest person—in the world." I sit on the edge of the fountain and weep. "I'm sorry, guys. This is the first time in my whole career that I've ever cried in front of my students."

James and the kids venture over to me, and before I know it, we're all huddled together in one giant hug. The kids pull away one by one as James and I continue hugging each other, rocking back and forth in a bubble of exhilaration.

"Thank you so much," I say over and over again.

When we finally stand up, I say, "James, how did you do this?"

"It's amazing what a few telephone calls and some compelling evidence can get you," he says, and looks like he's about to wink, but he doesn't.

"How did you get the kids to keep such a big secret?"

Raffey pipes up then. "Extra-special snack!" She rubs her belly and licks her lips.

"Ah, bribery," I say, laughing, and everyone joins in. A million thoughts are hurtling through my mind, a runaway roulette wheel. When it finally lands on a number, I say to James, "Why did you save all those old manuscripts?"

"Because," he says, looking into my eyes, "you wrote them."

I shake my head slowly and start crying all over again. Kylie hands me a clean tissue.

"Thanks, sweetie." I sob and ruffle her long ponytail.

James kisses me on the cheek then. "See? I told you everything was going to be okay."

"Are you guys going to get married now?" Max asks, looking up at us questioningly, and Nina says, "I told you."

I'm so over the moon right now, I don't even tell them to knock it off.

"Hey, James," Raffey says, tugging his fringe as we make our way back to the bus. "Make with the snack."

"Yeah!" scream the other kids.

# Chapter
## Twenty-two

*W*hen I get home, I am so excited to tell Kate the news, I can barely calm down long enough to get the key in the door. After dropping it about five times on the floor, I scramble into the apartment and start calling her name.

No response.

I would knock on her door, but I'm too excited, so I just burst in. She's sitting on her bed, tears streaming down her face.

And to think that this is the first time in what seems like months that I actually have some *good* news!

"Kate! What's wrong?" I ask, settling down beside her, Carolyn Conheady's business card bowing in my hand.

"It's the band! They canceled!" she wails. "What am I going to do?"

"Kate, I . . ." I don't know what to say. I've never seen my roommate in such a state. Crying jags are usually my territory. I rack my brains for something smart and soothing to say, something Kate would tell me at a time like this.

"They flaked, those bastards. I called the bassist today, and he didn't even know about the wedding!" She blubbers, honking into a stray pair of Casey's lime green–striped boxer shorts. "He said they were booked at some club on the Lower East Side. . . ." Kate falls over on her side, curls her knees to her chest in fetal position, and sobs.

"Kate," I say. "We're going to solve this. There are gazillions of bands out there."

"But the wedding's on Saturday! I won't even be able to get a DJ at this point. My mom is never going to forgive me."

Boy, she's good at this.

"Kate, do you know how many bands there are out there who would kill to play at your wedding?"

"Name one," she says, challenging me.

"Um . . . Well . . ." And then it hits me. "Spur," I say.

"Spur? Like on a boot?"

"Yeah, Kate," I say, getting excited all over again. "It's James's band. You saw them play, and you liked them. It's like you've already interviewed them! And they're good. You said so yourself. Remember?"

Kate doesn't say anything at first. She just stares at the ceiling, forlorn, thinking. I run to the bathroom and grab a roll of fresh toilet paper for her.

We sit on the bed silently. Eventually, Kate sits up and wipes her eyes, breathing calmly again. "Do you think they'll be able to make it on such short notice?" she asks, and I reach for the phone, smiling.

As I stare at my reflection in the ladies' room mirror, I realize that the last time I was this dressed up was at Nick's Christmas party.

The wedding's in DUMBO (an acronym, Stella informed us, that stands for Down Under the Manhattan Bridge Overpass), at BargeMusic, a permanently anchored vessel that hosts chamber music concerts and smallish weddings like this one.

As I sip from my flute of champagne, I wonder what Nick and Shelby will do to revive their careers now. I guess I'll read about it sooner or later. Not that I'm worried about them. But I am concerned for Lola, even though she is the only sane one in that whole scary family.

I adjust my bodice, standing up straight and sticking out my flat chest in an effort to fill out the tube of green silk and make my body look proportionate: small-waisted, long-legged, and as sexy as possible in my maid of honor's dress.

Kate rushes into the bathroom then, a blushing blur of cloudy white. Looking in the mirror, I tell her how breathtaking she looks, how beautiful the ceremony was, and how jealous I am of her.

"Thank you so much!" she says, gathering me into a hug. "Meanwhile, you saved the day, Maddy. You really did. Spur is so good. Everyone's talking about them."

We take turns reapplying gloppy lip gloss from my Smashbox Lip Illusions trio, blot on either end of a tissue-paper toilet-seat cover, and head back out to the dance floor.

James and the rest of Spur still have the floor packed. Kate's grandmother shuffles up to us and flashes her dentures. "Kate honey, I haven't danced like this since I was your age," she says, twirling and dipping in her husband's arms. Kate's grandfather emphasizes the point with a "Yee haw!" and they're off for another lap around the dance floor. Kate just takes it all in, a princess in a Penny Marshall movie.

Casey approaches us then, his silver tie loosened, his face flushed, golden curls plastered to his scalp with sweat from cutting the rug. He takes my wrist and says, "If it's all right with you ladies, I'd be honored to have this dance." Kate nods her blessing and turns to schmooze with the few remaining guests sitting at the orchid- and votive-festooned dining tables.

Casey glides me around the floor to "Teddy Bear." The crowd is eating up James's Elvis impersonation. This is the first time I've actually been drunk on life, instead of booze, at any party.

All the Spur guys look like they're having a blast, and they are fine-looking, too, in extra-long-sleeved black tuxedo shirts, unbuttoned at the throat, clean tapered trousers, and shiny black cowboy boots. For such a special occasion, they're even sporting clean hair and close-shaven faces. The only thing tattered and old is the brown felt cowboy hat that James always wears when he plays, somehow made all the more endearing by the fact that he and his band have turned into this wedding's most memorable element.

After a couple more dance numbers, James says, "This next tune is one of our own. We're slowing the pace and inviting all you lovebirds out there to show your romantic stuff."

As the band launches into a melodic ballad, Casey bids me adieu and trots off, looking for his wife. *His wife.* It sounds so wonderful. The single people start clamoring for seats at the edge of the dance floor, including me.

Kate and Casey begin to sway in time, and soon Casey's married friends from his editing job at *Brooklyn's Own* join in, as do Kate's colleagues from her fund-raising job. Even the puffy-haired older relatives get into the act. They all look so happy, the women leaning their flushed faces into their mates' silky lapels. I sigh, stroke the petals of my bouquet, which I somehow seem to be surgically attached to, briefly lament my singular status, and look at James.

*The first time I walked in the room*
*And I looked in your eyes*
*I already knew*
*But still out came my lies*

A white-gloved waiter comes by with a tray of champagne and I swoop one off the silver tray, the bubbles tickling my nose before the glass touches my lips. I need to busy myself as I sit here.

*And you were so right*
*To call me so young*
*But time has since passed*
*And I have since grown*

I tilt my head, listening, and look at James again. If I'm not mistaken, he's staring straight at me. I take a deep swig.

*She offered me friendship*
*When I knew no one*

*You called us lovers*
*This time, you were wrong*

*'Cause there was this feeling*
*That stood in the way*
*It would come over me*
*When I'd hear your name*
*Don't know how I didn't see it*
*Because now it's clear*
*Why I get weak whenever you're near*

Oh my God. He's singing about Rachel. And me. I look around, tears readying themselves to escape my eyes. Nobody is any the wiser.

*See . . .*
*It turns out I love you*
*And only you*
*Turns out I love all the things that you do*
*From the chalk on your shirt*
*Your secondhand shoes*
*The way that your lips feel on mine*

The tears are falling fast and furious now and I swipe at them with the back of my hand between sips of champagne. By the time the song is over, I've shredded my bouquet and emptied my glass, but my eyes are still overflowing.

"Thank you very much," James says when they're done. Everyone in the room applauds for him and the rest of the band. He grabs his bottle of Stella Artois from the floor and raises it in a salute. "We're going to take a little chow break, but we'll be back before you can say 'Happy honeymoon!'"

James places his guitar in a slim stand on the stage. My heart drops into my flesh-tone fishnets when I realize he's heading straight toward me. I can barely see his eyes underneath the curled brim of his cowboy hat—that is, until he sits down beside me.

"I guess I should've asked if this seat is taken," he says, lifting his hat to run a hand through his hair, then replacing it again.

"Oh, sure," I say, jittery with nerves, wiping away yet another tear.

"It's taken?"

"No. It's not taken. Sorry." As always, I am the essence of smooth. I'm afraid if I say anything else, I'll start sobbing.

"Nice bouquet," he says, gesturing at the pile of petals on the table.

"Heh heh," I say, feeling more like Beavis and Butt-head than the maid of honor.

"You wanna take a walk?" he asks, then reaches into his pocket and hands me a handkerchief.

"Wow. Thanks," I say, marveling at the monogrammed hankie. "I didn't know you used these."

He shrugs. "My grandmom sends them to me on my birthday every year. I like to pocket a couple on special occasions."

We maneuver our way through the forest of round tables, past the buffet, and head out onto the green diamond-plated iron deck, facing lower Manhattan. As we climb the steep stairs to the upper level, I can feel the boat sway gently with the current of the river. My heart, on the other hand, is more like a storm at sea. The sun hangs low over Miss Liberty's shoulder, a bright red ball, which makes James's cheeks look flushed, like candy apples.

I blow my nose and apologize for soiling his handkerchief.

"That's what they're for," he says. He doesn't question me about the tears, which I'm grateful for, and that makes me cry even more. He just smiles at me patiently.

"How come you waited so long to tell me that you and Rachel weren't together?" I ask.

"It never seemed like the right time. And if I'd brought it up, you'd probably have thought I was hitting on you."

I ponder this. "Yeah, I guess. Anyway, I was so blinded by . . . you know." I don't want to mention Nick's name, not now, not ever again. We're silent for some time, looking out over the water.

I feel at peace for the first time in what seems like years, even after everything that's happened. Maybe it is because the school year is over and there's more hope than ever, even though I have no idea what's in store for me.

"How come you didn't mention the manuscripts sooner?" I ask.

"I remembered them when we talked to Michelle's mom. But I didn't think she'd handle it right, so I kept quiet. And when I talked with Casey—"

"You talked with Casey?"

"Kate put us in touch. Publishing's a small community. Turns out he knows Carolyn. Word was all over the place about *Golden Ghost*. Anyway, I thought the best way to handle it was to have Nick and Shelby see the kids, see their work, see *your* work. And Carolyn was game, so . . ."

"Wow." I take it all in. "Wow," I repeat.

"You have great friends, Maddy," James says. "People who really love you."

"Yeah, I do," I whisper, a chill running through my body. "I'm pretty lucky."

We stand at the railing and listen to the river lap against the barge. I say a silent thank you for my amazing fortune.

"What was that bet we had?" James asks, finally breaking the silence.

"From way back when?"

"Uh-huh."

"I believe it was that if you stopped winking, I'd dedicate my book to you," I say, still looking across the river, a hint of a smile playing on my lips.

"And if you gave up your celebrity habit, I'd sing a song about you."

"A *nice* song," I add.

"In public," he says.

I nod. "It's beautiful, you know."

"I'm glad you like it."

"I love it," I say, turning toward him. "Thank you."

He smiles at me, warm and bright as the setting sun.

"Every word is true," he says, touching my cheek with his thumb.

I tuck a stray strand of hair behind my ear. James takes a step closer and removes his cowboy hat. He surrounds my face with his hands and leans down to meet my lips. The scent of patchouli fills my head and I reach up with my free hand to run my fingers through his hair. Our lips meet, and I know I could kiss this scruffy, winking twenty-five-year-old forever.

# Epilogue

*I*f this were a scene from the movie of my life, here is what the audience would see: a bedroom, not the neatest place in the world, mind you, but I'm not really at liberty to care at the moment. Guitars and other music equipment are scattered around; a keyboard here, an amplifier there. You'd hear some meowing from a cat named Kenneth, follow his furry footsteps over an undulating mountain range of sheets that most likely haven't seen the inside of a washing machine for quite some time.

On the floor, among scattered socks, strewn clothes, and sheet music, you'd see a copy of the latest *Celeb File Weekly,* a picture of Nick and Shelby Seabolt on the cover, holding hands at a premiere.

The headline reads ARE NICK AND SHEL HEADING FOR DISASTER? A smaller, grainier photograph shows Nick and Lainey kissing on a yacht. The smaller text says that Shelby's back in rehab and that Nick is having an affair with his personal assistant, Lainey Abrams, with whom he is launching a line of gourmet spices.

Lying beside *Celeb File,* there's a copy of *Brooklyn's Own,* with a photograph of me, Maddy Braverman, on the cover. The cover copy reads "Brooklyn's own golden girl, Maddy Braverman, makes it big with her debut novel." A smaller photo in the upper-right-hand corner of the magazine is of Michelle Zucker, who's starring in a successful play at the Brooklyn Academy of Music.

The camera pans slowly up the length of the bed, revealing Kenneth, now washing his paws, and then James and me, who are wriggling under the covers, naked and blissful, in a postcoital way.

Farther over, on the bedside table, a copy of *Golden Ghost* is opened to a dedication page. It reads "*For James. Without you, none of this would have been possible. I love you, MB.*"

Then you'd hear a lot of giggling and some kissing and slurping noises.

And finally, fade to black.